TAKING A CHANCE FOR LOVE

Blake Allwood

Trigger Warnings:
Car Accident
Death/loss/grief
Depression
Trauma

Blake Allwood
Visit my website at www.blakeallwood.com

Printed in the United States of America

First Printing: Mar 2021
Blake Allwood Publishing
ISBN: 9798744358631
AMZ

Thank you to the following people for their assistance:

Bryan Seranas – Developmental Editor
Christopher Miller – Copy Editor
Jo Bird – Line Editor
Ann Attwood – Final Editor

A special thank you goes to all my friends and family
who supported me, I couldn't have done it without you.

And finally, an extra special thanks to my husband
who continues to tolerate me, no matter how many of
these rabbit holes I keep going down.

Titles by Blake Allwood:

Aiden Inspired
Suzie Empowered
Bobby Transformed
|
Romantic Renovations
|
By Chance Series:
Love By Chance
Another Chance With Love
Taking A Chance For Love
|
Big Bend Series:
Love's Legacy: Book One
Love's Heirloom: Book Two
Love's Bequest: Book Three
|
Novella:
Tenacious
(Available at blakeallwood.com)

Preface

Being a foster parent for over twelve years gave my husband and I an opportunity to meet and parent several incredible and amazing young men.

Our first foster son was a seventeen-year-old young man with Asperger syndrome. As his father, I saw how emotions could trigger him. Not in a big way, but sometimes he'd just shut down. As you can imagine, this made romantic relationships difficult.

More than once, I watched as he navigated relationships with people who didn't understand... or more accurately, refused to understand how his mind works. Of course, that was because he was young and his love interests were also young; but even adults who are on the autism spectrum can struggle with romantic relationships.

As an author, I wanted to speak up for my son and other people who are on the spectrum. So, when I envisioned Taking a Chance for Love, I immediately knew Clay would be a good candidate to honor this community.

I truly hope this story helps to eradicate misconceptions and stereotypes that plague this group of beautiful people.

Prologue – Twenty Years Earlier

The trees were so heavy with fruit, the limbs barely swayed as the hot arid breeze drifted through their branches.

I screamed happily as my uncle found me hidden underneath one of the trees. "You're it!" he exclaimed, and ran as I chased him.

"I'm faster than you, Uncle Chris," I yelled, but my great-uncle was already hidden, even though he always hid in the same spot, making it easy for me to find him.

The crew working nearby glanced at one another, then chuckled as I ran by them. I lingered just long enough to hear them talking.

"Chris is crazy about that boy," I heard one of them say.

The response, however, was what any young boy who adored his uncle would want to hear. The comment left me feeling like I truly had a place in this life.

"Bet he ends up growing up just like him."

The first thick drops of the monsoon storm began falling, and Uncle Chris grabbed me from behind, causing me to squeal.

As we ran toward the house, he said, just barely out of breath, "Your mama's gonna skin us both if I get you back soaked to the bone again."

"Not me," I giggled, as I bounced in my uncle's arms. "But she'll skin you." And we both laughed when she opened the door, shaking her head.

"I swear you're just as bad as him," she said to Uncle Chris, as she moved back, allowing us both in, dripping on the tiles of her entryway.

"I've already left the towels there on the back of the chair. Make sure you take your shoes off before you come in," she said, no heat in her command. It wasn't needed, since both of us had gotten a good lecture the day before, when we'd come in tracking sandy sludge across her living room.

"When you two are done drying off, come on in. I've just finished making scones. You can both have one, and hopefully, it won't spoil your dinner."

Dad slipped in the back door when mom wasn't looking, and pulled her into a wet embrace causing her to scream, which ended in laughter. "I swear, the lot of you are gonna be the end of me," she exclaimed, before darting out of his arms, and returned to the marmalade I could smell cooking on the stove.

As we sat around the kitchen table, I was overcome with happiness and I looked between Dad and Uncle Chris, and said, "I'm the luckiest boy in Mesa," causing both men to smile.

Mom came over and rubbed my head, and replied, "I'd say we're all pretty lucky." She turned loving eyes toward Dad, whose smile reflected the same emotion back at her.

That's what I'd loved, and that's what I'd lost. Our life under the trees had been a place of happiness and peace, the kind that my entire family seemed to feel deep in our hearts.

Chapter One

Joshua – Present Day

"Are you Joshua Howard?" the man asked, as I stood staring at the casket at the bottom of the open grave. Most of the other funeral attendees had already left, but I'd stayed back, the shock of my Uncle Chris's death still swirling through me.

"Yeah," I responded, but didn't look his way.

"I'm Cecil Arlington with Arlington, Hush, and Langley," he informed me.

I turned to him then, wondering why someone would tell me his professional name, while standing next to a grave.

"Your uncle put you in his will. Can you come by my office before you leave?" he asked briskly, then handed me his card. "You can call this number and set up a time with my assistant."

I stared at the card as he left. What on earth did my uncle leave me? I guessed the better question was, why would my uncle leave me anything? It isn't like we were close—at least not any longer. I'd moved to Atlanta with my parents when I was a pre-teen and hadn't seen him again.

I'd wondered all these years why I'd never heard from him. Was he so angry with my father that he didn't want me in his life either?

I'd begun trying to find him once I'd gotten old enough to do things without my father looking over my shoulder, but I'd never had much luck. Finally, I hired my friend, Trevor, who worked as a private investigator, to see what he could find. Within a week he'd located him, and with the information he'd given me, I'd reached out. That was just a few weeks ago.

My uncle had seemed genuinely happy to speak with me. He never told me he was sick. Instead, all he seemed to want to talk about was when I was younger, running amuck around the orange groves where he worked. He promised to get back in touch with me, but he never did.

I tried calling his home several times, but never got through again. I figured he'd had his talk and was done with me, then a few days ago, I got a call from a woman named Melinda, who said she was dealing with his messages. She was the one that told me he'd passed away, and gave me the details of the funeral.

Depression overtook me. My uncle was the last of my family. My father didn't count. Not really. Even my friends called him a statue. I spent the next couple days managing my anxiety. I knew it was ridiculous to mourn someone I didn't really know, but for me this was the loss of hope that I'd ever have a family. If I was being honest, it really represented the loss of a belief I'd secretly held onto, that once I was reconnected with my uncle, I'd reclaim all the happiness I'd once had as a child.

After I'd navigated all my emotions and the initial shock, I called my father to ask if he wanted to go with me. With his ever-present stoic, businesslike politeness, he declined.

I took a deep breath, knowing I was gonna get lashed by his temper, but asked anyway, "Dad, what was the problem between you two?"

"Nothing that concerns you," he snapped, making it clear the conversation was over.

If my uncle was anything like my dad, they'd probably had a fight over who was more stubborn or willful. Apparently, my dad won, since here I was standing by my uncle's open grave...alone.

I looked at the card again and sat down on one of the plastic chairs the funeral home had put out for people to sit on. As I appeared to be alone now, I decided to have a final talk with my uncle, even though I knew he couldn't answer.

"Uncle Chris, what happened? Why didn't you tell me you were sick? Why didn't you—?"

I stopped abruptly when I noticed a man was walking toward me and the grave. When he was only a few feet away, he stopped and stood watching me. Had I not known better, I'd have said he was checking me out, although, I couldn't imagine a tear-streaked man sitting by an open grave and talking to a dead man in a casket was a very attractive sight.

I put my head in my hands and continued speaking, this time quieter since I didn't appreciate the audience. "Uncle, I spent so many years looking for you. I missed you all that time, but I didn't know how to reach you..."

I sat there until the funeral home's men came to fill the grave in. Not having the stomach to watch them, I walked back to my car. The guy who'd been there was now gone, which was good. I wanted to be on my own, and even if he'd known my uncle, I didn't want to hear about a man who hadn't been a part of my life, or worse, hear about how my uncle had been a mentor or father figure in someone else's life, a life that by all rights should've been mine.

I climbed into my rental and drove to a business parking lot nearby, where I let more tears fall. The tears soon turned to anger.

After losing my mom, I'd held onto the thought that even though my dad was an unfeeling jerk, I still had an uncle who loved me. Now he was gone too!

"*I HATE THIS!*" I yelled, slamming my hands on the steering wheel.

I laid my head back, and thought of my mom who would have known just what to say. I missed her. Life wasn't fair. All that was left was *him*... a dad who never showed emotion, excluding the occasional angry outburst when things didn't go his way.

Once I got my feelings under control, I drove to my hotel, and extended my stay. I then called my dad, leaving a message when he didn't answer... not that I expected him to.

"Hey, just got back to the hotel from the funeral. Call me if you want to know how it went. Oh, also, I was approached by an attorney about Uncle Chris's estate, so I'll need to stick around a little longer. I'll call you later. Bye."

I hoped saying what I did would at least spark some kind of emotion, even a greedy reaction would be better than nothing.

I lay in bed that afternoon, thinking about my childhood, and how happy it had been. My uncle was in charge of a huge orange grove somewhere in the Mesa area. I couldn't even find the property on a map now if I wanted to, but I remembered running down the rows of trees, and around Christmas, eating my fill of freshly picked fruit.

My mom had been big on canning things, and we'd had marmalade coming out of our ears. Those were the years my father would laugh. I couldn't quite remember what that sounded like, but I do remember how happy I'd been.

My uncle used to come get me to help with chores, even during the intense heat of the summer, but we'd always stop mid-morning and eat a homemade orange popsicle. He told me you needed to love the product if you were going to be any good at producing it, so we had orange-flavored everything when we were living next to him.

I was probably nine or ten when my father and uncle fell out, but even at that age, I'd understood my life was changing. My stomach rolled with memory and resentment. There was not a lot a kid could do to stop the wheels put in motion by their adults, even if those adults were being idiots.

We'd moved to Atlanta that summer, and I thought I'd die from the humidity. Mesa was hot as Hades, but nothing like Atlanta's heat. I kept asking Mom if I could go back to help Uncle Chris in the fall, and she always shook her head and looked sad, the way she did whenever I mentioned him.

After a while, I stopped asking, then she got sick, and within a few months, she was gone as well.

That was when Dad stopped being Dad. He disappeared into himself, and although he provided for me, kids needed love as well as groceries. That didn't seem to matter though, my dad had turned into an emotional shell. I was eleven when Mom died. I was so angry that I'd lost so much in such a short time. I'd rail at my dad, I'd throw tantrums... but no matter what I did, he never even seemed to notice, or care. Eventually, I learned to live without connections to other humans. My happy place became the memories of my past—the place I escaped to in my mind.

With Uncle Chris's death, all the hope I'd held onto for all those years was dead now too, and I felt lost, empty, and downright pissed off about it.

I arrived at the attorney's office early the next day, wanting to get this over with and get back to Atlanta. The sooner I was out of Mesa, the quicker I could move on from feeling so empty. I'd learned one thing from my father, being busy was a great way to avoid facing your feelings.

The office was a testament to how lucrative the practice of law was. I was immediately led into a conference room with lush thick carpets and gleaming mahogany furniture. The woman placed a bottled water in front of me, smiled, and said, "Mr. Arlington will be with you in a moment."

She was as good as her word and within seconds, the attorney appeared, carrying a folder full of papers.

"Hello again, Mr. Howard. Thank you for coming in."

He spread the papers across the table, walked over to the coffee machine, and poured himself a cup without offering me one, then came back and sat down.

"Did your uncle tell you his plans for the estate?" he asked.

I shook my head. "I haven't spoken to my uncle for a while."

The attorney nodded, but wasn't paying attention.

"Your uncle put a deed restriction on the property. It will have to remain an orange grove."

He looked at me, taking his glasses off, and placing them on the table.

"We can work on that," he said. "I've previously overcome similar deed restrictions in court with some success. The problem with yours is that your uncle made the inheritance contingent on your acceptance of those terms."

I stared at the man for a moment. When he didn't continue, I said, "I'm sorry, what inheritance?"

Mr. Arlington looked momentarily shocked, but quickly hid it.

"Your uncle owned a two-hundred-acre citrus grove in Mesa, Arizona. It is one of the last groves left in the city. Over the past twenty years, the city, state, local businesses as well as others pressured him to sell the property for development, which of course he didn't want to, and hired me in the late nineties to help keep it that way.

"I drew up this will ten years ago, and you were always the sole beneficiary, although two weeks ago he added the deed-restrictions. He was already very sick, so you could probably contest the change that way."

"Don't you have to be confidential about your relationship with him?" I asked, wondering why he'd be willing to talk to me, if he was legally obligated to keep his dealings with my uncle a secret.

"I did, but the will stipulates that I am to act on your behalf after he passed away, so my fiduciary responsibilities are now with you."

"So, I now own a two-hundred-acre citrus grove where the neighbors, municipality, and state are all contentious?"

The man nodded, a nasty grin crossing his ancient face.

"What's the property worth?" I asked.

The attorney pulled out an appraisal, similar to ones I was used to seeing while managing my father's properties.

I blinked at the zeros, the property was worth millions. "You can't be serious!"

The old man nodded.

"So, did my uncle provide a way for me to pay you? Plus, I can only imagine how horrific the tax costs are associated with an inheritance this large."

"The property is itself a corporation. You are inheriting your Uncle's *share, so that* will minimize the taxes." He placed a document in front of me that outlined my costs for acquiring the company and then another which showed the cash reserves.

The money was significant, but having worked through numerous estate transactions while working with my father, I knew the amount would disappear quickly.

"How much do you charge the estate?" I asked.

The old man pointed to the documents that outlined his costs, they were about what I expected, so I didn't complain. Besides, I didn't want to get on the wrong side of him, as I was sure to need his help with what lay ahead of me.

"So, tell me more about the deed restrictions and conditions of the inheritance."

The attorney picked up the papers that said Deed Restriction and pulled out a handwritten note from underneath.

"As I said, you must keep the property as a citrus grove. You may not develop it commercially. There are basic provisions for a home, but that is about the only development potential you have. The company owns the property, so the deed restrictions belong to the board, which I explained to Chris when he asked. As the new president of the board, if you contest the restrictions, the company shares will automatically be sold, and you will be shut out of ownership."

"What will happen to the money?" I asked.

The old man smiled his nasty smile again. "It goes to a variety of charities."

"So, obviously, my uncle hated me," I said.

"No, not at all," the attorney said. "He was just doing business. He felt strongly about the property, and didn't want it developed."

I didn't have anything to say about that, so I just looked down at my hands.

"Are there any other conditions?" I asked.

"Actually, yes. The property must remain your primary residence for a year, and you are to continue the employment of a Mr. Clay Masters who resides on the property. Masters must also approve any sale of the property, which means he basically has the final right of refusal."

I frowned at him, "Who is Clay Masters?"

A look of disgust crossed the attorney's face. "He is some guy your uncle took in."

"Your uncle was adamant that we put him into the conditions."

I just nodded.

"Now what?" I asked.

The attorney smiled. "Now, you decide what we do next. Shall we accept your uncle's conditions, or do we contest them? I warn you though, contesting them will not be easy, because I filled in every loophole I could find."

"I'm confused, didn't you just say that you're *my* attorney."

"I am now." The predatory grin on the old man's face made my stomach churn a bit. "The good news is my partners would enjoy trying to undo my restrictions and conditions, but it would cost you," he said, the ugly smile spreading even wider across his face.

"I see." I immediately recognized the greedy man in front of me. I'd had to deal with them in my work as a contractor. Come hell or high water, I'd never give this man an opportunity to milk me or my uncle's estate dry at least if I could avoid it. I quickly decided to change the subject. "Do I have a place to stay on the estate or did my Uncle give his home to someone else?" I asked.

The attorney looked pained. "You did inherit your uncle's place, but it isn't somewhere I think you'd want to stay. Your uncle lived in a travel trailer that looked to be from the sixties. He wasn't a worldly man but if he had been, then your inheritance would've been significantly less. There are also several buildings on the property, including barns, a restaurant, and commercial properties. One building also had a rental unit in it..." The attorney rummaged through the papers for a list of property improvements and nodded. "Yes, it says here the store has a rental unit attached to it. I dare say, you'd be better off staying there than the trailer."

"Can I take the paperwork with me to read through? I'd also like some time to look over the land and get to know Clay Masters as well. Maybe then, I can get some idea of why my uncle did what he did."

"Yes, that's fine," the attorney said, becoming distracted again. "However—" he abruptly added, before he got up to leave, "—you are restricted on time. You'll need to let me know soon whether or not you wish to contest the will and its conditions. It'll become more difficult the longer you wait."

I nodded, took the paperwork he gave me, and left.

I put the address from the paperwork into my GPS and let it guide me back to the place of my childhood. When I pulled up in front of the old camper the attorney had mentioned, I smiled. There was potential here that the old attorney had missed, because the camper was an old Airstream. I knew several people who'd purchased one, fixed it up, and then moved them to Florida as vacation homes. So, not all that bad after all.

I pulled out the keys went inside. The little place was dated, but clean.

I looked around the space, considering what I could do with it. I sat on the little sofa-table combo and pondered my situation.

Clearly, I had two choices. Give up and let the property be sold, or stay and fight.

My father had obviously influenced me over the years, because I knew I'd never give up without a fight. So, apparently, this was gonna be my new home.

"Sorry, Dad, guess you'll have to find another peon employee to push around," I said out loud.

I went about deciding on my priorities, and realized, first things first, I needed a new mattress, so went to a store and ordered one for same-day delivery, then bought some new bedding. I collected my things from the hotel and checked out, not knowing how long it would be before I got access to my uncle's money, and determined to make my savings to last.

I couldn't help but pray that it wouldn't take long, because my savings weren't significant and would run out quickly.

I got back to the trailer as the mattress was delivered, then did a tally up of what else I needed.

Luckily, due to my uncle being tidy and a bit of a minimalist, there weren't a lot of things for me to deal with, or throw away. The towels and wash cloths were nearly new, and the kitchen was fairly well-stocked.

In his cupboards, I couldn't believe it when I found the orange-related stuff I remembered from my childhood. It made me smile, like the man in my memories really hadn't changed over the years, and somehow I felt closer to him for that.

I began inspecting the cooking supplies, and soon realized my uncle must have never used the Airstream's kitchen.

I guessed the mystery of wherever it was that he ate would solve itself soon enough. Regardless of what he ate, unless the inheritance money came quickly, I'd be mostly eating Ramen noodles like I'd done in college.

Across from the property was a discount grocery store, so I chose to stretch my legs and wandered over. After purchasing some basics, I returned to the trailer and called my father.

"Hey, so I got back from the attorney. Seems Uncle Chris left me his estate, but it's full of deed restrictions that are almost impossible to overcome."

Dad didn't really respond, he just grunted a few times as I explained more.

When I could tell he wasn't going to offer any advice, I said, "Well, I'm going to stick around for a while, and see what I can figure out."

I knew the answer before I asked, but I was nothing if not a glutton for punishment, and asked anyway, "Are you going to be okay without me?"

As usual, he failed to show any concern whether I existed or not, and all I got from him was a noncommittal sound, before responding, "You gotta do what you gotta do."

Thanks Dad, you are such a great help, I thought sarcastically.

I went to sleep that night, feeling as lost as I had when I'd stared into the grave the day before. In my mind, I made a checklist of the things I'd need to know, before I decided what to do. Mostly, I wanted to know what the place looked like. I'd also make a point of meeting this mystery guy, and see if I could figure out what to do about him.

The next morning, I woke up to a knock at the door. I looked at my phone. Who knocked on someone's door at five thirty in the morning?

I pulled on my sweats and answered the door shirtless.

The light was dim, and I could barely make out the older woman in front of me. "Can I help you?" I asked.

The lady smiled. "No, but I can probably help you. I'm Melinda Fitzgibbons, your secretary and office manager. I saw you at the funeral, but you seemed...preoccupied, so I decided to let you get settled in, before I began harassing you with business."

"How did you know I was here?" I asked. She continued smiling.

"Our property manager came by yesterday to check on the Airstream, and noticed you'd settled in. By the time he got in touch with me, you appeared to already be asleep. After the funeral, we thought you could use the rest."

"I see," I said, although I really didn't understand in the least. I was seriously not going to be able to do much to help since I had no idea about the business yet.

"Let me get dressed, and I'll be right with you."

She smiled. "I think you'll want to *come* with me. This was your uncle's getaway space. You'll be much happier getting ready at the apartment attached to the store."

"Oh, that explains a lot," I said. "I'll grab my things. Do you want to come in?" I asked.

She nodded, so I walked to the back of the Airstream where I'd dumped my suitcase the day before, and collected my belongings. We walked out the front door. An ATV was parked in front of the camper, and the woman pointed for me to put my suitcase in the back.

We rode in darkness through the citrus trees towards God only knew where. After what felt like a long ride, we ended up in front of a large commercial building. I followed her around the back and through a door that faced the trees.

The entrance led to a stunning modern apartment that had been recently renovated. The décor was open concept, with a beautiful kitchen and tall cabinets with rich brown and light marble countertops. "Wow, this is different from the Airstream," I said.

Melinda just chuckled. "Your uncle had this redone for you," she said, matter of factly.

I looked at her and cocked my eyebrow. "For me? I hadn't spoken to him in over fifteen years."

"I know," she said. "But, when your uncle found out he was dying, he hired a local company to renovate the apartment. He told me he wanted to make it easy for you to stay."

"I have a lot of questions," I sighed.

Melinda looked sympathetic and nodded. "I'm sure you do, hon. I'll answer as best I can, but I warn you, your uncle wasn't a talkative man. He told me a little about you and the falling out he had with your father—no details, of course—but enough that I know you were *estranged*."

She said the word like it tasted bad in her mouth.

"He wrote you a letter, but I'm not supposed to give that to you... yet. He said he wanted you to learn everything, before you had to become responsible. He used to enjoy watching you play here. I guess he wanted to imagine the little boy coming back and playing here again."

I nodded, bewildered by the man who'd left me an incredibly valuable property with a million and one restrictions. It almost seemed impossible to reconcile the uncle I remembered with all that'd recently happened,

"You get ready, and I'll be in the store getting things put together. Your uncle gave me explicit instructions on how to manage your stay." She turned to go, then paused and looked back toward where I was standing. "This isn't going to be easy for a grown man to process. I seriously think the old man still thought of you as a child, but I've been given very clear instructions to follow. I loved your uncle, not only as an employer, but as a friend. I'll follow his last wishes to the letter, but please understand, I sympathize with the discomfort you're going to feel." She sighed. "You come get me when you are ready, and we'll go for breakfast. Your uncle even specified where." She chuckled as she left. "I hope you're hungry!"

I walked back into the renovated apartment, and dumped my few belongings on the king-size bed. My uncle must have hired a designer, because the place was styled like the pages of a magazine. I went into the master bathroom and gasped. The shower was the size of a small room with multiple showerheads. The place looked like an HGTV remodel.

The shower was so complicated that I accidentally soaked myself when I tried it. So, I locked the door and stripped down before I tried again, playing with the different knobs until I figured out which did what.

With all the different directions the water was coming at me, it took a moment to get used to it. When I did, I readily admitted I understood why someone would want to shower this way, the water massaged everywhere.

Someone had stocked the bathroom with shower gels, shampoo, and conditioner, like the ones in the ritzy hotel my father had been hired to build in Atlanta a few years back. I'd snuck around before the hotel officially opened. It was way swankier than I ever thought I'd use in my lifetime. Now, apparently, I owned something equivalent.

After getting dressed, I left the apartment to meet Melinda. I was in for my second surprise when I walked into the area of the building dedicated to the store. This wasn't the store I remembered as a child with concrete floors, and makeshift tables that held the bushels of oranges and lemons from the groves. Instead, this was a modern boutique with cute choochkies that represented the grove perfectly. I wandered around, looking at the merchandise, almost picking up a few items for myself, before I remembered I wasn't a customer, but the owner of the company that ran the store.

When I looked, I saw Melinda watching me with a smile.

"So, what do you think of the store?" she asked.

"It's really different from the one I remember."

Melinda's smile widened. "I'm sure it is. When you were a kid, this entire building was used as storage. The apartment was cold storage. At the time, a lot more people came to buy fruit. In fact, several of the smaller groves used to bring their fruit for us to sell. Things changed a lot after your family left. Smaller grove owners sold out, and our need for storage diminished. Your uncle got tired of living in the Airstream, and he refused to live in the house your parents had occupied, so he converted half of this building into his apartment."

She leaned back on the desk that held the register and smiled sadly.

"Over time, the citrus industry left Mesa. A few people still came to the grove to buy fruit, but it got to the point where we were sending most of our produce to the packing house downtown. The packing house shut down about ten years ago. It was either take our produce down to Yuma's packing house, or figure out a way to increase our own traffic.

"So..." She waved her hands around the shop. "With my help, of course, your uncle turned this into what you see today."

I could tell she was proud of the shop. "It is beautiful," I told her, turning around again and taking it all in. "When I first came in, I started shopping for myself, before I realized what I was doing."

"Then I did my job," she laughed, as she walked over to me.

"They'll be plenty of time for you to learn about the shop. Your uncle's plans are for you to work with me soon enough. He thought you could learn the value of what we do, by starting with the end product. Therefore, we're supposed to visit Linda Mae over at the Square Biscuit."

"Huh?" I asked.

"You'll just have to see for yourself," Melinda said mysteriously.

We climbed into the ATV and took off through the trees. The sun had still not risen, but I was able to glimpse rays of light between the trees on the eastern skyline.

We took what looked to be a well-worn path. Melinda was silent, and I didn't really know what was going on. I was still reeling from all the things I'd learned this morning such as owning a beautiful apartment and a remarkable store, all before dawn!

I could hear traffic as we came out of the trees, and before long we arrived at a main intersection. Melinda pulled the ATV into a parking lot that was much more crowded than I would expect for the time of the morning.

I was shocked when she pulled almost up to the front door. There was a plaque on the wall in front of the spot that read, "Reserved for Grove Owner."

"This is where we're going," Melinda said, and climbed out of the vehicle, smiling.

I followed her inside, surprised to see what appeared to be a nineteen-fifties diner filled with customers. Even the seats at the counter were full.

Melinda made her way through the crowd, and several people wished her a good morning. Finally, we passed through a side door into a busy kitchen. I had no idea where we were going, but apparently, Melinda did, so I followed her.

Melinda stopped in the kitchen, and the staff swarmed around us. Finally, an older woman who looked to be in her mid-eighties noticed Melinda, and frowned.

"Why are you in here, Melinda?" the woman asked crossly.

"Mom, this is Chris's nephew, Joshua."

The woman's face went from disdain to joy in a matter of seconds. Before I anticipated it, I found myself embraced in a hug.

"Oh, sweet boy, I haven't seen you in too long." She pulled back and looked me up and down.

The woman was about the same height as Melinda, but slightly slumped with age. Despite that, I could tell from the grip she had on my arms that she was still stronger than most old women.

Melinda looked at her mom. "So, as Chris instructed, you have him first. Joshua is to be fed a good meal, then he has to work with you for his first week here."

"What?" I asked. "I don't know anything about restaurants."

"Oh, you don't worry about that, honey," the woman said. "Old Linda Mae will teach you."

Melinda chuckled, but not so the woman could hear her.

I turned to Melinda. "I thought you said I was working with you."

"You will...at least, you will *later*. As I said, your uncle wanted you to learn about the end product first and the restaurant is where a lot of the oranges are used. She pointed to a machine sitting on the wall. "That's an orange juice squeezer and we use it a lot."

"I see," was all I could say.

Melinda smiled again. "No, you probably don't, but you will. Remember, this is all predetermined by your uncle. I recommend you roll with the punches. If you do, it shouldn't be as bad as you're probably thinking it is."

I sighed. "I don't really think I have much of an option."

"You're in good hands with Linda Mae. She's trained a lot of people. I'll be back to pick you up after closing time."

"When is that?" I asked.

"We only serve breakfast and lunch, so the store closes at two. You should be done and ready to leave by three."

I nodded. "I guess I'll see you at three."

Melinda was smiling broadly when she turned to back towards the dining room. If that was any indication, I was about to get quite an education.

Chapter Two

Clay

My morning started like normal. I dragged myself out of bed, showered, then pushed down the ever-present depression.

I'd never been a morning person, and until coming to Mesa, I'd never really had to be... That being said, there were benefits to this area as well. Growing up in Jersey, there were always people around, and I hadn't appreciated the simple joys of working in solitude, without interruptions, until I began working alone among the trees. The longer I lived in the relative peace of the groves, the more I healed. The pain didn't hit me in tidal waves any longer. Instead, it seemed to only wash over me early morning, or late at night.

This morning was like all the rest. I forced my eyes open when they'd rather stay shut. Feeling particularly proud of myself, however, I only hit the snooze button a few times, meaning, I got up a full thirty minutes earlier than usual.

I spent most of my time among the trees, which I didn't mind when I wasn't freshly showered. Melinda, however, had called last night to tell me to be at Linda Mae's early today though, so I knew I was going to meet the infamous nephew. I'd seen him by the graveside all tears and drama. I felt sick, knowing the old man would've been repulsed by all the attention. But I'd seen my share of dramatic family members. Even at my own family's funeral, people I'd never met, but was supposedly related to, cried like the people in the caskets were their own parents and husband.

Me, I didn't cry at all. The Asperger's probably had something to do with it. I functioned well enough emotionally. I mean I *have* emotions and could recognize those emotions in other people, but sometimes they confused me. Sometimes, I didn't react the same way others did. My mom helped me navigate the feelings, and without her, I often felt like a fish out of water.

A few family members told me I was a ticking time bomb, which I didn't really understand. I wasn't going to go off emotionally! I was *already* destroyed. The explosion had happened when the police called my cell phone, and told me I no longer had a family.

When I got to the restaurant, Linda Mae was in a typically sour mood. She did smile at me when I walked in, but I guessed that was more of an accident than her being happy to see me. It seemed to me Linda Mae spent most of her life looking like she'd eaten a sour orange. But, no matter the sharp disposition, the woman cooked like no one I'd met before. Sour oranges or not, I was always happy to see her. We were related. She was my grandmother by birth, but she didn't pretend I was anything more than one of the people that worked here. I know it was strange, but I sort of liked that about her.

Within moments of my walking in, Linda Mae plopped my usual breakfast order of biscuits and gravy down in front of me, then she followed that with the fresh orange juice this place was known for.

"Thanks, Linda Mae," I said. She just *hmphed*, but I swear I almost saw another smile cross her face. How on earth was it that I almost got two smiles out of the woman in one morning?

A moment later, I understood what was happening. Melinda walked into the restaurant with the man from the graveside behind her. *How is it that he's even better looking up close.*

Melinda strode through the restaurant, and the man followed behind her, eyes darting around the room and frowning. Shortly after they'd walked into the kitchen, I heard Linda Mae's voice carry. I'd never heard the woman sound so excited to see someone—not even *me*, and I was the prodigal grandson returned to the fold... at least after my adopted parents had... passed.

When Melinda came back out, she was alone. She crossed the crowded room and sat with me.

"This should be fun to watch," she said, with a mischievous grin.

"What's going on?" I asked.

"Oh, Linda Mae's got her clutches into Chris's nephew."

"That seems rather cruel. Didn't he just get to the grove yesterday?"

"Yep," Melinda replied. "Wasn't my doing. All this is what Chris asked for. He has the next few weeks outlined for the boy."

"That so?" I asked.

"You know very well he does," Melinda said with a chuckle. "I know you and Chris talked about it. In fact, he even told me that if something didn't work out, I was to come get you, so don't play innocent."

"I know there's an agenda, and I have instructions on what to do if he refuses to abide by the rules, but I don't know the particulars. It all seems a bit cloak and dagger to me."

"Well, it is, sort of. But you know Chris. He never did anything without a reason. From what he told me, he didn't know the boy very well. I'm guessing he wanted to see if he had what it takes to keep the legacy alive."

"Some legacy," I said, shaking my head.

The grove had been steadily losing money for the past five years. At least since I'd arrived. Yes, it still turned a profit, but the days of running this place, as it had been in the past, were about over. I'd tried to explain that to the old man on more than one occasion, but he kept putting me off.

Chris had some magical idea about this nephew of his. "He'll know what to do, we just have to make sure he has enough time to get his bearings."

From the display I saw at the graveside, I seriously doubted that, but who was I to contradict? I assumed he was acting like people expected him to that day and his ridiculous good looks and tight little body made me guess he got most anything he went after... I forced myself to shake the judgmental thoughts out of my head. I didn't know the man, and even my jaded brain knew better than to judge a book by its cover.

As usual, Linda Mae ignored Melinda, but one of the servers brought out a plate of eggs and bacon as well as French toast. Melinda's usual breakfast.

"How long are you two going to be at each other's throats?" I asked.

"Mom is a master at holding grudges. Last time I pissed her off this much, she didn't talk to me for several years. She's still talking to me, though, so I'm guessing it'll take less time than last."

"You going to tell me what you did this time?"

Melinda leaned over the table and patted my hand. "Nope."

"Suit yourself," I replied, not really caring one way or the other.

Shortly after that, Linda Mae came out of the kitchen with the nephew close behind her. She was talking a mile a minute. I made out something about squeezing oranges, and how his uncle wanted him to learn the old-fashioned way first, before he switched to the machine.

The look on the pretty boy's face was worth the early morning start. His expression held both embarrassment and worry at the same time. Linda Mae led him through the crowded room like no one was there, dodging customers and chairs as she went.

The nephew took significantly longer to get through the crowd than the experienced restaurateur. When Linda Mae turned to talk to him, he was still only halfway across the room. He'd got stuck behind a group of men who'd stood to go, and were still hugging each other. Linda Mae returned to pull him through the crowd with her.

They disappeared into the cold-storage area, and reemerged with the nephew carrying a large box of oranges. If navigating the crowd was hard for him before, this would be amusing. I half expected Linda Mae to turn her full temper on him like I'd seen her do to other new staff. Instead, she walked with him, helping him navigate the room, until they were both back behind the counter.

I looked over at Melinda. "What on earth has happened to your mother?"

Melinda was clearly as stunned as I was, and instead of responding, she merely shrugged. "I think hell must have frozen over."

"Apparently," I replied, and we both turned our attention back to Linda Mae and whatever his name was. Neither of us had touched our food, both too interested in watching the show.

"Wanna make a bet? I say Linda Mae bursts a blood vessel before closing today. No way my mother can be nice all day long."

"Oh no, I'm not taking that bet. I don't want to give you money for something obvious."

"I seriously have no idea what's got into the woman," Melinda said. "When I read that Chris wanted his nephew to work for Mom the first couple of days, I thought it was because he was trying to scare the kid off. You don't suppose Chris talked her into being nice, do you?"

"Anything could happen, I guess. Did Linda Mae seem surprised when you introduced her to him?"

"Yeah, actually, she was in a typical bad mood when I walked in with him, but the moment she saw him, she lit up like a light bulb. Totally out of character for her."

We both turned back toward the two of them, riveted by what might happen next. Neither of us believed Linda Mae would keep the pleasant attitude up for long.

As we watched, the older woman gave the man an apron. She then sat him behind the counter, placed a cutting board in front of him, and proceeded to show him how to cut the oranges and use the juicer. "Make sure you don't have your hand in the way of the machine. I've done that a couple times myself, and it hurts, let me tell you!"

Linda Mae was chatting away like she'd been snatched by aliens and replaced with a different person.

"Okay," Melinda said. "This is getting creepy."

"I agree," I replied.

After a moment of staring at them, I asked, "Why are they using that old thing? I thought it was for decoration only."

"Well, Linda Mae threw a fit when Chris put the automatic Vevor juicer in, although, it's cut her work time down by fifty percent. I haven't seen her train anyone on that old thing in years, but she keeps it clean and shiny. When I had to fill in here, she made me clean it every day."

"Well, it seems she is training the guy the old-fashioned way."

"Do you not know his name?" Melinda asked, noticing I'd avoided saying it since she'd sat down.

"Yeah, Josh or Joshua, something like that. Chris told me, but after seeing him at the funeral, I figured he wouldn't last long enough for me to need to remember."

I looked back over at the man who was cutting up his oranges, and squeezing them just as Linda Mae had shown him.

"Maybe I'm wrong. I haven't heard him complain... yet."

Melinda shrugged. "He's been like a deer in headlights since I picked him up this morning. Who knows? Only time will tell."

We finished eating and left the diner. The sun had just come up when we walked out of the restaurant together. "What are your plans today?" she asked.

"I'm running the dogs this morning. I'm hoping to deal with the voles. They've taken over the western groves again. I swear those rodents are going to be the end of me."

Melinda nodded with sympathy. It was a subject she must've heard year after year in the orange groves. Voles and disease were two of our greatest concerns regarding the trees.

"I've got Dude in the kennel behind the store," she said. "Little brat tried to bite me again this morning."

"Yeah, sorry about that, I'll stop by to get him later."

I waved as we went our separate ways.

When I'd first arrived at the groves, Chris had just come back from surgery. He'd been bedridden for at least a month, and the orange groves were in bad shape. I'd spent some time on a grove that belonged to my late husband's family in Florida, so I had some understanding of how to manage pests.

My late husband's family had a Jack Russell Terrier, who did an amazing job. So, when I arrived to find the voles had destroyed over a third of the orange trees, I went online to learn about the breed. As fate would have it, there were two dogs at a local shelter, and so I volunteered to foster them until they found them a permanent home.

It took a bit for them to know what I wanted them to do, but when the little female got scent of one of the rodents, they both took to managing the pests like fish take to water.

Over the years, we've collected several dogs. Most were fostered to families around the groves, with the exception of three nasty little beasts. Dude, Buddy, and Clip.

Those three cantankerous young males weren't able to be in a family environment. All three bad boys had a variety of nasty habits. One was a biter, one peed on everything, and one destroyed furniture and shoes.

No matter how many foster homes we tried, none worked. So, Chris took one, and I took the other two. Melinda had agreed to take Chris's pup, Dude, after he got too sick to take care of him, but that one was the biter, and she was always complaining he tried to attack her customers. I knew I'd need to take Dude off her hands before long, but as it was, my two, Buddy and Clip, were almost more than I could handle.

I picked Dude up on my way. Luckily, our three troublemakers loved to work the groves, so I seldom had problems with them, while they were working at least. I'd built a kennel on the back of my ATV to put the dogs in when I traveled between areas. Each of my workers had the same setup, and they were all assigned a team of dogs to accompany them while they worked the trees. The three troublemakers were always assigned to me.

Dude, Buddy and Clip always greeted each other by circling around and trying to pee on the same spot the others had. If they weren't so freaking difficult to manage, they'd be cute to watch, but ever since I'd had my first pee spot to clean up, and Clip had dispatched a pair of boots I'd just bought, I wasn't as inclined to see them as cute.

I was working on a broken irrigation system in the eastern part of the groves when Melinda called and told me she was swamped at the store. "Can you pick Joshua up from Linda Mae's?"

"Um, I don't have a clue where Clip or Buddy are at the moment. It might take me a while before I can round them up."

"No problem, Mom said she has some extra work for him to do, so just get there when you can."

"What do you want me to do with him once I get him?" I asked.

"Show him a good time," Melinda teased.

"Yeah, right. I need a man like a fish needs a bicycle," I recited.

That had become my favorite mantra since Melinda found out I was gay, and took it upon herself to fix me up. Melinda and I had a great relationship, except for the fact that she was obsessed with finding me someone, which drove me nuts. I never wanted to date again. I'd had my perfect marriage, and now that part of my life was done.

"I'm swamped, Clay. And we just got word that a tour group is coming in at four. My shelves are almost bare from the morning rush. If you can entertain him, I'd appreciate it."

"Okay, okay, but don't expect me to be all weird like your mother. If the man is going to be here, he can work like the rest of us," I grumbled.

"Just remember, that man is technically our boss."

"Yeah, I can quit and leave him to fix this outdated irrigation system and chase down the devil hounds if he wants to be the boss."

"Oh, don't get your panties in a wad," Melinda responded teasingly. "Just go get him. If he wants, you can take him back to the apartment or the Airstream. Either way, I can't really deal with him right now."

"Okay, I'll get him. Then you owe me! Wanna grab a beer tonight at Luey's?"

"Not tonight, honey, I've got a date. Remember, I told you about him."

"Oh yeah," I sighed.

"Why don't you take Joshua with you. I'm sure he'd like to get out."

"Yeah, right, no thank you," I replied. "I think I'd rather stay at home and drink alone."

Melinda laughed, but quickly broke off. I could hear her talking to someone in the background.

"Clay, I've got to go, the next wave is about to hit. Apparently, the group is an hour early. God help me."

"Go," I said. "I'll handle the pampered nephew."

When Melinda hung up, I exclaimed. "Like I've got time to deal with nonsense, I bet if I say boo, he'll be bawling his eyes out like he did at the graveside," I said out loud. Reaching into my pocket, I pulled out my secret weapon for dog retrieval.

I'd been working on whistle training the three, and it worked well for Buddy, who was food motivated. The other two seemed to come maybe a third of the time, but all of them ignored the whistle if they were on the scent of a vole.

I sent up a silent prayer and blew the whistle.

It only took a couple seconds, before Buddy burst through the trees ready for his treat. I was just about to give it to him, when the other two appeared as well.

"Well, I'll be, when was the last time all three of you came after just one whistle?"

The dogs sat watching me with a *duh* look on their faces.

"Oh, I get it, you're excited to see me deal with the nephew. This is a conspiracy, I tell you. Don't think I don't know you're all ganging up on me!"

Clip jumped up and barked at me, causing me to laugh. Well, at least the dog's antics had shifted the sour mood I'd developed at having to deal with the new guy. I looked over at the dogs who were staring at me, and shook my head. I'd swear sometimes those dogs seemed to know what I was saying. The conspiracy comment wasn't just a joke.

I put the three into their kennel on the ATV, and gave them each a treat, then drove over to pick up Joshua.

When I arrived, Linda Mae and Joshua were sitting behind the restaurant, while Linda Mae smoked a cigarette. "It sure took you long enough to get here, I've worked the socks off this poor boy. I'm sure he'd like to get home and cleaned up."

"Mrs. Linda Mae, it wasn't bad at all. I enjoyed it more than anything I've done in a very long time," the nephew said.

"Your daddy always was a dictator," Linda Mae replied. "That man..." She shook her head. "...he almost made me cry once and I don't *ever* cry."

"Well," Josh or Joshua, or whatever the crap his name was, replied, "He hasn't changed much, I can tell you, but I've never minded hard work. It makes the day go quicker."

Linda Mae clearly liked that answer. "You do him and your uncle proud, young man." She wiped a tear away, not even trying to hide it. Since when did the rusty iron lady cry in public? "I just couldn't bear to go to his funeral. Your uncle was like family to me."

Joshua put his arm around the older woman and pulled her into his side. "I wish I'd been able to spend more time with him," he said.

I could tell he meant it. Maybe the remorse I'd seen had been more than just trying to make an impression.

Linda pulled away. "Okay, you get on with your day. I'll see you bright and early tomorrow. I only get you for a few more days, and I want you to have a chance to wait on a few customers before Melinda sweeps you away to play in that cutesy little store of hers," she said, with an effort to look contemptuous, but instead, the pride for her daughter seeped out. Even Joshua seemed to notice it.

"Well, I don't know what she and Chris planned for me, but if you ever need me, you just let me know. I'd love to learn more about the restaurant. This was my first time ever working in one."

Linda Mae looked shocked. "Really?" she asked. "You seemed to take to it well enough."

The man smiled. "You're just being nice. I was a total klutz, and we both know it."

"Fat chance," I heard myself say, before I realized I was speaking out loud.

Linda Mae looked at me with her *I could squish you like a bug* expression. She turned back to Joshua and said, "He's right, I don't give out compliments that aren't deserved."

"Now, the two of you run on. I'm going home to put my piggies up for a rest. We'll see you tomorrow morning, Joshua."

With that, Linda Mae put out her cigarette, and went back inside.

"Appears you've been dismissed," I said to the man, who watched her disappear.

"Well, that was fun," he said, then he turned back to me. "I thought Melinda was picking me up."

"She was," I replied. "But she got caught up with a tour group at the store. Apparently, I have nephew duty now."

"Nephew duty?" he asked, and cast a sideways glance my way.

"You," I replied, my sour mood returning, now that the shock of seeing Linda Mae being nice to someone was wearing off.

Just as I was about to really be nasty, the man noticed the boys in the back of the ATV.

"What have we got here?" he asked, and all three dogs began to clamber at the kennel door.

"Aren't you the cutest little monsters in the world!" he exclaimed, and to my horror, he opened the door and reached in.

Before I could move, he'd pulled Dude out of the cage and was holding him way too close to his face. Luckily, the man seemed to know to shut the door before the other two escaped, but the inevitable nip was just over the horizon. And sure enough, Dude chomped on the man's finger before he could get another word in.

Like a burst of lightning, the man had Dude on the ground, with his hand held gently to the dog's chest.

"No bite!" the man said in a stern voice.

Dude was squirming around trying to get loose from Joshua's grip, but although it was clear he wasn't applying much pressure, the dog was stuck in a subordinate position on his back.

Dude growled and kicked, and tried to scratch, but the man didn't give.

Finally, he sat down next to the dog, not moving his hand.

"What are you doing!" I finally asked.

"What you should've already done," the man replied, with just a touch of venom in his voice.

"You can't have a dog that bites people. Have you not done any training with him?"

I was so shocked by his comment that I didn't know how to reply.

"That's a working dog. He's trained to hunt voles, and he wouldn't have bitten you if you hadn't taken him out of the kennel without permission."

"That's true, and I apologize both for taking him out without permission, and for snapping at you, but that doesn't excuse his behavior."

Dude grew calm, and although he was shaking like a leaf, he'd relaxed on the ground, looking away from Joshua.

"That's good, that's much better. Are you ready to get up?" Dude growled again, but this time he refused to look Joshua in the eye.

Joshua let up his hand, and the dog sat up and was about to run. Before he could pounce, Joshua put his hand on the dog's back and ordered, "No, stay!"

To my surprise, Dude did just that.

Joshua put him back in the kennel. Clip and Buddy, having watched the entire scene go down, were cowed in the corner.

Joshua eyed the dogs as he put Dude back in with his friends and closed the door.

"You don't have much of a training program with these dogs, I see. Do you not watch the *Dog Whisperer*?" he asked.

"The what?" I replied.

"You know the show, *The Dog Whisperer*?" Joshua stared at me for a moment, then shook his head. "You should Google it. If you're going to own Jack Russell Terriers, you should have a better understanding of what it means to be the alpha dog in your pack. Otherwise..." Joshua held up his bloody finger so I could see. "...this happens."

Joshua looked at his own finger. "I assume they're current with their vaccines, especially rabies?"

"We aren't totally incompetent," I replied, although I could hear the childish way that sounded. He'd rubbed me the wrong way, insinuating that I had somehow neglected my duties as a dog owner, because my dog bit him. Dang, it was him that reached into the kennel in the first place.

"Well, that's good to know," he said. I could see he was shutting down now that the adrenaline had passed.

"Can you drop me off at the apartment? I could use another shower."

I should have probably said yes, but the guy had pissed me off, and since he didn't have a clue what was on his uncle's agenda, I decided to give him a workout and see what he had in him.

"No, I'm sorry, but you won't need a shower for what we're doing."

I drove us both back over to the broken irrigation system, released the dogs back into the trees, and showed Joshua what we were working on.

The old irrigation system had been clogged before it broke, and it needed to be washed out. Now, nasty clogged drains were something of a legend in these parts. You'd think the slime in a system would just dry out under the intense heat of the desert, but that was often not the case. The clogs would often sit in the system and fester until they were a disgusting, slimy, decaying mess. That was the situation with the system I was working on today.

I handed Joshua the snake we used to clean out clogs, and said, "Your job is to remove the debris, while I get the water working. When you're done, we'll connect the joints and get it back up and running."

To my surprise, the man picked up the snake, went to the pipe I'd pointed to, and without further instruction, began to snake out the clog. The job usually took me a while to get the mess out, but I watched in amazement as Joshua pushed the snake in then did some weird trick where he flipped the snake around two or three times. When he pulled it back out, a huge mass of black festering goo slid out of the end of the pipe. The smell was so intense, I almost gagged. When I regained my composure, I looked at him. He was over at the water faucet washing off the snake. He didn't seem fazed by the nastiness at all.

"What did you do?" I asked. "Clearing out these clogs usually takes me an hour at least."

Joshua looked at me over his shoulder, and smiled. "I'm a licensed plumber, at least in the state of Georgia. That's a little trick one of my buddies taught me. You have to use the clasp at the end to gather up as many angles of the clog as you can, and if you get lucky, you can pull it out all at once. Don't get your hopes up though, it doesn't work all the time, but when it does, it's impressive, no?"

"Yeah, pretty impressive," I replied, sort of dumbfounded.

"I'm just about done cleaning this snake. Want any help with the valve?"

"Um, I probably have it, unless you have another trick up your sleeve to make it faster."

Joshua looked at the pipe connections in my hand, and smiled. "Nope, unfortunately, there's no faster way to connect pipe than what you're doing, at least not any I'm aware of."

I just nodded and continued with the job.

Joshua was sitting under one of the trees watching me work. "We haven't been introduced yet, so I don't know your name. You've been calling me the nephew, so I'm assuming you might not know mine either. I'm Joshua."

I looked at the guy for a moment. "Yeah, I know your name. I'm Clay."

I'd swear the guy's eyes opened wide at the mention of my name, then he looked at me funny like he was trying to figure something out.

"*You* are Clay Masters?" he asked.

I looked up from my work, and replied, "Yep."

Chapter Three

Joshua

Clay Masters was one heap of handsome, masculine, angry male, who seemed to handle his job very well. So well, in fact, that he pressed every button in me. *God, I'm hopeless...*

He might not have a clue how to train and handle dogs, as was indicated by the bite marks hidden under the band-aid on my finger, but he seemed competent enough to manage the other things he was working on. But, I could tell he was a take-charge kind of guy. My stupid sexually deprived brain could just imagine how it'd feel to have him take charge in the bedroom. Now, *that* was a fantasy worth having...

Before we started working, I used his first-aid kit to clean and bandage the bite. The dog had already had its shots, but I'd call the drugstore later to see if I could get a tetanus booster. I knew I was due for one, and working in construction, you never let that lapse, and if you did, you got any wound covered immediately.

I was shocked that he let the dogs run wild after we'd arrived at the job site. Jacks were notorious for being runners, but I kept my counsel to myself, especially after the biting incident.

I sat under the tree, thinking about the man who held so much power over me and my inheritance. I'd learned long ago, to keep my libido out of things that had to do with business. So, I ruthlessly ripped my sexual attraction for this guy out of my mind, and thought back to what the attorney had said. Expansion depended on this guy's approval, and although I still had no idea what I was dealing with here, I doubted I'd ever be a full-time orange farmer. So, at some point, we'd have to deal with one another, professionally.

He was clearly a jerk, but I decided I should try to get to know him a little better anyway. If I could get on his good side, it might help matters in the future.

"I probably should get a tetanus booster for this bite. Do the drugstores around here do them?" I asked.

"I'm not a doctor, so you'll have to figure that out on your own," he replied, without looking up.

So, this was how we were going to do this.

"Okay, I think I'll go figure it out then." Maybe it wouldn't be so easy to get on his good side after all.

I walked off in the direction I'd seen the dogs go, although I had no reason to believe I'd run into them. By now they were probably in Flagstaff.

I pulled my phone out and did a quick search for drugstores that had urgent-care clinics and made the call. I silently thanked the universe that Mesa had grown up around the groves, or I doubted I'd have had enough cell coverage for this call, much less the data for a search.

The first place I called was located less than a mile from where I was standing, so I booked an appointment for what I thought would be less than a thirty-minute walk.

I went back to where Clay was still working. "I found a place just down the road. I'm going to run over and get a quick shot."

"Yeah, do what you want," he said.

I could be wrong, but I thought there actually could be something going on with the guy's head, or maybe he was just a jerk. I couldn't tell, and I didn't care or rather I was convincing myself not to care. *No matter, I'll just do my thing and let him do his.*

I was sure a mile walk along a sidewalk would've been thirty minutes. Heck, I knew from experience that was what it took, but this was no sidewalk. I was darting through trees, up ravines, and at one point, I found myself stranded on the side of a canal that ran down the middle of the groves. I walked forever before I found a bridge, then that much more time before I got to the clinic.

I arrived just moments before they closed, but luckily, the nurse practitioner had gotten the shot ready when I called.

"You look like you've been wandering through a forest," she said, when I sat down for the shot.

"Yeah, that's because I have," I replied. "I was in the middle of the orange grove across the street when I called. I had no idea what I had to go through to get here. That's why I'm so late."

The woman nodded, but I could tell she didn't really understand what I'd gone through. I doubted many people in the Mesa area had actually walked through a two-hundred-acre orange grove.

I called a taxi to pick me up after I was done with my shot. I asked the driver to take me back to the apartment, and I went in without letting Melinda know where I was. It had been a full day, and I was feeling more than a little done with it.

I walked in, went directly to the shower and climbed inside.

Now, the shower had been nice this morning, but after working with Linda Mae earlier, and that dragon man this afternoon, as well as walking aimlessly through orange trees, the water from the massage jets was amazing. I know I moaned like I was in the middle of an orgasm as the jets hit my tired back and legs.

I crawled out of the shower, dried off, fell onto the bed, and instantly into a hard sleep.

Chapter Four

Clay

When I took Dude to drop him off with Melinda, she was just closing the store. "So, how did Joshua's rest of the day go?" she asked.

"Fine, for the time he was with me. He left after an hour, though, and I haven't seen him since."

Melinda looked at me like I'd grown a horn. "What? He left you to go where? When?"

"Melinda, what's the big deal? He's a grown man. He can go where he wants."

Melinda continued to look at me for a long moment, before she asked, "You pissed him off, didn't you?"

"No, well... I don't think I did. He was worried because Dude bit him, so he wanted a shot, or something."

"*What?*" Melinda all but yelled. "Dude bit him?"

"Yeah, but not badly. It was just a scratch."

"It was something he was concerned enough about to go get a shot. Where did he go?"

I shrugged. "I'm not sure. He said something about going to a drugstore."

"Dear God," Melinda said under her breath. "Clay, how did he get to the drugstore?"

"I... I don't know. I assume he walked."

Melinda looked like her head was about to explode. "Clay, please tell me you didn't make that man walk all the way to the drugstore that's clear on the other side of the grove."

"Um, well..."

Melinda pointed to a chair beside the storage-room door. "Sit here. I'm going to go see if I can find him. You better hope he's in the apartment, or else you're going to get to spend your evening looking for him, and hope to God he isn't lost!"

I sat, knowing that when Melinda was mad, no one in their right mind crossed her. I had to resist doing my number game. The one where I counted up and down my fingers over and over to self-soothe. I tried to resist doing it in public, because it made people uncomfortable, but when I was nervous, or had gotten into trouble, it was my go to for calming down. I counted to fifty and took several deep breaths.

After a few minutes, Melinda came back, a look of pure anger etched across her face.

"You stay right where you are," she said. "I'm going to cancel my date, and you and I are going to have a heart to heart."

"W-wait, Melinda, you can't cancel your date, you've been looking forward..."

Melinda held her hand up to stop me. "You're right. I've been looking forward to this for a long time, but tonight your stinking attitude needs to be dialed down a bit, before you wreck all our worlds. So, wait there!"

She left me and went into her office. I could see her talking on the phone, and as she spoke, I felt my heart break for her.

Melinda was my birth mom. She'd given me up for adoption at birth, but the adoption was open, and I'd known about her since I was little. We corresponded on and off, especially when I was in high school. At that age I'd hated everything to do with my parents, but Melinda wasn't much help, continually telling me about how evil Linda Mae was, and how lucky I was to have parents who didn't hate me as much as I hated them.

To my surprise, Melinda ended up being more of a best friend than a parent after I'd moved to Mesa. I'd lost my entire family, and been asked to leave Florida by my late husband's parents. Melinda never asked for the details.

We'd never really discussed the adoption either, or why she decided not to keep me. I was never strong on emotions, so I was happy we'd developed the friendship, despite our familial connections. Unfortunately, at the moment, the woman was spitting mad, and I knew I had some very uncomfortable moments waiting for me.

I had no idea what I'd done that was so bad she needed to cancel her date, but Melinda was never melodramatic. If something had upset her, there was a good reason.

When she came back, her face was even more furious than it had been before.

"Come with me," she said, and walked toward the back door.

She got into the driver's seat of the ATV, and motioned for me to get in.

We rode across the grove in silence toward Luey's, the bar we liked to go to sometimes after work.

When we went in, Melinda yelled to the server to bring two beers over. "What kind?" the girl asked.

"It don't matter, whatever is cheapest," she replied.

There was music to face, and I knew that from the moment Melinda canceled her date, but God help us, if she was drinking cheap beer, I'd really stepped in it. Melinda was an alcohol snob. She didn't usually drink beer, but if she did, it was always imported, and it was always expensive.

"Melinda," I said with a sigh. "Is it really that bad?"

"Yes," she said matter of factly.

Usually, when we went to Luey's, we sat at the bar, or at a table up front, so we could socialize as people walked in. Luey had a room in the back where the occasional couple would go to neck, but mostly it wasn't used for anything. Melinda led me into the back room, sat down at a table far away from the rest of the crowd, and gestured for me to sit across from her.

The server brought our beers over. "You might as well bring another round in a moment." The girl looked shocked. Melinda could spend an entire evening at Luey's and never buy more than one beer. Although the young woman was still new, she knew our routine well enough to know if Melinda was buying rounds before we'd even started talking, it was a big deal.

"You're scaring me, Melinda. Was the man hurt or something?"

"Or something," she replied.

She then looked around one last time, leaned back in her chair, and sighed a deep sigh. After taking a long sip of the cheap beer, she put the glass down with a slam and said, "You are screwing things up."

"What? Screwing what up?" I asked.

"Joshua," she replied. "You are messing up the plan that Chris worked out."

"What plan, and how am *I* messing it up?"

Melinda sighed again. "Chris didn't want it to be public knowledge, but he had this all planned out. Clay honey, you're a part of those plans, I know he discussed them with you."

Melinda paused, and for a moment, it appeared she was going to cry, but she shook herself out of it, and said, "You loved Chris, right, like the rest of us?"

I nodded.

"You've also worked here long enough to know that Chris never did anything without a plan, right?"

I nodded again.

"Then you need to listen to me very carefully, because you are on the verge of undoing Chris's last wishes, and if you do, we are all screwed." She took a deep breath.

"Joshua and Chris were estranged. Chris hadn't seen his nephew since he was a boy. Joshua's dad and Chris got into it over something, and hadn't spoken since. Joshua was Chris's heir, so he kept tabs on him, but because the dad wouldn't talk to Chris, he had to do it through private investigators. I remember when he first got information about the boy. He came over to Linda Mae and me, and showed us what he'd found out. I'll never forget how proud he was. Joshua was still really young then. He'd graduated from high school with honors, and Chris had an article about him being the salutatorian of his class, as well as several other honors. He got into a really good school in Atlanta. There wasn't much more information about him until he graduated. Chris wanted to see him graduate, and reached out to his father, but the dad was a total piece of work and told Chris not to come. Chris went anyway, but the boy never knew he was there."

Melinda paused briefly, and then continued, "As I said, Chris made Joshua his heir a long time ago. When he heard from him a couple weeks before he died, he was concerned that the boy's dad had heard Chris was sick, and was trying to home in on the property, so he could develop it. When Joshua inherited, that's exactly what he could do, so during the last two weeks of his life, Chris came up with an elaborate scheme to convince the boy to stay and to keep the property as a grove." Melinda sat back.

"That's all very interesting, but what does that have to do with me?" I asked.

Melinda looked at me again with an odd expression. "You really don't know?"

"No, I really don't know. Chris told me his nephew was coming to stay, and I was to show him the ropes and help guide him, but that was about all he told me."

Melinda sighed again, this time with a look of shock mixed with frustration. "Well, it's a lot more complicated than that. You play a really big role in this, but I'll trust Chris knew what he was doing by not telling you."

She thumbed her fingers across the almost empty glass as she thought. The server brought two more pints and left them on the table while Melinda remained silently thinking.

"Okay, here's what you need to know," she finally said.

"Joshua is inheriting the orange groves, the store, and the restaurant. There are conditions on his inheritance, but they're not issues that can't be overcome. If Joshua decides to sell, we will all be out of a job. Do you understand me?"

"Yeah, but I already knew that."

"Well, blockhead..." she replied. "If you help Joshua feel comfortable here, he might decide to keep the grove, not develop it..."

It was my turn to sigh. "Melinda, the groves have been slowly decreasing in profitability year after year. The state has begun gouging us for water, and the city and community want the land to be developed as something besides agriculture. I don't think it's even a possibility that it will remain an orange grove."

Melinda continued to tap the side of her glass. "Let me ask you this," she said. "Do you want Chris's last wishes to go disregarded, because you've already given up?"

I had to admit, the woman had just hit my soft spot. After losing my family, I'd wanted to avoid my friends, and the sickening sympathy in their faces every time they saw me. The only people who seemed to accept me as I was, were Melinda, Chris, and Linda Mae. Chris had taken me into his life and the grove without hesitation.

"Okay, I'll play. What do you want me to do?"

"First off, don't force him to wander alone through the orange groves to get medical treatment when he needs it." I flinched. I was annoyed with him and was honestly glad to see the back of him earlier. I didn't think about how he was going to get to where he was going. Basically, I blew him off, and although not intentionally, I knew—now that Melinda was forcing me to look at it—that was exactly what I'd done.

"Okay, I'll try to be more sensitive in the future."

"Good," she said. "Chris had his day set up. He was supposed to go hang with Linda Mae this morning, then come help me at the shop this afternoon. Unfortunately, as you know, I got swamped. I thought hanging with you would be fine, and you could give him a tour, or something. It didn't include siccing the dog on him before sending him to the doctor on foot."

I was just about to argue, but Melinda put her hand up again. "Clay, when I went into the apartment, I found him face down on a made bed, fast asleep. We're supposed to be helping him learn to love the groves, not wear him down to the point he can't hear people calling his name."

I sighed. "Yeah, so I screwed up. I get it, what do you want me to do?"

"I want you to stop being your typical, bullish self, and try to be nice to the guy. Have a little empathy. He's lost almost everyone in his family. Chris told me he'd talked to the boy, and he sounded excited to be coming back to see him. Joshua arrived just in time for Chris's funeral. That has to have been a shock, even if he was just coming for the inheritance.

Melinda looked off toward the entrance. "I remember him from when he was a boy. He was this scrawny little thing who loved playing in among the trees. Chris and Joshua were inseparable. His mom had to almost pry him away from Chris in the evenings."

She chuckled, before she continued, "Chris was still a player back then, but he'd skip a hot date if Joshua wanted to hang out, or go get ice cream. No matter what this guy is like now, he loved Chris at one time, and Chris adored him."

I shook my head. "I'll try, but I'm not really a socializing kind of guy. If you need me, I'll help out, but if you need him to feel cozy and comforted, you and Linda Mae had better manage that. You know me, I'm just as likely to tell him to go to hell as to say something positive."

"Yeah, you get that from Linda Mae," she said. "You can't fight genetics... but if you let that devil dog bite him again, you take him to the doctor. You don't make him walk, agreed?"

"Agreed," I said, and drank down the rest of my beer.

"So, am I forgiven?"

"No," she replied, but there was a smile on her face.

"Ah, Melinda, you know you love me."

"Yeah, like I love being stung by a scorpion."

"You always have such a way with words," I said, and we both laughed.

Chapter Five

Joshua

I'd had the same dream since I was a little boy. Running through the orange trees, gleefully singing and dancing. Tonight's dream was a little different. I was both my current age and a little boy again. It was hot like I remembered back when I was little, and I sat with my back to the trees, staring out into the grove. Unlike my other dreams, there were Jack Russells running circles around me. The breeze blew past me, alleviating some of the heat, but it carried the distinctive musky smell of the orange trees.

I woke up from the dream with a feeling of freedom that I hadn't experienced since leaving the groves so many years ago, but I was still exhausted like I hadn't slept at all.

When the reality of my situation forced itself back into my head, the happiness of the dream melted, and the stress, frustration, and anger associated with my contacting my uncle after so many years only to find he'd died, caught up with me. When you added the fact that my uncle seemed not to trust me, and wanted to mess with my head with all his restrictions, made me want to scream and throw things across the room.

Instead, I lay in bed, looking up at the dark ceiling. I took deep breaths allowing the anger to die down. I'd loved it here once, so I needed to keep my uncle's mistrust to the side, until I worked through enough of the details to know what I was actually up against.

Linda Mae had been a hoot. Growing up in Atlanta, I'd had my fair share of strong women in my life, and Linda Mae was certainly going to be one of those. I hadn't spent enough time with Melinda to figure her out yet, but I guessed she was going to be more or less like her mom. I actually found myself excited to get to know the two women better. I'd loved working in the restaurant. It was challenging, and the smell of the pressed oranges brought back memories of my early childhood, and how happy I'd been in the groves with Uncle Chris and his crew.

Clay... well, that was a totally different story. The man seemed like he'd rather I fell off the side of the earth than have to deal with me.

Apparently, whether I liked him or not, was irrelevant. He pretty-much had control over me, due to the way my uncle had written his will. I'd have to try to get along with him in one way or another, otherwise, the entire thing could turn into a total nightmare.

Of course, he was easy on the eyes. He was nicely built. Yeah, I'd noticed that even through his surly attitude. His arms were his best feature. They started with long fingers attached to big strong hands, with muscular forearms. And then, oh God, his biceps were huge balls of delight. Of course, the rest of him I hadn't really seen, since he was dressed, but I could tell he had a broad chest that tapered down to a thin waist. I'd thought he was handsome when he'd driven up to where Linda Mae and I were sitting. Fawning over a straight guy was probably a bad idea, especially since I was technically now his boss, so besides using him for eye candy, it'd be best to just keep my observations of his looks to myself.

When I'd learned he was Clay, guilt hit me first, because I sure didn't want to be fawning over a guy with disabilities, but clearly, he'd been mislabeled. So, here I was lusting after one of my straight employees... not that lusting after an employee was a lot better.

I sighed to myself and got up, turning the light on. I couldn't see a clock on the wall, so I pulled my phone from my jeans. I'd forgotten to plug it in last night, so it probably didn't have any charge. Sure enough, it was dead. I rustled through my bag until I found my cord and plugged it in.

There was no way to know what time it was, but I guessed it was pretty early. I'd fallen asleep after the shower, and I figured that was six or seven in the evening. That was nine or ten o'clock Atlanta time, so I wasn't surprised. My usual wake-up time was six o'clock, and Mesa was two hours behind, so it was a good guess to say it was around four in the morning.

I fell back onto the bed and stared at the ceiling, letting my thoughts drift to Clay.

I'd always had a problem with straight guys. It wasn't like I'd chase them or seek them out, but since my dad went into construction, that was who I usually ended up around. Oh, and yeah, I had a thing for rednecks. Not a recipe for romantic success, I knew.

I didn't think I'd classify Clay as a redneck per se, but he was definitely blue collar, not only because his physique was that of a man who worked hard for a living, but watching him repair the irrigation equipment, I could tell he liked doing it. That was a turn on for me.

I dragged myself out of bed, and headed into the shower. By the time I was ready, my phone had charged enough that I could turn it on and get the time. Five on the dot. Okay, so Melinda would be knocking on my door in about thirty minutes if she stuck to the same time as she had the day before. I had just enough time to check my emails before she got here.

Like clockwork, Melinda was at my door at five thirty.

We rode up to Linda Mae's, but today Melinda was much chattier. "So, how did yesterday go?" she asked.

I filled her in on my time at the restaurant and how much I enjoyed working with her mom. That made Melinda laugh. "Don't get used to it," she said. "Linda Mae was clearly in a strange mood yesterday, but she'll probably be back to her surly self today."

I shrugged, I couldn't imagine that sweet woman being anything other than pleasant, but I didn't argue.

"I also met Clay," I said.

"Yeah, about that, I'm sorry I was too busy with an unplanned group visit to pick you up yesterday. Clay did me a favor. Just so you know, your uncle didn't plan on you working with him until much later. Clay is a great guy, but well, it takes a while before he warms up to you."

I laughed. "Yeah, I figured that out on my own. It's all good. I liked seeing the groves after all these years. I'd forgotten how quiet it can be underneath the trees. If I hadn't been in such a hurry, I'd have enjoyed just sitting there."

I was waxing nostalgic, and when I turned back to Melinda, she was smiling.

"You really did love it here, didn't you?" she asked.

I smiled, a little embarrassed I'd showed so much emotion.

"Yeah, those are my best memories. I remember hanging out with my uncle while they worked on the trees, or harvested the fruit. Once, I almost got struck by a rattler that had slithered into the trees to cool off... it didn't even slow me down. I just loved it here."

We pulled up to Linda Mae's before I could get any more nostalgic, thank God. Melinda put her hand on top of mine as I was getting out of the vehicle. "It would make your uncle so proud to hear you say those things. He loved this place a lot, and when you and your family left, it broke him a bit."

I wanted to ask her more about that, about him, but she jumped out and headed inside, so I followed her.

Linda Mae had a list of things she wanted me to do that morning. "Do you know how to make biscuits?" she asked.

"I don't think so," I said, laughing out loud. "I can make toast, and I can order breakfast when a server asks what I want. That's about the extent of my cooking skills."

Linda Mae shook her head, but not in an ill-tempered way. "You kids these days can't tend to yourselves to save your lives. I don't have time to teach you how to cook this morning, but you can take this to the bank, young man. I'm gonna teach you a thing or two soon enough. For now, I gotta get these biscuits on. We ran out of flour, and I had to send Lola over to the grocery store to pick some up. For now, you go back to your juice-squeezing duties. I'll come get you when I'm done, and teach you how to use that modern contraption."

Melinda flashed her typical smile at me, and then left. I saw her sit down at the table across from Clay, just as they'd done the day before. Lola, the woman Linda Mae had pointed at when she told me about the flour, brought them both a plate of what looked like biscuits and gravy.

Linda Mae came out, her apron covered in flour. She showed me the modern juicer and how to use it. "Be careful with this, she's sensitive, and if she breaks, you'll be right back on the manual squeezer. Takes them a couple days to get out to fix her, so best to treat her with kindness."

I nodded. The machine wasn't complicated. Fill it with washed oranges, and press the button. Linda Mae sighed when I turned out the first glass in a third of the time it took to do it manually. "It's quicker," she said. "But, if you ask me, you lose a little of the love by using a machine." I agreed with her, and I even noticed the crowd who'd watched me before, had lost all interest since we'd switched to the machine. Oh well, as busy as this place was during the mornings, I figured they'd have to hire someone full time to do the orange juice if they didn't have the automatic squeezer.

"I want Lola to have you waiting tables this morning. When someone orders juice, that's your department, but until then, you're training with her." Then, Linda Mae disappeared through the back door.

Lola came up to me shortly after that, and said, "Alright, guess you're mine now."

Lola was closer to Melinda's age than Linda Mae's. She was short and pudgy, and her face had that ruddy glow you'd expect for someone who served greasy breakfast foods every day. She wasn't overly friendly, but we got along well enough. She confided in me that she hated to squeeze orange juice, and it was a crappy day when the machine broke, and she had to use the manual. I didn't tell her that was my favorite part, but the fact that I'd taken that chore off her hands seemed to please her.

Clay and Melinda left shortly after I started working with Lola. Clay did make eye contact and even nodded at me, though I could tell it took a deliberate effort for him to do so. That was progress, I guessed. No one could fault him for trying, at least.

The morning went quickly. We were busy right up until the minute Linda Mae locked the doors. "They'd keep coming if we didn't lock them out," she said. "I told Chris time and time again, these people want a dinner menu, but he never listened to me. 'Oranges are a breakfast meal,' he'd say. Truth is, I knew he was just trying to give me my afternoons and evenings off. But, I'm gonna tell you what I told him, this place could double its money if you'd stay open at least a few nights a week."

She, Lola, and I busied ourselves cleaning up the front and setting the place up for the following morning, while the two cooks in the back did the same with the kitchen. Linda Mae and I went out back like we had the morning before, and she struck her cigarette, while I leaned back, letting my tired feet rest.

"When I'm done with this," she flicked ash off the end of her cigarette. "I'm gonna show you how to make marmalade. We do that twice a week. We have to make it that often because that's the only jelly we serve here, and it goes really fast."

"We make our own marmalade?" I asked, sort of shocked.

"Well, of course we do, son. You didn't know your uncle very well, if you thought we'd use store-bought. The man was a lamb ninety percent of the time, but when it came to his citrus, he never compromised." Emotion flooded her vision for a moment, before she reeled it in. She looked at me as she took a long pull from her cigarette, and let the smoke drift out. "I respect your uncle for that. His work ethic and demand for quality, it kept this place afloat while the other groves slowly disappeared from Mesa."

She finished the cigarette, stamped it out on the ground, then picked up the butt, and put it in the trash. "Follow me inside. Have you had any of our marmalade yet?"

"No, Ma'am. I don't really like it to be honest... store-bought doesn't have much flavor."

She laughed. "That's exactly right, it's like eating plastic with orange flavor. Good marmalade starts with a different kind of orange. Not the kind we eat or squeeze for juice, but one that's too bitter to do anything with, other than turn it into marmalade. In fact, Christopher Columbus, the jackass himself, brought sour oranges to the island of Haiti and the Dominican Republic."

Linda Mae went over to the large refrigerator that sat in the corner of the kitchen and pulled out a huge metal box full of biscuits. She pulled back the plastic lid and took out two biscuits, putting them on a napkin she'd placed on the table.

She put the other biscuits back into the refrigerator and pulled out a large black plastic container of marmalade. "The biscuits aren't really warm any longer. We save them to use for biscuit pudding on Saturday and Sunday, but you can still taste the marmalade, and it's best on a biscuit, even if it is a bit cold."

She split each biscuit in half and laid them back on the two napkins., scooping a large helping of the marmalade onto each biscuit, then she put the tops back on. I winced inwardly, thinking it was going to be a dry mess, and I'd have to pretend to like it just to keep from making an enemy of the woman I'd begun to think of as a friend. But I was pleasantly surprised when I took a bite, and the flavor exploded in my mouth. First, the sweetness caught my taste buds and was quickly met by an intense, sharp, orange flavor.

I was so shocked by the deliciousness, and with my mouth still full, I said, "Oh, my... this is delicious."

Linda Mae's eyes sparkled from the compliment. "I told you, son, the only good marmalade is made with sour oranges."

"You weren't kidding," I replied, and took another huge bite. "Do we grow those here?"

"She chuckled," No son, those are a dime a dozen around town. We have several families who donate them to us every year, and we always have way more than we can use."

The two of us worked side by side, putting the recipe together, which remarkably simple, all things considered. We started off by cleaning the oranges, then zesting them, a word I'd heard before, but never really understood. Then, we put the skinned oranges through the juicer. Linda Mae had pulled out a teaspoon of the juice and encouraged me to try it, which I naïvely did. I seriously thought my mouth was going to collapse in on itself, the juice was so sour. Linda Mae laughed and laughed at the sight of my puckered face.

"It's going to take a while before I trust you again," I told her, when I was finally able to speak again. That caused her to laugh even harder.

We worked steadily, her showing me how to make the marmalade. When it was done, she turned the stove off, walked over to shelves, and pulled out four large containers similar to the one in the refrigerator.

She placed them all on the table next to the stove. "Now, we have to let this cool before we put it in the storage containers."

She went back to the refrigerator, pulled out two plated lunches, and put them both in the microwave.

"I hope you like meatloaf," she said. "I had Lola make us a couple plates before she left."

"Yeah, I like it fine," I replied.

Linda Mae nodded, came over, and handed me a glass. Go out front and get yourself something to drink from the soda machine.

"Do we have any iced tea," I asked.

Linda Mae grimaced a bit. "Yeah, but it's crap. You'd be better off with soda or water, or I can put on a pot of coffee," she said.

"No, not a problem I'll do soda."

I didn't realize until just then how much I missed sweet, iced tea. I'd have to run to the grocery store when I got back. Then, I realized, I hadn't picked my rental car up from the Airstream.

We sat down across from each other and ate our lunch, while we waited for the marmalade to cool.

"Do you think Melinda will be around later?" I asked. "I need to go pick up my car from the Airstream."

"Who knows with that girl. She's had a mind of her own since she came out of me." Linda Mae sighed. "I swear that girl is always running around."

I almost choked when she called Melinda a girl. The woman was at least mid-forties, maybe more, but I guessed your mom would always see you as a kid, no matter how old you were.

"Why did you stick around this long? You could be one of the snowbirds at this stage of the game."

Linda Mae eyeballed me for a long moment, making me squirm.

"Child, if I didn't remember you as that cute little boy that used to run around here like a demon from hell, I'd box your ears for saying such nonsense. I never had any interest in all that driving around. My people lived here and have farmed this valley since before Christ. I sure don't plan on leaving it anytime soon, and this here is *my* restaurant. It may have belonged to Chris, but I opened it, and I've run it since the beginning. I'd rather be here than sitting at home in some old rocking chair. Besides, I can still run circles around anyone who works here."

"I know that's true," I said, and I meant it. I'd been impressed by the energy this little woman possessed. She seemed to be in every part of the restaurant at once.

"You know what impresses me the most about you, Miss Linda Mae?" I asked the still peeved older woman.

She eyeballed me again, and I knew if she didn't like what I was about to say, I was going to get to see the personality Melinda warned me about.

"What's that," she asked suspiciously.

"What impresses me most is that after all these years, you still seem to love being here and working at the restaurant. I don't think I've ever loved a job, at least not like you seem to."

Linda Mae studied me for a moment before she responded. "I wouldn't say I love working, I've always worked, it's just who I am, but I do love my customers, and I love seeing this place buzzing with life every morning." She turned to me then, and said, "And I love seeing a new younger generation coming in and enjoying the kind of food we prepare here. When Chris approached me all those years back, he said he wanted to create a diner where the fruits of the groves would be a part of the menu, where freshness was just second nature. Other folks I'd worked for always wanted to cut corners, or use cheaper ingredients, but never Chris. He wanted quality... in fact, he demanded it. I'd say that's why after all these years watching places come and go, we are still here."

I nodded. "Yeah, this place is impressive, and so is this meatloaf. It's different, tastier."

Linda Mae smiled. "There's a secret ingredient, we use pork rinds instead of breadcrumbs, and we add just a little grapefruit juice as well."

"Wow, I've never made meatloaf, but I've eaten my share, and this is better than most."

"Well, finish up," she replied, pride clearly showing on her face. "The marmalade should've cooled down enough now for us to put it away."

I was surprised the marmalade just went straight into plastic containers and was put in the refrigerator. "I thought you had to seal marmalade in jars. My mom used to do that."

"Well, if you were going to keep it for a long time, you'd have to, but here, it doesn't last long enough for all that."

"Have you ever thought of having some canned to sell to customers?" I asked.

"Sure, we talked about it a few times, but it seemed like a lot of trouble, and we'd have had to create an entirely new system to ensure the cans were sealed properly and all that. It just didn't seem worth it."

I nodded but decided I'd do a little research online about it.

Once we got the marmalade covered and put away, we cleaned up the mess and went back outside to sit on the chairs.

I liked Linda Mae. She was a hard-ass, no doubt, but the woman was full of spirit. I hoped that once I got to be her age, I was still enjoying life like she did.

We sat while Linda Mae smoked, and we shot the breeze, until Melinda finally showed up. She was clearly in a hurry. "I hate to rush you, Joshua, but I have another tour bus coming this afternoon, so we need to get back ASAP."

I hugged Linda Mae when she stood up with me. When I looked over at Melinda, she had a shocked expression on her face.

Linda Mae hugged me back, and told me she'd see me early tomorrow. We had to make the biscuit pudding, and that was specifically in the directions Chris had given to her.

"Yes, Ma'am," I said. "What time do I need to be here?"

"Melinda will set all that up, I'm sure," was all the older woman said, as she turned to head back inside.

"See you tomorrow, Miss Linda Mae."

"You can just call me Linda from now on, son. That's what everyone else calls me," she said, as she disappeared through the door.

Melinda stood spellbound next to the ATV.

I climbed into the passenger side and Melinda got in next to me.

"That is *not* what people call her," she said in a hushed voice. "It's either Linda Mae, or Mrs. Fitzgibbons. She must really like you, and she doesn't like anyone, what have you done?" Melinda asked me. "Are you drugging my mother, and if you are, what are you using, and where do you get it? I fully plan to buy stock in the company."

"No, I just think we appreciate each other, that's all. And, I think she remembers me from when I was little." I looked at Melinda as she started up the ATV. "I have to admit, Melinda, I don't really remember many people from back then. I know you all remember me, but I only remember Uncle Chris, and I have vague recollections of some older men that worked with him, but that's about it."

"Well, I'm not surprised," Melinda replied, as we drove along the well-worn path under the trees. "Your parents weren't really social. Your mother liked having dinner on the table at a certain time, and she expected the men in her life to be at that table at that time. She was a strong woman, your mother." Melinda looked at me and smiled. "I always admired how she whipped your dad and uncle into shape. Occasionally, I'd see her out in the trees picking fruit alongside the men, or working in the warehouse, but like I said, she wasn't really, social, and seldom talked to anyone. I think the only reason I ever talked to her was because I was dating your uncle before they left.

"Did my mom enjoy living here?" I asked, feeling emotional all of a sudden.

Melinda thought for a moment. "I honestly don't know, Joshua. I'd only been here a short time when your parents left. I'd taken the job with Chris, because I lost a secretarial job. I'd tried working for my mother, and that went over like a lead balloon. So, you see, I only saw your mother occasionally." She thought a moment more. "I can tell you this though, when I did see her, she was usually smiling, so if I were to guess, I'd say she was happy here."

I didn't think about my mom much anymore. Dad had put a strict moratorium on discussions about her, and I'd pushed the pain aside, hidden in a closet to be ignored. Sometimes, when I couldn't sleep, I wondered what she would've thought about me being gay. Dad didn't seem to care or notice, and when I'd told him he just grunted and said something rude about sleeping with a hairy-assed man, but besides that one comment, he'd never reacted. I guessed he just didn't care. He'd have had to give a crap about me to care about my sexuality. As it was, I just wasn't worth the effort.

Melinda must have noticed the wave of melancholy that came over me, and she patted my knee. "I can't imagine she would've been surprised you ended up back here. You were always supposed to inherit the place."

I realized she thought I was wondering if my mom would approve of my being back. I didn't really want to pursue the conversation any further, so I smiled and thanked her.

"Oh, Melinda, I need to get to the Airstream and get my car. I also have some groceries there I need to pick up and bring to the apartment. Can you drive me over?"

She thought for a moment. "Honestly, Joshua, I doubt I'll have time this afternoon. Maybe after we close, but that'll be eight tonight. We're open later on Friday and Saturday nights. Can you find your way back there yourself?" she asked.

"No, it was dark when you brought me over here, but I'm sure I could hire a taxi."

Melinda laughed. "It's less than a few blocks from here, so I'll see if one of the men can take you over. Once you see it in the daylight, I'm sure you'll be able to find it by yourself."

"No problem," I said. "You have things for me to do this afternoon, right?"

"Yes, but not all that I'd like. This is our busy season, of course, and with Chris being gone, I'm doing double duty. I'm going to have you help with some of the categorizing, so you know how to do it when the oranges begin to ripen. Things will get even busier then."

"Good, I was afraid you were going to make me do a tour or wait on customers, or something. I'm afraid I'm still really ignorant about this whole operation."

Melinda smiled. "You'll learn. Trust me, come April, you'll be an expert."

It hadn't really sunk in that I'd still be here six months from now, until she said that. I was glad she wasn't looking at me, or she'd have noticed me freak out. Could I really handle being here a whole year?

When we got back to the store, I excused myself. In the apartment, I changed out of my grimy restaurant clothes, and put on a fresh pair of jeans. I didn't have many clothes with me, so I'd need to do laundry soon, or go shopping for more. I wondered if I should fly back to Atlanta to pack some stuff and let my dad know I wasn't going to be coming back to work. We didn't really have any big projects coming up, until after the New Year, so he had plenty of time to replace me before things got busy. Even if my dad mostly ignored me, I didn't want to leave him in the lurch.

I finished off the day working with a teenager who was still in high school. She was in charge of teaching me how to separate the fruit. The cooler was a lot bigger than expected. The back corner had boxes and boxes piled all the way up to the ceiling.

"Is this whole thing filled with fruit?" I asked the girl as I turned in circles.

"Oh, yeah," she said. "They fill it during the harvest, but they have to refill it several times throughout the year."

"Do you know where they store all the extra fruit?" I asked.

"No, somewhere off-site," she said.

I wondered if my uncle knew all this would cause my business mind to wonder about the nuances of the groves. I'd always been curious about how systems worked. Even as a kid, I remembered asking questions. Most adults got perturbed by them, but Uncle Chris always seemed to answer me when I'd ask him something.

Weeding through the fruit wasn't really all that complicated. The best went into boxes labeled, A-grade, if the fruit was fine, but had a few small blemishes, they went into a B-grade box. Then the boxes were put out in the store for people to buy. The B-grade sold for about a third less than the A.

The fruit that was still good but too ugly to sell went into boxes that were put aside in the cool storage. "What happens to these?" I asked the girl.

"I think they go over to Linda Mae," she replied.

That made sense. I'd noticed that the oranges we squeezed were pretty ugly. At the time, I figured it was because they were grown here on the farm. I'd seen organic food from local farmers, and they were seldom perfect. Now that I thought about the system, I thought it made perfect sense. The fruit that was still good, but ugly was unlikely to sell, but using them in the restaurant as squeezed orange juice was genius. Ugly oranges apparently still made delicious juice. The juice I'd squeezed myself was beyond delicious, and I never heard one customer complain, not that anyone who knew Linda Mae would be brave enough to, at least not where she could hear them.

There was also fruit we couldn't use. Either it was too small or damaged. That went into a large cart, and after we were done replenishing the stock, we pushed the cart out back behind the store where it was dumped into a compost bin.

"Cool, we compost?" I asked.

"Yeah," the young lady said. "The compost is used around the orange trees in early spring when they flower. I think Linda Mae has a compost bin over at the restaurant too."

"Cool," I said again.

When we were done sorting and stocking, I went up to the counter to let Melinda know I was heading out to see if I could find the Airstream, provided she could point me in the right direction."

"Oh, sorry, I meant to find you, Clay is coming by to drop off the demon dog. He said he could take you to the Airstream."

"Oh," I replied, feeling exhausted all of a sudden. I wasn't sure I had the energy to deal with his surly attitude after such a long day. Melinda seemed to notice my reluctance, and quickly added, "You should ask Clay to take you to Luey's for dinner. It's where we usually hang out after work."

"Yeah, thanks," I said. "I'm going to wait in the apartment until Clay gets here. I need to make a few phone calls, anyway, so can you have him knock when he arrives?"

A customer had just come up, wanting Melinda's attention. "Sure," she said. "I'll send him over when he gets here," then she returned her attention to the customer.

When I got back into the apartment, I went to get my phone I'd left plugged in by the bed.

No messages. *How can a twenty-six-year-old guy be gone for over a week, and have no messages?*

I dialed my dad's office, and when his secretary answered, I asked for him.

"Honey..." That was how all Dad's secretaries addressed me when they were putting me off. "Your dad is in a meeting, can I take a message?"

This sugar-sweet fake-ass Southern accent put off, always set my teeth on edge, and I had to bite back the smart-ass comment that wanted to slip out every time.

This time, I did let a bit of my frustration show. "Yes, you can tell my father that I'm going to be out here for a lot longer than I anticipated. Let him know I'm going to send him an email specifying everything."

"Okay, honey. I'll let him know." Again, with the 'honey' garbage. Long ago, I'd figured out that these women had very little brain power in their heads. Secretaries never lasted long with my dad. I had no proof, but I always suspected 'secretary' was another word for 'the woman I'm dating at the moment' for my dad.

There was no way I believed the woman I spoke with would tell my dad what I'd asked her to, and I doubted I'd get him to answer my call anytime soon, so I pulled my computer out and sent the email.

> *Dad,*
>
> *It's going to take several months to work through Uncle Chris's will. You will need to replace me before the New Year rush. I'll let you know when I will be back home for good.*
>
> *Joshua*

My father wasn't particularly good with messages, phone conversations, personal conversations, or any type of communication really, but I'd learned if I kept my emails short and to the point, most of the time he'd read it and sometimes he'd even respond.

I figured my being here had peeved him a bit. Technically, he should've been the person to inherit the place, but the days of my dad and Uncle Chris getting along were over, and I suspected Dad always knew I was Uncle Chris's beneficiary.

To my surprise, my dad responded within a few moments of my sending the email. Of course, it was a typical dad-style one-line response, but I was still surprised I got that much.

We've got things under control here, take your time.

Well, that was taken care of, at least. Now, to figure out what would come next.

I was about to give up on Clay and take out across the groves to find my own way, when there was a knock at my door.

Clay stood on the other side, hands in his pockets when I answered.

"Hey, Melinda said you need a ride over to the Airstream."

"Yep, do you have time to drop me off?"

"Sure," he said, turning to leave.

"Give me a second to find my keys, and I'll be right out."

"Take your time," he replied.

That struck me right in the gut. It was at that exact moment I realized how much this guy reminded me of my father. Sure, hard worker, strong and handsome, but emotionally stunted. Not for the first time, I was struck by how I tended to be attracted to guys with a lack of emotion.

I found my keys and headed out the side door. One thing was for sure, I was *not* going to date a guy like my father. Even if the guy was gay, I sure wouldn't end up living the rest of my life with someone who couldn't give a crap about me, or at least show a little emotion when I was around.

I'd worked myself up into a tizzy by the time I got to where Clay was waiting for me in the ATV.

I tried to smile, but I was sure it came out more of a grimace. We rode in silence as Clay drove me through the trees, turning back and forth, until I was utterly lost. There was no way I could've found my way to the Airstream without help. I was lucky I didn't try to do it on my own.

The email exchange with my dad was still festering inside me, when Clay finally tried making small talk.

"So, you're from Atlanta?" he said.

"Yep," was my only response. In normal circumstances, I'd have corrected myself, knowing not to be rude to someone that was just trying to be friendly.

Clay nodded and drove on in silence.

We finally came around a corner, and I could see the Airstream in the distance. The tension between Clay and I was humming.

As we pulled up to the camper, Clay stopped and turned to me. "Hey, I know I was a jackass yesterday. I really didn't mean to be, just sometimes I..." I could tell he was at a loss for words, but I wasn't in the mood to help him navigate them.

"Yeah, don't worry about it," I replied, as I hopped out of the ATV, hoping to put an end to the awkward conversation, and put some distance between myself and the man I wanted to unfairly take my frustrations out on.

When I went to open the Airstream, it was locked. I didn't remember locking the door. In fact, I was almost sure I'd left the keys inside when Melinda had picked me up the day before.

I looked back toward Clay. He was climbing out of the ATV and walking toward me.

"Yeah, sorry about that," he said. "Your uncle used to make me drive by and check to make sure he'd locked up. We had a homeless man take up residence in there once, and the guy sued us when we told him to leave. Apparently, if someone takes up residence, even if they're trespassing, it's a bitch to get them out. We ended up having to pay him a few hundred just to get him to leave. Since then, we try to keep it locked when we aren't here."

Clay unlocked the door and opened it for me.

"You have a key to my door?" I asked, ignoring the whole story about the homeless person.

Clay looked around nervously. "Um, well, yeah. Your uncle asked me to... um, he wanted me to make sure it was always looked after."

I stared at the man for a long moment, weighing my words carefully. I knew managing my temper wasn't my best skill, and I told myself just to walk away, but unfortunately, I didn't heed my own counsel, and responded before thinking.

"Who were you to my uncle?" I asked.

Clay thought for a moment. "Um, well, I guess you could say I was his caretaker."

I felt my eyes narrow a bit. The frustration with my dad, the crap about the will, and complete lack of control over my life all swirled inside me.

"Well, I don't need a caretaker. You can give me the keys to *my* Airstream, and I'll make sure it stays locked from now on."

Clay looked like I'd hit him. I should've regretted my response to him immediately, but I didn't feel it.

He took the key off his keychain and handed it to me. Looking both pissed and wounded, he turned around, got into the ATV, and left.

Chapter Six

Clay

You know, most people liked me. I knew I didn't rub everyone the right way, but for the most part, I was a likable guy. Yeah, yesterday I screwed up with the new dude, but to be honest, I didn't think a grown man needed me to hold his freaking hand.

The reaction to me having a key his uncle had *given* me, when he asked me to keep an eye on the camper, well, that shouldn't have sent the gorgeous twink into a dither.

It took a moment for me to register that I'd actually thought the words 'gorgeous twink' regarding Chris's nephew. I guessed I was at least five years older than him, maybe a little more. Paul had been that much older than me.

Well, this was something new, I hadn't thought about another guy since my late husband. I hadn't dated, or even looked at another man, the pain had just been too much. Clearly, he was getting under my skin.

I flipped back over my memories of the day before, and I couldn't think of anything other than being standoffish about the dog. He'd insinuated that I wasn't training the dogs properly, and that had stung, because it was true. I sucked at training dogs. I tended to give in to them, instead of holding a firm hand. I knew that, the dogs knew that, and now it seemed, so did the pretty nephew.

I drove back over to the store and sat on the chair beside the storeroom, knowing I'd be out of the way, while I waited for Melinda to have a break.

It didn't take long for her to notice me. "So, what's up?" she asked, looking a little concerned.

I looked at her and shrugged. "I don't seem to be able to do anything right with that one," I said, noticing the whiny sound of my own voice.

"What did you do?" she asked.

"Nothing. I tried making small talk like you wanted me to, then when we got to the camper, and he realized I'd locked it like Chris had told me to, he got pissed and took my key away from me. Told me he didn't *need* a caretaker."

Just as I finished, we noticed Joshua pull up outside the back door and head into the apartment. Although he didn't slam the door, you could almost feel the frustration radiating off him. A few moments later, he came back out carrying his stuff with him. He got back into his car and drove off.

"What was that about," Melinda asked me.

I shrugged. "No idea."

"I have an idea," she said. "He's a grown man, and the way Chris is manipulating him with all these requirements, I bet he's feeling like we're treating him like a child. I know I sure would be pissed if I was thrown into this kind of situation."

"What exactly does Chris have him doing?" I asked.

Melinda looked at me. "Again, Clay, I'm not supposed to discuss it with you, or anyone else for that matter. Let's just say, it's a lot of nostalgic stuff, designed to spark memories of his childhood here in the groves."

"I see," I replied. I knew Chris was as committed to this place as anyone could be, and his nostalgia ran deep. Once he told me how his nephew, Joshua's father, had wanted to sell the place, and he'd refused. They'd got into an argument about it, and Joshua's father moved the family out east to get away from Chris. As far as I knew, they hadn't spoken since.

We both looked in the direction that Joshua had driven off. "I guess you'd better have a talk with him then, because I do nothing but make him angry."

"Yeah, I think it's probably best if you stay away for a while," Melinda agreed. "I'll talk to Linda Mae and see if she has suggestions about what to do to make Chris's directions less childlike, and more on par with the man Joshua is."

I agreed, then left and went to Luey's. "You coming over to have a drink?" I asked before I left.

"Not tonight," Melinda replied. "I have to finish up here, then do some inventory. We sold a lot more stuff this week than I anticipated, and the weekend is coming up. I probably need to put in an order, unless I want to run out of merchandise by the middle of next week."

"I'll leave you to it then. Hey, Melinda, one last thing before I go. Do you know if Joshua is gay or in a relationship?"

Melinda's left eyebrow arched at the question. "Why do you ask?"

"Because, if he is, then that might explain the cold shoulder. He might think I'm coming onto him, or something."

Melinda laughed out loud. "I seriously doubt he thinks you're coming onto him, Clay," she replied. "But, to answer your question, yes, his uncle said he wrote an article in his school paper about coming out to his father."

"Is he seeing someone back in Atlanta?" I asked.

Melinda smiled and shook her head. "Not sure about that, Romeo. You'll have to ask him yourself."

I shrugged, but inside I was cursing. Now Melinda thought I had the hots for the guy. I didn't get the hots any longer. It wasn't in my DNA, was it? Nah, it was just me being paranoid. Melinda got me riled up over Chris's last wishes and all that. Best to let the feelings pass and get on with my life. I'd rather pull every tooth out of my head, than face the bitterness and sadness I still felt about my family and Paul. It wouldn't do me any good rehashing the past. The only thing left there was darkness.

I quickly debated going home and working through some particularly difficult mathematical equations I'd been trying to solve. Ever since I was a child, and had learned I had an innate ability to solve math problems, I'd learned doing really complicated math helped to calm me. I decided, however, math wouldn't be enough to distract me tonight. What I needed was alcohol, and copious amounts of it.

With that thought, I pulled into Luey's, and went inside.

Chapter Seven

Joshua

I know I should've felt bad about being a jerk to Clay. He was trying to be decent, but I was sick of men like my dad. I was sick of being controlled, and my feelings being ignored. And I was sure as heck tired of my uncle controlling me from the grave by sticking some hot man in my path. Now that I thought about it, I could almost see Clay's hot self sitting over at the local bar, having a good laugh about how Chris's ignorant, backward, gay nephew was out here being led around on a wild goose chase.

I bet they were all having a laugh at my expense. I drove over to the apartment, grabbed my things, and drove back to the Airstream. My uncle could go suck it. I didn't want to be in his fancy apartment any longer, and I didn't want to have to depend on people who had all the control, while I was just supposed to do what I was told.

I called the store, and when someone answered I didn't know, I told her to let Melinda know I'd drive myself over to the restaurant the next morning.

The woman who'd answered acted nervous. "Does she know how to reach you?" she asked.

I left my number, and asked her to have Melinda text me the time I was supposed to be there.

I figured my lousy attitude was seeping into the conversation because the poor woman simply said, "Yes, sir," in response.

Regardless, I was still too pissed to feel bad. My uncle might still be pulling the shots, but that didn't mean I had to play by *all* his stupid rules.

I did a search for hardware stores, and after several calls found out they didn't carry exterior locks for the Airstream. Finally, the last one I spoke to referred me to an RV store. I just managed to reach them before they closed, and they were able to have the part waiting for me when I got there.

It took some effort, but after a couple YouTube videos, I managed to figure out how to change the lock.

It was dark when I finished, and after brushing my teeth, I fell into bed and slept until my alarm went off. Luckily, I'd remembered to set it after getting Melinda's text about my whereabouts for the next morning.

I got ready, and after looking up the restaurant on my phone, I let it direct me to where I was going. I was surprised how long it took to get there by road. The acreage seemed like a world away from the busy streets of Mesa when you were in among the trees, but when you were driving outside the groves, it seemed like they just disappeared. I guessed most people drove around us and never knew we were here.

Luckily, the work of changing the locks and a good night's sleep seemed to have alleviated my peeved attitude, which was good, because Linda Mae was in rare form when I walked in. She snapped at me first, and I noticed Lola smiling from across the room. So, I'd finally become just one of the family, it appeared. The honeymoon was over.

The freezer was on the brink of breaking down, and Linda Mae was trying to reach someone at the repair shop. Of course, at five thirty in the morning, few people were at work yet.

"Um, Linda Mae, I can have a look at it. I did some classes in HVAC. If it isn't a huge problem, I can probably fix it myself."

I could see the war inside the older woman, between wanting to rage at me for making such a stupid request and the need to get the thing fixed before it shut down and ruined all the food. "Do your best then get back here, I have to teach you how to make biscuit pudding today," she said, in a huff.

It only took a couple minutes before I found the problem. Someone had shoved a large box up against the intake, and the machine wasn't getting enough air circulation. I pulled the box away from the unit, checked the temps to see where they were, and did an inspection around the unit's compressor and other intake areas. For the most part, the cooler was in good shape. It definitely needed some cleaning, but from my cursory look, it appeared to be fine.

When I went back in, the temperature had returned to normal. I knew whoever put that box in that corner was going to get a tongue lashing, and I felt sorry for them. I found Lola and asked if she knew who the culprit might be, and she immediately pointed toward a young cook who was putting bacon on the fryer.

I went over and said in a low voice, "Hey, come over here. I want to show you something." When I showed him the box that had been blocking the intake, he literally paled. "Yeah, I'm guessing if Linda Mae found out, you'd be in a world of hurt. You can't put anything in this corner, or you'll cause the cooler to malfunction, okay?" The guy nodded, but the color had yet to return to his face. "Hey, I got your back on this one, just don't let it happen again."

Linda Mae walked back into the kitchen, just as I was finishing the conversation.

"Linda Mae, all's good. I just needed to clean the dust off the intake, and it was good to go."

The older lady was shrewd, and she looked at me and then over to the young cook, who was refusing to make eye contact with her. I thought I'd see anger in her face, but instead, I saw amusement. "Just some dust, huh?" she asked.

"Yep," I replied, knowing my jig was up, but happy she was letting it go.

"Well, that's good," she said. "Now, get your scrawny butt over here and let me teach you about making biscuit pudding."

My entire day was wrapped up in learning the basics of the recipe. After the last customer had left, and we had the place cleaned up and ready for the next morning, Linda Mae and I went to our back-door area, and sat down while she smoked.

"So, does it really make sense to have someone making the pudding all day long?" I asked.

Linda Mae sat for a moment, smoking and thinking about my question. "We make more money off that pudding than we do in one full day of work," she replied.

My eyes grew big, and I looked over at her. "Really? Biscuit pudding makes that much money?" I asked, not really believing her.

"Yep, that's one of our best moneymakers, and the fact that we sell it on Saturday only, or Sunday if we have any biscuits leftover, makes it special, so we can sell it for a little more money than we'd normally be able to."

Linda Mae looked over at me. "I know you're a businessman, and we haven't really talked much about the financial side of things, but that's because Chris didn't want to bog you down with the details of that right away, but we don't have much overhead in the ingredients, and because it is such a novelty, we double the price of the dessert, charging about what we do for a regular meal."

I just shook my head, letting that little piece of information sink into my business sensibility.

"Why did Uncle Chris want to keep me in the dark about the business stuff?" I asked. When I turned to Linda Mae, I could see she was going to recite the whole line about not wanting to overburden me. "Before you say it was to let me have fun, or some other nonsense, be honest. I don't understand the charades here."

Linda Mae sighed. "Your uncle was a peculiar man. He always had his own way of doing things, and those ways inevitably crossed folks the wrong way. But, let me just say this...I worked with your uncle for over fifty years, and he was smart in a different way than other people. Look around..." The woman waved her hands out over the street. "When we started this whole thing, this restaurant was in the middle of nowhere. Orange groves were all around us. Now, we're one of the only one left. The others went under, because water prices went up, land began selling for insane amounts of money, and the citrus industry shifted away from here to places where it is less populated, and cheap labor is easier to be had. If your uncle thought the traditional way about things, we'd have gone under years ago. I know it's hard to trust him, especially since you didn't know him these past few years, and you're having to trust a man who isn't with us any longer, but after all this time, I can tell you I don't really remember a time when your uncle was wrong about his approach to an issue. Give him a chance, Joshua. Play this game by his rules, at least for a while longer, and see if it doesn't make sense to you in the end."

I looked toward all the commercialization that surrounded the groves. "Tell me this, Linda Mae, is it really worth it to fight that?" I pointed toward the commercial development across the street from where the restaurant stood. "Aren't we just delaying the inevitable?" I asked.

She looked out at the same development I was looking at, and said, "I honestly don't know, son. There were times when I felt like we were swimming upstream, but then I thought about how my ancestors worked this land for thousands of years, and how your ancestors worked it for the past century. History is important, something to hold on to, because once it's gone, it's gone forever. I think that's why your uncle worked so hard to preserve this place. It's one of the last vestiges of what Mesa used to be—one of the last things that ties it to its past. I can't say what the future holds, but I'm an old woman whose days on earth are limited. I think holding on to parts of our history, and who makes us who we are, is worth preserving..." She looked back over at me and made eye contact. "...if you can."

Chapter Eight

Clay

I took my own advice and drank several drinks too many. I knew I was looking at a depressing night. That guy was stirring up feelings in me I'd thought were long dead, and alcohol was a great way to black out memories I was working to avoid. Of course, there were two problems with drinking your memories away. First, it would magnify all the emotions you didn't want to have, and second, the next morning was always a bitch.

Oh, for me, there was a third. After my third or fourth drink, I began to share my woes with the entire population of the bar. I'd made a point to leave my tragic life in the dark since arriving in Mesa. If people didn't know anything, they wouldn't bring it up. That was no longer the case with me and the twenty or so other occupants of

Luey's last night. My only hope was they'd gotten as drunk as I had, and would forget the whole thing.

There was one consolation...none of the other crew members were with me, and Melinda hadn't been out either. That didn't mean they wouldn't hear about it, but at least I wasn't the one spilling my guts out to them.

Usually, on Saturday mornings, I'd wander over to Linda Mae's for leftover biscuit pudding, or if they were out, have a large breakfast. One of the perks of working at Chris's place was Linda Mae offered free breakfasts if you got there early enough. Chris told me early on that the best way to get your crew to work on time was to feed them.

Today wasn't going to be one of the days I made it to the restaurant in time. Instead, I brewed some of the nasty pre-ground mess I bought at a discount store. I didn't spend much on coffee, because I usually had mine at the restaurant. That being said, I sometimes overslept and just needed a hit of caffeine. No need to keep the good stuff for those rare occasions.

After I'd taken several Tylenol and drunk copious amounts of nasty-flavored caffeine, I sat down and turned on the TV. I couldn't remember the last time my TV was on. I preferred to be outside working, than staring at my big screen. Sometimes, I'd invite the guys over for the game, but that too was rare.

I finally settled on a kids' channel and would you believe it, there was the *Dog Whisperer*. I'd swear, someone was messing with my head. I'd never heard of the show, until Joshua mentioned it to me a few days back.

I turned the volume up so I could hear it, and watched as they worked with a particularly nasty little dog, who wanted to keep its owner's boyfriend out of the bed. At one point, the little bitch even bit the guy... Caesar, I think, was the guy's name.

I watched in amazement as he worked to train her to share the bed and stop biting. As soon as that one episode finished, another one came on. This time, Caesar had dogs at his farm in the desert. He was working with a pack of them, talking about how you needed to be the leader of the pack, and that dogs reacted based on what you did. When a dog misbehaved, the owner was the one who needed to be trained.

It wasn't lost on me that it was basically what Joshua had insinuated when Dude bit him.

After the program was over, I turned the TV off and called Buddy and Clip over. I began working with them like I'd seen Caesar do on TV. Of course, I had absolutely no luck. I tried getting them to lie down, and Buddy just kept growling at me. After thirty minutes, my headache was coming back, so I gave up and went to lie on the couch.

I must have fallen asleep because I startled when Melinda knocked on my door.

I stumbled off the couch, and when I pulled the door open, Melinda was standing there with a thermos.

"I didn't see you at the restaurant this morning," she said.

"No, I slept in. What's up?" I asked.

"Well, I got a call from Suellen, saying you had quite an eventful evening at Luey's last night."

"Dang, why can't Suellen mind her own business?"

"Cause she thrives on gossip. That's the main reason the woman waits tables there." Melinda chuckled to herself.

I just shook my head.

Melinda put the thermos on the table. In the kitchen, she pulled out a bowl, and poured out what appeared to be soup.

"Mom sent some of her chicken noodle soup. I figured you were hungover, so I thought soup might help."

I nodded, walked over, and sat down. "You not joining me?"

"No, I already ate," she replied. "So, since you spilled your guts to the town gossip, you might as well tell me about it. That way, I can defend you when the grapevine goes into full swing."

I sighed, pushing the bowl away and laid my head down. "I'd really prefer not to talk about it, Melinda."

"Oh, I'm sure that's true this morning, but unfortunately, that's not how you felt last night." I looked up through what had to be bloodshot eyes, and gave her my most hateful stare. "You aren't intimidating me, Clay. Spit it out. I promise not to say anything until you're done."

"I'm sure you already know, if Suellen called you."

"I do, but I want to hear it from you. That woman invents stuff to make her stories more interesting. I prefer to know what's true and what's not."

I stood up and stretched. Knowing I was going to have to come clean, I asked her to give me a minute.

There was a small opening in the floor of my bedroom where a radiator probably used to stand. I'd found it one day when I was refinishing the floors. I'd put my pictures and personal belongings that had been Paul's and my parents' into a box that I kept hidden there. It was not like I had a lot of visitors, but having that part of my life hidden helped me keep the two worlds separate. Now that I'd caused them to collide, I guessed it was best to pull it out. I could show Melinda what she wanted to know, and not have to talk about it.

I brought the box to the table and sat down next to Melinda. There was an article I'd saved that described the accident that had killed my parents and Paul. I pulled that article out and handed it to her.

"You can read this, it tells you everything you need to know. I'm going to take a walk."

Melinda unfolded the paper as I left.

When I came back around twenty minutes later, Melinda was still sitting at the table, looking through my pictures. When she saw me, she put them all back in the box, along with the article, and closed it.

I couldn't bear to look Melinda in the eye. Instead, I walked into the living room and sat down facing the opposite wall from where she was. She came and sat across from me on the sofa.

"I knew your parents had died in a car accident. I'd looked that up myself when you showed up here. I also knew you'd lost someone you cared about, but I didn't know they had died together. I suspect you don't want to talk about it, huh?"

I nodded.

"That's fine, and you don't have to, but I need to ask one question, because people will ask me. Where were you when they had the accident?"

"I was in Scotland," I replied.

"Why were you in Scotland, Clay?" she asked.

"I'd rather not talk about that," I said, crossing my arms in a futile effort to keep her out of a part of my life I'd worked so hard to keep tucked away. Early on, even in my teenage years, I'd felt like I needed to keep my birth mom and my adopted family separate. Melinda never challenged me on it, and my birth parents never asked. I hadn't ever confided in Melinda about Paul. It just seemed wrong somehow.

Melinda sighed and stood up. She came over and put her hand on my shoulder. "I'm not going to pry any further, Clay, but unless you want to talk this out, I recommend you avoid Luey's for a while."

I nodded again, and Melinda leaned down and kissed my head. "If or when you're ready to talk, I'm always here, Clay, but you already know that."

I nodded. "Yeah, I know."

She patted my shoulder again and walked out the door.

I decided to leave the liquor alone, although it was more than a little tempting. Instead, I went out to the back shed and found as much work as I could to keep me busy, and my mind off all this crap. How the heck did I let myself get into this situation after all this time. I thought I'd be able to keep it hidden for the rest of my life. Facing the wall, I yelled, "Screw you, Joshua Howard!"

Chapter Nine

Joshua

Melinda called the next morning, asking if I could be ready to meet her by noon. I flat-out told her no. "Melinda, I need some time to process all this. I don't mean to be rude, but Uncle Chris's plans can wait until Monday."

She said that'd be fine, then she left me alone to brood in peace.

I opened the windows and door to the Airstream to let it air out, and read the last will and testament from my uncle all the way through. I was thankful for my business law class I'd taken in college, cause at least I could decipher most of the legalese.

Mr. Arlington had been correct. From what I could tell, the will was pretty ironclad. I debated sending it to my dad to see if his attorneys could navigate through it, but then I remembered how my dad reacted to Uncle Chris, and I wasn't quite ready to get him involved.

I read over the part about Clay Masters again, trying to glean from what little information was there about why he played such an important role in my inheritance. Again, I was left with a feeling of being completely at the man's mercy. I couldn't for the life of me understand *why* my uncle would have such an odd requirement, unless he was just screwing with me.

I was also intrigued by who sat on my uncle's board. Linda Mae and Melinda were no surprise. There were four other people I hadn't met and didn't know. From the addresses, it appeared all of them lived locally. Six board members and me... I guessed I was the tie vote, although since I owned most of the shares, I was pretty much the main vote.

Because Clay seemed so important to the property, I was surprised he wasn't listed as a board member. I'd have to ask the attorney about that next time we spoke.

I heard scurrying up the steps, and jumped, afraid of what I was going to see when I looked up. Right in front of me was one of the Jack Russells. "Hey, what're you doing here?" I asked, and was just standing up when the little brat began to lift his leg.

"Nope, nope!" I said, as I rushed over, and scooped him up before the pee began to flow. "You'll be doing that out here!" I said, and put him down on the ground, sitting in the doorway to block his access.

"Where're your buddies?" I asked, under my breath. "Worse, where's your hunky owner?"

The dog didn't look the least bit perturbed by my kicking him out of the camper. Instead, he pranced over to the tire and lifted his leg there. "Why did you think you needed to come into my camper to pee, when you've got an entire grove?" I asked. He didn't even look at me, instead, he traipsed off into the trees.

I shook my head, but I couldn't help the chuckle that escaped. "Naughty little beast," I said, and went back inside.

I was feeling antsy after reading the will, so I decided to wander through the groves I'd driven around on my way back from Linda Mae's the day before. Two hundred acres was a significant amount of property in the middle of the city. We were surrounded on all four sides by commercial and residential development. With the exception of a derelict property—some sort of resort with what probably used to be rental cabins—most of the development around us looked to have been built in the early 2000s. The area certainly wasn't high end, more middle class, but I completely understood why the city and state wanted the property to go into development. I knew my father would've been on cloud nine if he could've gotten his hands on a prime piece of undeveloped land like this in the middle of a city.

I took off in the opposite direction to the day I'd gone to urgent care. It seemed like I walked for miles wandering through the trees. I was met by the three dogs, but none of them stayed with me for long. I recognized the one that'd bitten me, and

I patted his rump, avoiding his mouth. "Once was enough for me," I told him.

Just like in my dream, I was struck by how restful it was among the trees. The fruit was still too green to pick, but many of them were the size oranges should be. I enjoyed the quiet of the grove, especially once I got to the part furthest from the streets. The feeling of being lost was more welcome than fearful. I knew I'd find my way back, and if all else failed, I could always call a taxi.

I thought about my youth. Back then, I seriously doubted there was much development yet. We'd left a couple decades ago, so the building boom would've just been starting. For the life of me, I couldn't remember a lot of building happening at that time. I only remembered the trees and the feel of the sandy earth beneath my often-bare feet.

As I wandered, I could hear the traffic getting louder. I had no idea where I was headed. Finally, I came to an area where the trees stopped. I thought maybe I was on someone else's property, but as far as I could tell, with the exception of Chris's buildings, the only thing attached to ours was the derelict resort.

I was about to turn back, but curiosity got the better of me. I wondered if this open land belonged to someone else, why it hadn't been developed, and if it belonged to us, then why there were no trees? As I walked, there were occasional clusters of trees here and there among the barren landscape, which caused me to think that maybe this was our property. I still couldn't see the other developments, and from the street, the dead land wouldn't have been visible either.

Finally, after a long walk in the open, I came to another grove of trees. I walked through them and found myself right on the edge of the derelict resort. The property looked like it had at one time been whimsical. There was an old, battered sign that announced natural hot springs. My curiosity got the better of me, so I decided to see if they were still open.

As I approached the main building, I passed several abandoned cabins. A few of them had roofs that had collapsed entirely. The closer I got to the main building, the cabins looked to be in better shape.

Finally, as I reached the main building, it became clear the business was no longer open. I was about to leave when an elderly lady stepped around the corner.

"This is private property, young man," she said, her face fierce with frustration.

"Sorry, Ma'am," I said. "I was just walking through the groves, and since your property backs up to ours, I thought I'd see what all this was about." I waved my hands toward the signs.

"You said 'Our land'," she replied. "Do you work for Mr. Howard?" she asked.

"No, Ma'am, not exactly, Chris Howard was my great-uncle."

"Oh my goodness!" she exclaimed. "Are you Margaret and Sam's son?"

I smiled. She knew my parents. "Yes, Ma'am, I'm Joshua Howard."

"Oh, I remember you from when you were small," she said, chuckling. "You used to run away when you were just a wee thing and end up over here. My husband used to collect antique toys, and you were obsessed with them. I thought your mother was going to skin you alive on more than one occasion when she'd find you over here sitting with Larry in one of our main rooms looking at his collection."

I smiled, even though I didn't recall the memory. I seemed to have forgotten more than I knew about my early childhood. I wondered what a therapist would say about that.

"Well, I'm sorry to have bothered you, I'll get out of your hair."

"Nonsense!" the older woman all-but yelled. "You come in here and tell me what you've been up to all these years. I sure wish Larry was still around, so he could see how handsome you grew up to be."

I smiled, and for some reason I didn't understand, I felt quite emotional. I didn't remember Larry, but hearing that one more part of my childhood was lost to me caused me to feel intense loss. "I'm sorry to hear about your husband. Did you hear we lost Uncle Chris too?"

"Yes," she said. "Your uncle had been sick a long time. He sure fought it, though. It would've taken a lesser man many years earlier. Why don't you come on in? I was just about to have some lunch. If you like bologna like you used to, I can fix us both a sandwich."

I was just about to decline as an image of sitting and eating sandwiches with an older man flashed in my mind. It might not be a real memory, but it was something I wanted to prolong, to see if maybe I could learn more.

The building was dilapidated. It needed so much maintenance I was amazed most of the building was still standing. We walked past desks that had clearly been the check-in area, and then through a great room that must have at one time been a dining hall. It wasn't until the woman opened the back door that we arrived at an area that appeared to have been maintained.

The little apartment was neat and clean, and unlike the other parts of the building, it had been freshly painted. Even the furniture appeared to be newer and in good shape.

The woman showed me to her table and told me to sit and wait for her. When she came back, she had two paper plates, each with a sandwich and chips on the side.

As we ate, we talked companionably.

"I apologize, I don't remember your name."

"I'm Lucy James," she said, smiling.

"I have to be honest, I don't remember much about my childhood. I'd love to hear any other stories you can tell me."

She regaled me with memories of my impromptu visits with 'Mr. Wawwy'. Apparently, he'd been close to my uncle, and since I'd been Uncle Chris's shadow, I'd become almost one of the family.

She smiled at the memories. "Those were good days, young man. Some of my best memories are when your family still lived here. Not that we had time to do much socializing back then, business had boomed during the winter months, and we were so busy, I could barely breathe.

She looked down at her hands, her smile fading. "Larry's been gone about eleven years now. Since then, I haven't had the resources to keep the place going. We closed down about three years ago. It's too much for me, but then I don't really have it in me to sell. I couldn't bear everything to be torn down and another strip mall put in its place. I know that's silly, but I'm an old woman, and I don't have many years left anyway. Once I'm gone, they can do what they want with it."

She stood up and took our plates and put them in the trash.

"Do you ever eat over at Linda Mae's?" I asked her.

That brought a smile back to her face. "Linda Mae used to be my competition." She chuckled again. "I cooked a mean breakfast back in the day. I probably would've been able to beat her, had she not had that blasted biscuit pudding she serves every weekend. I tried to steal her recipe, but she threatened to shoot me."

The older lady sat back down, a mischievous grin crossing her face. "She could never beat my pies, though. No matter how much she tried, I still took all the pie and dessert business."

She sat for a moment letting her thoughts settle. "To answer your question, I haven't been there since we closed. I usually stick to myself these days. I have to keep a close eye on the place to keep vagrants out."

"Is there anything we can do to help?" I asked.

"No," Lucy smiled and patted my hand. "The police help out and come fairly quick when I call. I'm doing okay."

I made a mental note to speak to Melinda about having the crew come over and help secure her fence. All I'd had to do was step over it, and I was right on the property. I was amazed that she didn't have vagrants living in the derelict cabins.

By the time we were done talking, I felt closer to the woman. I just wished I had retained my memories of this place, of her, and her late husband.

When I finally left, she hugged me and asked me to come back and visit her. "Now that we're neighbors," she said. I got the distinct impression it was more about helping alleviate some of the loneliness she must have been feeling on a huge run-down property that once used to be full of people.

"Well, Mrs. Lucy, I'd love to come back. Maybe I can convince you to come to breakfast one morning with me at Linda Mae's." Lucy just smiled. I would totally be doing that.

After I left, I felt like I had a semblance of direction for the first time since setting foot off the plane. Lucy had given me just a momentary glimpse of my childhood, and not in a loaded way like the stuff with the inheritance. I still had no idea who was in charge of the groves, but it sure wasn't me. I would ask if we could use the crew to help restore the fence around Lucy's property, but if not, I could hire a crew myself.

That thought put a spring in my step. Direction was important. Having it, made the difference between floating around being pulled like a balloon, and being able to achieve something.

I immediately texted Melinda and asked about the crew. She texted back a few minutes later, and said I'd have to discuss that with Clay, since he managed all that.

Well, by god, if I had to face him to get this project done, then face him, I would. Now, I just had to figure out how to find him.

Chapter Ten

Clay

After Melinda left, I found myself in the old machine shed behind the house. That might not have been the best place to go. Chris and I used to work together there. When he got too sick to help, he'd sit on an old armchair we had in a corner and watch me as I worked or, as he put it, kept me company.

I hadn't been back in there since Chris last went into the hospital. Now, not only were the ghosts of my past haunting me, but being in the machine shed added Chris's ghost to the mix. I was just about to leave, when I spotted a bottle of Jack sitting in Chris's old chair. I went over and picked it up. There was a card addressed to me underneath.

I wasn't sure I had it in me to read it right then, but I threw caution to the wind and opened the envelope. I immediately recognized Chris's handwriting. It was wobbly, indicating he wrote the note close to the end of his life. I wondered who he'd asked to drop it off in the chair. My guess was Melinda, and I also guessed she'd be the only one willing to do it exactly the way Chris told her to.

Dear Clay,

If you are reading this, I'm no longer alive. I've always wanted to write that line, since it was the beginning line of a movie I watched years ago.

By now, you probably know my nephew Joshua has inherited the property. I haven't seen the boy in over fifteen years, so I can't speak for his character. That's why I'm going to have to depend on you to check him out for me.

Joshua was a great kid. I loved him like my own son, but his father put up every wall to keep me from seeing him. As a result, I have no idea what kind of person he is. Development of the groves is probably inevitable, but I've put some significant roadblocks in the boy's way. If he's anything like his father, this is going to make him angry as a nest of rattlers. I'm sorry to put you in the path of that, but I really don't have much choice at this point. Mr. Arlington will have read the will to him, and your name is mentioned in it.

My deepest desire is for the property to be maintained at least partially as it's been for the past century. If Joshua decides to fight you, I'm giving you enough control to negotiate part of the property to be placed in trust along with the storefront. Joshua doesn't know this, of course. As far as he's concerned, if he fights you, he'll lose it all. That isn't what I want either, but I need to incentivize him to stick around long enough to remember how much he once loved the place.

Melinda has my plans in her possession in the event a time comes you need to make a compromise. The long and short of it is, that if the property can't be an agricultural pursuit, I want at least part of it to survive as a museum.

Now, on a personal note, these past five years, you've been my family, and I've leaned harder on you than I should've, but unfortunately, with this hateful cancer, I didn't have much choice. You will inherit the house you are living in. Cecil Arlington has a sealed envelope at his office, and one year from the time I die, that envelope is to be opened. Part of the provisions of that envelope gives the home to you.

Melinda has another envelope, and in that are my provisions to Joshua. Provided he stays on the property for a full year, without fighting you, he'll be given full rights at that time. My only hope is if he lasts that long, he'll be as in love with his ancestral home, as I was.

Finally, I know I'm putting a lot on you, and just after I deserted you. That's what the Jack Daniel's is for. My hope is that you and Joshua will get close enough to make at least one toast to me, but regardless, have a drink on me and remember, I appreciate you for all you've done and for helping me preserve my family's heritage.

I love you, son. Be a good lad, and don't drink all this at once.

Sincerely,

Chris Howard

I sat in the armchair, staring at Chris's letter for a long time. I understood a little more about the attitude Joshua had thrown at me now. I was the only thing standing between him and what must be millions of dollars.

I wasn't intending to drink, but Chris had made it too tempting. I poured myself a shot, toasted my old friend and boss, and downed it. I did it again three more times, until the buzz kicked in. I seriously considered another full out drinking session, but remembering last night, along with Chris's letter, I decided I'd be happy with the buzz.

I turned on the old radio, still sitting on the countertop. The station Chris listened to was even programmed in, and although I was never a fan of country music, I let it play, and allowed myself to enjoy the memories of hanging out with Chris.

The music was loud enough that I didn't hear the car pull up, or the door open. I had my head back against the chair, letting the memories of my family and Chris flow through me. I didn't even know I was crying, until Joshua cleared his throat. The man looked as beautiful as ever, and crap, if that didn't put me in a pickle. Alcohol loosened my tongue, and I was still holding the letter from Chris that I was supposed to keep secret from him.

I put the letter on the floor, and the bottle of Jack on top, then turned to the man who was clearly embarrassed at seeing me in the state I was in.

"What can I do for you, Mr. Howard?" I asked, knowing that by all rights, I was the one in his territory.

"Um," Joshua stammered for a moment. "I c-can come back later if this isn't a good time."

"No, now is as good a time as any," I replied, although technically I wasn't working, so I could've and probably should've sent him on his way.

"Are you okay?" he asked.

"I'm fine, why wouldn't I be?" I asked with a snarl. This guy was really beginning to mess with my buzz.

He looked at me for a moment, then must have thought better of the visit, because he turned to go. "I'll talk to you about this tomorrow," he said, as he headed out the door.

I still was not sure what came over me. Before he got all the way outside, I was out of the chair, and when I reached him, I took his arm and turned him around to look at me again.

"I said this was as good a time as any." Joshua looked at me, shocked. I was surprised by my own actions. I must have had more alcohol than I thought, and I let his elbow go. "I'm sorry," I said. "I didn't mean to touch you."

Joshua continued to stare at me before I saw a light flick on inside him, and his temper flared. "How dare you grab my arm and turn me around like I'm a child? My uncle might have given you all the cards in this stupid game we're playing, but I'm not going to let you jerk me around like some disobedient kid." I could almost see the cartoon flames coming out of his ears as he stood up to me. "I have no idea what you and he planned for your enjoyment, but I'm done playing, you hear me? If need be, I will call Mr. Arlington tomorrow morning and begin undoing your little game. Maybe the charity will get everything, but I'd rather end up with nothing, than be pushed around by you and a dead man who, just like my father, didn't give a crap about *me*!"

He turned to go, and my slightly drunk brain couldn't think of anything I could do to stop him, other than grab him and pull him to me. I held him to my chest as he struggled. "Shh, it isn't like that. I'm not here to hurt you, and this isn't a game. Your uncle loved you, I'm sure he did."

The man finally stopped fighting me, but he was still stiff in my embrace. I slowly let him go, and he pulled away. There were tears in his eyes now, but I could tell they were more from frustration than sadness.

"Why did you do that?" he asked.

"Do what?"

"Why did you hug me?"

"Um, well... I don't know. It just seemed like the right thing to do."

Joshua turned to leave again, and I couldn't help myself. "Please don't go," I said.

Joshua turned around and faced me again. "Tell me one reason why I shouldn't leave, Clayton Masters." My name came out of his mouth as a sneer.

I wasn't going to admit to this beautiful, angry man that I wanted him to stay, because he was the first man in over five years my broken heart had noticed. Instead, I stood like an idiot, staring at him with my mouth agape.

"That's what I thought," he said, and started walking back to his car.

I reached out for him again, but when he turned around, I kissed him, and not just a chaste kiss. It was a full-out kiss, tongue and all. Even as I was kissing him. I was reeling with the shock of what I'd done. I mean, probably because of the Asperger's, I over thing every emotional response I make. I would never, *ever* kiss someone unless they made the first move.

At first, the shock kept Joshua still, but the longer the kiss lasted, the more he relaxed into it.

Within seconds, he was giving as much as he was taking, and it felt as if the two of us were going to devour each other.

He pulled back first. "Wait, wait, I can't do this. I still don't understand any of this! What's going on with you and my uncle, and the freaking will, and all the charades I'm being put through. No, I can't add you kissing me to the equation."

When I tried to reach for him again, he all but yelled, "*NO!*" Then, he pulled back.

He got in his car and drove away without looking back.

"*CRAP!*" I said out loud, as I watched his car disappear down the driveway. What had I just done?

Chapter Eleven

Joshua

I know I ran away from Clay like a school kid, but I'd thought the man was straight. Was he really that drunk? Maybe, and if so, hopefully, he wouldn't remember it. Regardless, I was sure as hell not going to get involved with some straight dude that allowed his drinking to give him permission to experiment. *And* I wasn't going to play *closet pet* for another man as long as I lived.

The memory hit me like a hammer. I'd been eighteen, and my dad had employed a man seven years older than me. The guy was supposed to be his protégé or something and as a result, he was over at our house quite a bit.

The man was ruggedly beautiful, in a southern redneck sort of way, and I was... well, I was just scrawny. Everyone knew I was gay, even before I was officially out, so the redneck was aware.

He and I had gotten along fine, until I'd moved to the pool house. The redneck—I still refuse to say his name, even to myself.

One afternoon, my dad came home early and stumbled on us kissing. My dad didn't really give a crap about me, or what I did, but that wasn't the case with his employee. The idiot ended up lying and telling my father I came on to him, and he was afraid he'd get fired if he didn't go along with it.

Luckily, that was the year I'd begun thinking about being in a band, and I was recording the day he made a pass at me. I actually had a recording of him telling me it'd be cool if we could date from time to time. When my dad jumped down my throat that night about how I was going to get them sued for sexual harassment, I went out, burned the conversation onto a CD and handed it to him the next day.

He never apologized, of course, my dad didn't do apologies. But I didn't see the guy around his office again. I'd always wondered what would've happened if I hadn't accidentally recorded that conversation. Would the idiot have screamed sexual harassment? Worse yet, would my dad have kicked me out with no place to live? I knew the answer to both those questions was, probably, yes.

From then on, I swore I'd never date a guy associated in any way with my dad's business. The exception was my dad's architect, Peter. We'd kissed a few times, and were making out behind the same pool house when my dad caught us. Of course, he'd fired him, and that was that. Peter had moved to Atlanta for the job. I felt bad about that, and I'd apologized profusely. He didn't mind. He hated my father as much as I did. In the end, we became best friends.

I thought about my history and felt the usual clutch of my stomach. It both embarrassed me and infuriated me that I'd been such an idiot the first time and stupid the second. Even though Peter ended up on his feet, I still felt guilty for getting him fired after moving to Atlanta to work for my father.

I shook my head at my apparent pattern. Of course, I immediately thought the situation with Clay was more like the redneck. It had to be a stupid ploy for Clay to create some sort of chaos surrounding the transfer of the property.

The next morning, I texted Melinda that I had business to attend to and wouldn't be available. When business hours rolled around, I contacted Arlington's office to see when he was free. Luckily, he had an opening before noon, so I headed there to see him.

When I had him in front of me, I asked him the question I was most concerned about.

"What does Clay Masters have to do with this entire process? Would he legally stand to inherit anything if I failed at my uncle's little games?"

The old man shook his head. "There is only one thing the old man left to Clay in the will, but if anything, he has to help you succeed to inherit it. So, no, there is nothing I can think of."

I explained what the guy had done the night before, and the attorney shook his head. "I mean, there's always a sexual harassment claim, but in this situation, he actually has more power than you. If you came onto him, he could make your life a living hell, since to inherit, you can't actually fire the guy."

"So," I asked. "There really isn't anything that would put *me* in jeopardy?"

The older man had the same look of disgust on his face as he thought about it. "No, you're fairly safe from the charge of sexual harassment, I think, but I'd watch my back regardless."

I nodded. "You have nothing to worry about there. Tell me, Mr. Arlington, if I can't fire him, can I at least kick him off the property or assign him some menial task to keep him away from me?"

The attorney shook his head. "The more you do to antagonize him, the worse this whole thing could go for you. I recommend that you not be alone in his presence, and that you make it clear to him and everyone else you aren't interested in him...in that way." The man's face almost twisted into itself from the revulsion.

"I can tell you don't like the man. Why?"

Mr. Arlington looked at me, surprised by my question. "I almost had your uncle convinced to let the property go into development just after he got sick. That's when Clay Masters stepped in. The idiot advised him he could keep the agricultural business going. It was bad advice, and he all but screwed your uncle with it. Dang it, son, just look around the property! There's nothing agricultural for miles around. It's time to give up the fight and let reason win."

"I see," I told him. "Well, I'll make my decision soon, but at the moment, it's looking more and more like we should be discussing how to best develop the property. And if I can't sell it, Mr. Arlington, you and your partners need to figure out a way for me to develop it myself."

The man looked startled. I assumed he thought I was a nitwit like most people who first met me. The truth was, business came second nature to me. I'd been trained by my father since my mom died, because that was the only thing he and I ever talked about. The groves were in a perfect part of Mesa, not far from the major highways, and close to well-established middle-class families. I'd already done a house-price search and found the values were about double the average for the city.

"We'll look into that for you," he said, and looked like he was about to dismiss me.

"One more thing," I said, before the man could leave. "My uncle has set up a bunch of ridiculous hoops I'm having to jump through. I need to know what happens if I refuse to keep jumping."

The man looked at me, and for the first time since I met him, he looked, if not impressed, then at least a little less disdainful. "Well, son, it isn't like you have a lot of choices. You've seen the will and read the parts that he laid out. There is a possibility that things could change this time next year with a sealed envelope your uncle gave me before he passed away, but I wouldn't rely on that very much. If this comes down to a judge's decision, the more you do to follow your late uncle's directions, the better it'll look."

I was shocked by the revelation of the sealed envelope. "Um, what sealed envelope?" I asked.

The man sighed. "I wasn't supposed to let you know about that. It was in Chris's terms that I keep that a secret, but even the partners have told me I should let you know it exists. I wasn't sure I'd tell you until now."

"You have no idea what's in this envelope?"

The attorney shook his head. "And I can't give it to you until the terms of your uncle's request have been met. Of course, you could try to force the issue, but I'll remind you if you don't play along with Chris's rules, you could lose the property altogether."

"I won't be forcing the issue, but if you have any clue as to what's inside that envelope, I'd like to know."

He shook his head again. "I'm sorry, young man, I don't. As I said, the old man came in just before he went into the hospital, and handed it to me along with very clear directions of when it was supposed to be opened, and how we were to go about it. That's all I know."

I left more perplexed than when I'd arrived.

As I drove back to the property, I thought of my uncle and his feelings about the groves, and what it meant to his... to my family's heritage. Although I agreed with Mr. Arlington in principle about the development of the land, and how it couldn't be avoided forever, I thought it must have been hard for my uncle, who wanted to preserve the property, not to have any advocates. Learning that Clay had stood up for my uncle, even as his own attorney was pushing him to go in a certain direction, impressed me. I still didn't trust Clay, but the attorney's admission did the opposite of what he'd probably intended. Clay had my uncle's back, and loyalty was and always had been very important to me.

When I got back to the Airstream, I texted Melinda.

I met with Mr. Arlington, my uncle's attorney this morning. Can you, Linda Mae, and Clay meet me this afternoon or tomorrow? I want to discuss some issues with all of you.

Melinda texted me back right away and said she'd let me know when she'd spoken to Linda Mae and Clay. It took around half an hour before she got back.

We can all meet around three at Linda Mae's. Should I come pick you up?

I replied immediately.

No, I'll drive myself over.

I knew I was going to have to continue to play by Chris's rules, but one thing was clear, the old man thought I was still a child. I was not. So, at least in that regard, things would definitely have to change.

When I arrived at Linda Mae's, the three of them were sitting in the dining room, waiting for me.

Linda Mae smiled at me, and winked. That wasn't the reaction I'd expected, but I didn't let it distract me. Instead, I sat down across from them.

"I thank y'all for meeting me on such short notice. Melinda has probably already told you, I met with my uncle's attorney this morning, and well, there are some things we need to iron out."

I turned to Melinda. "Uncle Chris gave you clear guidelines for me to follow if I'm to inherit the property, and although I've felt like I'm being pulled around on a string, I was informed there isn't much I can do about that. Melinda, I have a degree in business, and I've worked with my father's company for the past five years. I'm not the preteen child my uncle remembered when I moved away, and I'm not a teenager to be controlled. Starting today, I need access to the books, all of them, if I'm to operate as the new owner of the company."

I could see she was going to protest, and I raised my hand to stop her. "I know Uncle Chris didn't want that to happen right away, but I don't care. This is not negotiable. I need to know what's going on with the property, and I need to know sooner rather than later. Linda Mae, I'm impressed with the restaurant thus far, but I need to know if we're operating in the red or the black. When I inspected that cooler, it looked like it hadn't been serviced in over a year, maybe two. I'm guessing you need resources, so if you get me a list of things that need doing, I'm going to work with Melinda to figure out what monies are available."

Before she could respond, I looked over at Clay, and sighed. "Clay, how long have you managed the property and the crews that work here?"

"Five, almost six years," he replied.

"That's what I thought. I know you and my uncle had an agreement, and I'm going to respect that..." I looked him in the eye, and said, "...for now. It seems my uncle gave you a lot of control over me and the company, whether I like it or not, but let's get one thing very clear. I am the owner of the company, and at the end of the day, I'm the one responsible for the success or failure of the business."

I looked at all three of them, before I continued, "I don't know anything about running a citrus grove, a restaurant, or a shop, but I do know this property has been in my family for over a century, and it's not going to go into ruin because of me. From what Arlington tells me, we are up against the wire, because everyone from local communities to the freaking state want this place to be developed. I ain't promising I won't agree with them before this is all said and done, but I will honor my uncle's request to get to know the business, before I allow the outside world to influence me. As for the four of us, well, that's going to be a bit tricky. Until Uncle Chris's plans are acted out, you are, in essence, my teachers. That's cool as long as you understand I'm not someone you can walk all over or control. Respect me, and I'll respect you." I intentionally looked at Clay when I said that.

When all three nodded, I turned back to Clay. "I'm not sure what happened yesterday, but if you're technically my employee and at the same time my supervisor, that can't happen again. You clear on that?" Clay's face, which had turned red the moment he saw me, grew redder, and he looked down at his hands and nodded. "Good, now one more thing. I met Mrs. Lucy James at the old resort on the edge of our property. I noticed while I was there that her fences had fallen down, and she said she's having difficulty with vagrants and trespassers on the property. Clay, do you think we could carve out some time for the crew to go over and help her get them repaired?"

"Um, Chris tried several times," he said, with surprise. "She refused his help every time. Did she ask for help?"

"No, she didn't, but if she won't let us help, we can at least put the fences back up along our property line. Besides, I think I can bribe her once we get the crew over there working."

Linda Mae looked at me out of the corner of her eye. "Lucy James is the most stubborn, thick-headed woman to ever cross this earth. If you go over there with a crew of men, you'll end up with a broom handle sticking out of your ass."

The irony of Linda Mae calling someone thick-headed almost undid me. I was close to laughing, but I wanted to maintain the air of authority for a moment longer. "I already figured out that might be hard to manage, but I have a couple tricks up my sleeve. Clay, when are you and the guys available to go over and help?"

"Um," he replied, scratching his head. "The truth is, unless we're dealing with irrigation or repairing stuff for Melinda, we don't have much to do this time of year. We could be there tomorrow."

I thought for a moment. "I'm not sure that's enough time for me to work my charms on Mrs. Lucy. I'll go over there right now and see if she's available. Meanwhile, I never got yours or Linda Mae's mobile numbers. If I'm going to be working here, I should at least have a way to get in touch with you two."

They nodded, and each of them texted me their numbers. I almost said something about Linda Mae's evident ability with her mobile, but something in Melinda's expression warned me not to comment, so I dropped it.

"Okay, like I said, I'm going over to Mrs. Lucy's now, and if she's open to it, I'll text you, Clay."

I'm not quite sure what I expected to happen in the meeting. Part of me thought they would all three give me crap about pushing my weight around, but I was pleased that none of them seemed to mind. Melinda looked concerned about the financial records, but once I put my foot down, she seemed to surrender to the idea.

I drove over to Mrs. Lucy's, through an unlocked gate and pulled in behind her old Chrysler. By the time I got out of the car, she was at the door with a look of frustration on her face. Luckily, when she saw it was me, she smiled.

"You're back sooner than I thought. Got time to come in?" she asked.

"I do. In fact, I wanted to talk to you about something if that's okay."

The woman looked at me dubiously. Linda Mae was right, I would have to navigate this carefully.

When we sat down at her table, just like we had earlier, I sighed.

"Mrs. Lucy," I began. "I was informed that my Uncle had a vagrant living in his Airstream, which, as you know, isn't very far from here. I've decided to stay in the Airstream instead of over at his old apartment for privacy reasons, and I'm a bit concerned about safety."

The woman was watching me carefully, I knew she was waiting for the other shoe to drop.

"I also just came from meeting with Clay, and he told me his men have a little too much time on their hands. We both know idle hands are nothing but trouble."

I finally got a nod out of her, which gave me the prompt I needed to continue to the sales pitch.

"I figured it would do us a lot of good, and help you too, if you'd allow my men to put your fence back up along *our* property line, and around the front where your cabins sit."

At first, she shook her head no, which I'd expected.

"Now, before you completely reject the idea, here's what I had in mind. If I can keep my guys busy between now and when the fruit begins to ripen, they'll be fitter for harvesting when the time comes. I have a list of chores for them, but to be honest, I just don't have enough to fill that amount of time. I was able to step right over your fence yesterday onto the property. If I can do it, so can vagrants, and before long they're going to start a fire and burn down your place *and* mine. I just can't afford that kind of risk right now, when everything is up in the air. So, I'm asking you for a favor. Will you let me use the repairs as a way to keep the men working?"

She looked at me for a long time. "I wasn't born yesterday, son," she finally said. "Your uncle tried to get me to let him help around here since Larry died. The truth is, I don't like being a charity case, but what you said is true, nonetheless. I had one of those guys start a fire in one of the cabins last year, and it burned to the point the roof fell in. If you help me get the fence put back up properly, it will indeed benefit us both. But, I'll not be letting you do it for free. I still have some insurance money from when the cabin burned, so I can put that toward the costs."

"That's fine. The only cost will be for the concrete. I've seen several bags of quick concrete sitting inside one of the sheds by Melinda's shop. It's sort of an eyesore, so I'll want the guys to use that first, unless you object, of course. If it's designated for anything else, you can pay for that, but if not, we'll just use those."

Mrs. Lucy smiled. "You are a smooth cat, aren't you, young man?"

"Why, Mrs. Lucy, I have no idea what you are talking about," I replied, with the thickest southern accent I could muster.

She chuckled. "Okay, you win this one, but I'm not a charity case. I may be an old woman, but I'm not without a few resources. You have to promise me you will let me know the costs."

I stood up and crossed my heart. "I promise not to try to deceive you, or turn you into a charity case."

Mrs. Lucy chuckled. "Now get along with you, I have work to do."

I laughed too. "Is it okay if I have the guys start tomorrow morning? I wasn't joking, Clay said they don't have nearly enough to do."

"Of course, not that I can turn those puppy-dog eyes of yours down anyway. I'll see you and the crew tomorrow morning."

"Yes, Ma'am," I said, as I walked out the door.

It sucked that my dad had dragged me out of Arizona, and the life I loved as a child, but he gave me a gift when he put me in a world where I learned how to speak with a southern accent. I'd learned through the years, there was no more powerful tool to move a stubborn person off their high horse, than turning on the southern charm. Not that I'd ever admit that to anyone who asked, but those of us from the south... we knew.

Chapter Twelve

Clay

Linda Mae, Melinda, and I remained seated until after Joshua had left. Once he was gone, the two women turned to face me. "So, you going to tell us what happened yesterday?"

"I'd prefer not to," I replied.

"Well, I don't think I remember asking you what you *prefer*," Linda Mae said, accenting the last word.

I sighed. "Well, I found a letter Chris had left me on my chair, or..." I looked at Melinda. "Melinda left on my chair in the machine shed along with a bottle of Jack Daniel's. I was already feeling sorry for myself. Reading Chris's letter put me over the edge. I'd had a few shots just before Joshua came in. Before I knew what was happening, he was yelling at me about something, and the next thing I knew, I was kissing him."

I looked down at my hands, but I could tell both women were staring at me.

"And..." Linda Mae said. "I'm sure there's more to it than that."

Melinda reached across the table and put her hand over mine. "Tell her, Clay."

I looked up at Melinda, and my head was beginning to spin.

"I-I can't Melinda. I need to forget all this. I-I need to get away from it."

I stood up to go, but Linda Mae pulled me back down into the chair.

"Honey, we all have stuff that's happened to us, but you need to be brave. It seems to me you let your emotions get the better of you, and it caused some problems between you and that young man." She pointed to where Joshua had just left. "If you don't get a hold of those emotions, they're going to cause you to do something stupid, and this time, maybe worse than kissing your new boss."

I knew she was right, but that didn't make it easy.

Melinda came over, sat next to me and put her hand on my shoulder, letting her arm rest on my back. "Sweetheart, you can trust Linda Mae, she might be a demon from hell most of the time, but she is someone you can depend on to keep your counsel."

I looked up just in time to see Linda Mae give Melinda a nasty look, before she turned back to me.

"You two don't understand. I haven't told anyone about this, not since it happened."

"Well, not until last night, I'm sorry, honey, but the cat's out of the bag, so to speak."

I sighed and stood up. If I were going to tell them what happened, I'd have to do it while pacing.

"I lost my parents and my husband on the same night. I was in Scotland getting an award for some work I'd done as a collaborative agreement between the university I worked for, and one in Glasgow. When they were driving to the airport to come to my award ceremony, a drunk driver crossed into their lane of traffic."

I sighed. Once again, I waited for the waterworks to come. Usually, I couldn't even say the words 'husband' or 'parents' without shutting down, but I was somehow able to stand in front of these women, my birth family, and tell them about the family I'd lost.

"I know that was tough, honey," Linda Mae said. "But, I guess I'm confused about why that caused you to kiss Joshua."

"Well, that's the thing. I haven't been attracted to anyone since..." I drifted off, the feeling of guilt swamping me.

"You think, because you're attracted to Joshua, that you're somehow being disrespectful to your late husband?" Melinda asked.

I shrugged. "Melinda, I have no idea what I feel. Seriously, I haven't even thought about another man that way in such a long time. Those feelings, I thought, were all over for me. I was just caught off guard when I first saw Joshua."

Linda Mae smiled a sad smile, and said, "I know a little about that myself. Sit down here, and I'll pour us all some coffee.

When she came back, she placed three cups down in front of us, and grabbed some creamer off the countertop.

"When Edmond passed away, Melinda was only twelve. We were both unprepared to deal with a life without him, but especially back then. You gotta do what you gotta do, so I threw myself into work. Melinda suffered the most, because Edmond was the emotionally supportive one. I grew up hard on the reservation. We were forced to live in the schools where the schoolmarms saw us as savages. They thought the best way to get the savage out of us was to beat us. I learned early to put my emotions away and not deal with them."

Linda Mae looked at her daughter, and sighed. "By the time Melinda hit fourteen, I knew I was really screwing things up. I had to teach myself to open up to her. I waited too late, of course. Having emotions, and even harder, expressing them is tough."

Linda Mae took another drink of her coffee, then turned to her daughter. "Melinda and I have had to have several heart-to-hearts since then. Neither of us were any good at letting the past go, and as a result, we didn't see or speak to each other for several years." Linda Mae looked back at me. "Those were wasted years, Clay. Good times that we both threw away and mostly because of me. When the heart is hurt, people like you and I want to build walls to protect it, keep it safe from being hurt again. But, that's the kind of thing fools do, because inevitably, when you keep yourself locked away, you hurt not only yourself, but those you love the most."

Linda Mae put her hand over Melinda's, and they smiled sadly at one another.

"I remember when Mom started trying to hug me more, or pay attention to me more, but by then, I was so angry," Melinda said. "I was so hurt that my father had died, and I didn't quite understand why or what had happened to him. I blamed Mom for his death. When she tried to show affection, especially after not being an affectionate person before, I just figured she felt guilty for his death. We really did throw a lot of good times away, times we needed each other, and all because we'd been hurt."

Linda Mae turned back to me again. "As I see it, you need to go find that boy, apologize to him, and try to explain why you lost your head."

Melinda added, "You also need to stop letting all this stuff *stay* in your head. You need to talk to someone, and I know, because we're your birth family, we might not be the best ones for the job, but there are several good therapists within walking distance of here. Regardless, find people to talk to, and I don't mean at Luey's!" We all three chuckled at that.

Melinda came over and hugged me. "There are several stages of grief, unfortunately. You're gonna have to let yourself feel the emotions before you can get through them. Call me anytime, okay? I'm here for you."

She hugged Linda Mae too, which was an odd thing to see, but I guessed baring their souls to me struck a chord with them as well. "I've got to get back to the store."

"Hey, before you go, shouldn't we discuss what happened with Joshua?" I asked.

Melinda sighed. "Chris was unfair with what he was asking Joshua to do. Expecting him to follow our rules like a child was bound to blow up in our faces sooner or later. I'm actually proud of him, for standing up to all of it, before it got any worse."

"Are you going to keep up with all of Chris's directions?"

"Yep, because there really isn't another option. Those were the rules Chris set out for Joshua to inherit the place, so we all need to play along."

Linda Mae patted my hand. "Don't worry about it too much. The boy has a strong head on his shoulders. He'll let us know when he's had enough. We all know Chris was prudent. It may seem like this is all a game, but he wouldn't have put it together and asked us to follow through if he hadn't really thought it was important. By what Joshua said this afternoon, I think deep down even he knows it."

She turned to Melinda. "Melinda, we can't keep treating him like a child, though. You need to write out a schedule, so he knows where he's supposed to be during the week. Also, if he says he needs to do something else, like fixing Lucy's fence, we need to support that too. He's right, he is the heir to the property. Making him feel like he works for us, instead of the other way around, won't do anything but chase him back to Atlanta."

We all agreed, before Melinda left. I stood up to help Linda Mae take the cups back to the kitchen.

"Thanks for the talk," I told her.

She looked at me for a moment without responding, then she sighed. "Genetics is what they are, baby, and unfortunately, you seem to have inherited mine. Here's my advice from someone who is too much like you. Don't try to get through life on your own. If you don't open yourself up, you'll wake up one day, and realize you're alone."

"Can I ask you one more thing?"

Linda Mae smiled. "You want to know why I never remarried?"

I nodded.

"Well, it's not like I didn't date again, but I like my freedom. Men are delightful things to play with, but once you move them in, the fun can run out pretty fast." She chuckled at her own words.

"Did you ever fall in love again?"

She smiled, "Yeah, but it isn't something even Melinda knows. Chris's father, Arthur, was quite a lot older than me. He and I dated for a long time, which is how I came to know Chris. I fell for the man pretty hard, and we even talked about getting married, but Melinda was still living with me at the time, and we were struggling to navigate the emotional landmines. By the time Melinda moved out, Arthur had developed the same cancer that ended up killing Chris. So, instead of getting married, I became his nurse. I don't think Chris or Melinda ever knew there was more to it. After losing the only two men I'd loved to cancer, I decided to stop trying."

"Do you regret it?"

Linda Mae looked at her hands for a moment, before responding, "Yes and no. It's difficult to be alone, especially at my age, but then I know a lot of couples my age who are together and are miserable. I don't really regret it, but sometimes I wish I'd allowed myself to be open to the possibility. The best advice I can give you is to let yourself feel the emotions that come your way. Just because we feel them, doesn't mean we have to act on them." She elbowed me in the ribs. "But, at least you'll know you're alive."

I looked up at her, sort of shocked by what she'd said. I'd thought to myself several times over the past few years that I felt dead inside. Linda Mae seemed to know exactly what to say. The feelings swirled around inside me, but for the first time in a very long time, they didn't feel quite so overwhelming, like maybe having spoken to Linda Mae and Melinda might have somehow helped me control them. That was definitely a good surprise.

"I wish I'd opened up to you and Melinda earlier, and to Chris too, I just couldn't..."

"No, honey, you probably couldn't at the time. Now you have. Right now is the perfect time. And, if by some miracle, you end up falling for Joshua..." She pointed again toward the door he'd walked out of earlier. "...you'd be a lucky man. He's something special, that one. I knew it when he was little, and nothing I've seen since he got back, has convinced me he is anything less now."

After that, Linda Mae shooed me out of the place, so she could lock up and go home.

I really wanted to go to Luey's, but after my drunken confession, I sure didn't have it in me today.

I drove the ATV back to the house. As I walked through the front door, I got a text from Joshua telling me he'd convinced Mrs. Lucy to let us help with the fence. *"That's a miracle,"* I said to myself.

Before I could respond, he called. "Hey, I thought this would be easier over the phone than trying to text."

"No problem," I replied.

"What do you have planned for all that quick concrete in the shed by Melinda's shop?"

"Nothing, it's what we had left over from a project we did a couple years back."

"Good, I convinced Lucy to let us use that, instead of buying new. I'm guessing she has a limited budget."

"Yeah, I think she does. Chris tried to get her to let us help, but she is... well, as Linda Mae said, stubborn."

Joshua laughed. "Yep, that's an example of 'it takes one to know one'."

"For sure," I chuckled.

"So, do you want to meet me over there and look at what she has that's salvageable? I can make a run to the hardware store to pick up whatever else we'll need."

"S-sure," I replied, a bit embarrassed by my stuttering.

"Cool. I'm at the Airstream now. Why don't you pick me up on your way over? I think I'm on your way."

I laughed. "You aren't too far out of the way. I'll see you in a moment."

I was afraid it would be awkward between us, but Joshua was waiting, and jumped right into the truck when I pulled up.

"I was hoping we could salvage as much of the fence as possible to keep the costs down. If I can get an inventory of what's needed, I can run over to

Habitat for Humanity's ReStore to see what I can find."

I let him talk about supplies and where to get them, enjoying hearing him talk about something I could see he was passionate about. When he finally paused, I asked, "You really like this sort of work, don't you?"

He thought for a moment. "It's part of me, it's what I've grown up doing. Besides, I like Mrs. Lucy. She said I used to come over to the resort a lot when I was little."

"Do you remember it?" I asked.

"No, not really, I think I have some buried memories. I got glimpses of memories when she was describing how I'd sit with her late husband Larry, but it could all be made up in my mind. Regardless, it feels good to have some connection, even if I don't really remember it.

I nodded, although I wanted nothing to do with my childhood home where memories of my parents and their loss felt like they would overtake me.

We arrived at the fence and walked along it. Most of it was still salvageable. A few of the posts were bent beyond repair, but it just looked like time and Mesa's strange weather were the real culprits.

"I counted a hundred posts that need to be replaced if we do the entire perimeter," Joshua commented.

"Yeah, that looks about right to me too. There's a building out by the machine shed that had some fencing in it from before I arrived. We could check that out to see if any of it could be used."

"Cool," Joshua replied, but I could tell he was avoiding eye contact. The machine shed must have brought back awkward memories of the day before.

"Listen, Joshua, about yesterday—"

"Please," he interrupted. "I really don't want to hash that out. You and I have to work together. I'm not sure what that was all about, but let's just put it behind us." I tried again to apologize, but he interrupted me. "Seriously, let it go," he said again, and walked away.

I sighed, but it was no good forcing the issue, the man didn't want to talk about it, and if I pushed, it would be more for my sake than a real apology.

"Joshua, wait up! Okay, I'm not going to bring it up again, just know I'm sorry."

"Got it," was all he said, as he climbed back into the truck and waited for me.

Chapter Thirteen

Joshua

Clay didn't seem too surprised that I'd called him out in front of Melinda and Linda Mae, but he did look appropriately chastised, which made me feel a little better. If the kiss was truly an emotional response, and not some conspiracy to undo me, that would go a long way in making it easier for us to work together as a team.

I was pleased that our afternoon looking at Mrs. Lucy's fence went as well as it had. I sort of thought Clay would sulk or be upset, but instead, he was very professional and pleasant to be around.

When he mentioned the machine shed, he must have noticed my awkwardness, and tried to bring up the subject. Putting a stop to the discussion was the only way I knew to make sure it didn't happen again. I was not gonna lie to myself, and not admit that I was terribly attracted to the man. He was tall, dark, and the muscles in his arms bulged when he lifted or moved things. No, it would be too easy to fall for him, and that wouldn't do. In fact, until I knew more about what my uncle had planned for me, the best option was not to get involved with anyone. I was even afraid to try a hookup app. Things were just too up in the air.

When we pulled up, the same awkwardness fell between us. Instead of acknowledging it, I got out and walked behind the house toward the shed. I hadn't really noticed the house that much, but as we walked through the property, memories flooded me, and I began remembering my life here as a child.

My mother loved cacti, and if I remember correctly, she grew wildflowers among them. There were several huge saguaro cacti proudly standing around the property. I wondered if they were there originally, or if my parents collected them from the desert. Grief flooded me, as I realized that the people who would've been able to tell me that were no longer living, except for my father, and I doubted he knew or cared.

I'd seen pictures of when the house was adobe style. Uncle Chris had given the home to my parents after I was born. I assumed it was, because he wanted to entice them to stick around, since he didn't have kids of his own. The two of them turned the house from an adobe to a ranch style. Now it resembled so many other homes built in the early eighties with little character but lots of space.

I remembered a small area behind the house, not far from the shed, where we'd sit out under the citrus trees and eat picnics. I didn't recall much about the inside of the house except that my bedroom was painted in bright colors, and the ceiling fan had glow in the dark stickers on it that would mesmerize me at night.

Clay had followed me around the exterior as I silently reminisced. I'd honestly forgotten he was there, or what our mission was. When I turned around and saw him standing a short distance away, I chuckled. "Sorry, I was going down memory lane."

"You grew up in this house?" he asked.

"Yeah, well, until I was ten, and that's when we moved to Atlanta."

"I bet it's a lot different from what you remember."

I looked at the house again. "Yes and no. My memory isn't that great, but the color seems different. I thought I remembered it being plain white."

"Yeah, the siding was dead when I moved in. I completely replaced it with vinyl."

Clay must have seen me cringe, because he laughed. "I know, not the best choice, but I didn't expect to live here long, and your uncle only gave me a tiny budget to work with. Vinyl was the least expensive option."

"My mom tried to spruce up the place with her cactus gardens, but even then, I remember thinking it was ugly and pretty at the same time." I laughed. "The opinions of a preteen aren't always diplomatic."

"I bet this is so different from Atlanta, how did you adjust?"

"Not well at first," I admitted. "I struggled with the move, and shortly after we got to Atlanta, my mom got sick and passed away. In fact, she was probably sick before we left, but no one knew it at the time."

"Do you think your dad would've stayed if he'd known she was sick?"

"I doubt it. Once my dad makes up his mind, he doesn't change it."

Clay stood quietly after that statement.

"So, you said the fencing was in the shed behind the house?"

"Yeah, I'll show you. Watch out for snakes though, I've had to have three removed already this summer. The sheds provide a refuge from the heat. I try to keep an eye out for them, but they're here, nonetheless."

I cringed at the thought. I'd lived most of my life without snakes around. The idea of rattlesnakes living in sheds around the property sent shivers through me.

Clay went up to the shed, slowly opened the door, and turned on the light. There were no rattle sounds that I heard. So far, so good. He walked in and looked around, still nothing. "I think we're in the clear," he said. "But be careful looking around."

I decided to let Clay do the looking around. He was much more adept at snake wrangling than me. We walked down the aisle until we reached the back, and sure enough, there were several panels of fencing.

"These appear to be the same height as Lucy's."

"Yep, perfect," Clay replied. "Although we don't have enough to do much of the perimeter, we can use this to fill in the areas where the fencing is damaged."

"It'd be nice if we could do the project without having to cost Lucy or us any money. It's a good possibility. Although I don't think we have enough poles, they aren't that expensive to replace. I'll have the guys pick these up and bring them with us tomorrow morning."

Clay drove me back over to the Airstream, and I watched as he drove away. For the first time since I arrived, I felt like I had some control of my life, and that felt really good.

Chapter Fourteen

Clay

I had the guys meet me in the shed first thing in the morning, and we picked up all the fencing.

When I called Joshua, he answered immediately. "Hi Clay, I'm ready when you are."

"I'll be there after we drop off the equipment, and I get the men started. We don't have room in the truck on the way over. Do you want to go over to ReStore since you didn't have time yesterday?" I asked.

"Perfect," he replied, and hung up.

I was glad we were on better terms. Lucy's fence might actually be the bridge between our differences.

By the time I got over to pick Joshua up, the guy was ready. Unfortunately, ReStore didn't have what we needed, but the lady at the counter told us about another place that sold used lumber and fencing equipment further out of town.

When I put the address she gave me into my GPS, it said we were thirty minutes away. "Wanna go check it out?" I asked Joshua.

"No, I'd prefer to get back and help with what we've got. Maybe after we're done, we can go over. She said the guy that owns it lives there, so hopefully, there'll be someone available to help us when we arrive."

I liked his plan, and we headed back to the project. The guys were really tackling the fencing, and an entire section had already been replaced.

Joshua, to my surprise, grabbed the posthole digger and held it while one of the workers, Jimmy, drilled the holes. The guy had clearly done this before, and although it was dusty and dirty work, he didn't seem to mind.

By the time we were ready to go for lunch, Mrs. Lucy had shown up and invited us all over for sandwiches and lemonade.

"Yes, Ma'am!" Joshua said for all of us.

When she was gone, he looked over at me and the guys. "If you need to take your break, you can have time after we're done eating at Mrs. Lucy's, but I need y'all to go over with me, so she feels like she's contributing."

None of the guys objected, and in fact, I knew none of them needed a longer break since none of them ever left for lunch anyway. The fact someone was providing lunch, even if it was sandwiches, was more than they were used to getting.

Mrs. Lucy was an entertainer. I could see why the hotel had done so well for so long. She teased the men while they ate, and at one point, looked down Jimmy's shirt to see if he was stuffing the sandwiches down there, because surely he wasn't eating all of them. Before she was done with us, she'd accused all the men of having hollow legs.

We left in great spirits. I pulled the men back toward the worksite, and Joshua hung back to talk to Mrs. Lucy after we were gone.

He joined us a few minutes later, smiling. "She said we can do the entire perimeter, Clay, do you have time to walk the rest of the fence before we go look for supplies?"

I nodded, and the two of us walked off, while the men continued working on the fence where it was in the worst shape.

"How did you get her to agree?" I asked.

"I simply said if she could supply lunch, that'd go a long way toward keeping the men on task."

"She doesn't have to do that!" I exclaimed. "Isn't she on a fixed income?"

"She probably is, but she's also someone with an immense amount of pride. You can't just expect someone like her to accept charity, without giving something in return. Besides, did you not see how happy she was today?" he asked. "I watched her come alive, and you should've seen her face when she agreed to make sandwiches for the men. She has served the public all her adult life, you know she has to miss it."

I just sighed. The man clearly understood people better than I did. Luckily too, because Chris and I had done everything short of sneaking over at night to put her fence up, and she flat-out refused. She'd even threatened to call the police if we showed up. Of course, Joshua had sweet-talked her less than a week after arriving on the property. Linda Mae first, now Lucy... he must be some sort of magician.

Chapter Fifteen

Joshua

As the weeks passed, the three of us began to fall into a rhythm. Uncle Chris's agenda felt less and less onerous as time passed. I wouldn't say Clay and I were becoming friends, but we were tolerating each other better and better.

The project putting up Mrs. Lucy's fence brought me closer to the men also. I ended up going out at least once a week to Luey's to have a beer and shoot the bull.

I'd learned while working with my dad, the guys needed times when you were their equal, and not their boss. It seemed to help level the playing field, and even encouraged them to feel comfortable coming to you, when there were problems.

Clay did that automatically, but I had to force myself to do it. My father was a dictator. *"Do it my way, or you're fired."* I knew for a fact we had lost a lot of good men who didn't work well under that kind of leadership.

Working with Clay's men was better. They liked each other, and the typical bickering I'd experienced in my dad's company wasn't present among these men. I asked Clay a couple weeks after we'd finished Mrs. Lucy's project what his secret was, and he laughed.

"Your uncle hired these guys years ago, long before I got here. The most recent hire has been here for twelve years. They were all migrant workers moving from grove to grove, but when the business dried up, your uncle gave them all full-time jobs."

"How do we afford that?" I asked.

"We don't," he replied. "They cost us double what we'd normally pay, but before you get all wound up, it's impossible to hire a crew now the groves have disappeared. If we didn't have these guys full-time, we'd never find anyone to harvest when the time comes."

I sighed. "Is there anything about this business that isn't sucking money?"

Clay shrugged. "Nope," he said, and wandered over to another pipe we were having to repair.

Well, luckily, because of Melinda's store and the restaurant, we were still in the black—barely. We had a couple hundred thousand dollars in expenses flowing out of the groves. Most of it was going to the state for water, labor, marketing for the store, and general upkeep of the property. Oh, and the taxes on the property were outrageous.

Arlington wasn't joking when he said the city and state had put a lot of pressure on my uncle to sell.

After expenses, we'd made just under a hundred grand in profit. Which wasn't bad, but that's what was left for my uncle to live on.

I'd moved out of the apartment in what I thought of now as my 'get to know you temper tantrum'. Part of me was still pissed—more, because my uncle had blown a ridiculous amount of money modernizing the apartment, when he could've spent the money on innovative treatments to cure his cancer. I mentioned that to Melinda, and she laughed.

"If you'd known your uncle, you'd never have thought that. He believed the best cure for his type of cancer was work, and he must have been onto something. He lived ten years with it, and he only got really sick right at the end. Besides, the apartment was his gift to you. He knew you were going to have an uphill battle, and that was his way of making it better."

"So, I've been kicking a gift horse in the mouth. That's what you're saying, right?"

"Honey, that's what I've wanted to say, but since you're the boss, I've just kept my mouth shut."

I gave her my most, *Please, you know I'm not the boss*, look, and when she chuckled, I left her to go back to the Airstream, pack up my stuff, and move back into the apartment.

I announced to the group that we needed to Airbnb the Airstream. "We've got to increase revenue, and I have no idea how to do that. By my calculations, we can bring in around five grand off that."

No one cared really, but I wanted them to see I was making some headway at least. As could've been predicted, the rental hit heaviest and hardest just as the harvest was about to come in. "Y'all could've warned me," I told them, sitting down for breakfast at Linda Mae's one morning.

"Like you'd have listened," Linda Mae chuckled.

As it was, I was the only expendable person, so it was left to me to get the trailer cleaned and ready each day for the next guests. So much for being the boss.

My relationship with Clay improved daily. I think that was more about becoming part of the tribe of men who worked on the groves than the initial attraction we'd both had for one another.

At first I kept a wary eye on him expecting him to grab me at any moment and kiss me again. Then, after thinking about it, I felt disappointed he didn't. *Crap, if I'm not a total airhead queen.* It was just, the more we worked outside the more buff he got, and his tan—that he'd clearly inherited from his Native

American ancestry—seemed to glow from being exposed so much to the sun.

My resolve to remain professional with Clay hung precariously by a thread, which only became thinner as my physical attraction was coupled with a new appreciation I had for his work ethic, love for his men, and his commitment to the groves. There were days, I couldn't keep my eyes off him, but on those days, I intentionally went to Melinda's store, or Linda Mae's restaurant and helped them. I clearly couldn't turn my growing attraction off regarding this man, but I could certainly distract myself when they became too intense to manage.

Harvest became the ultimate distraction as it was intense and amazing at the same time. The guys were experts, and although we didn't use any fancy, new harvesting equipment, they could harvest large sections in record time. I intended to help, but quickly learned I was more in the way. I kept to the sidelines, so I could learn, but not hinder progress. The guys teased me mercilessly about being slower than their dead grandma. I resorted to flipping them off.

Many of the oranges were deliberately kept on the trees to keep them from spoiling. I was told by Clay this was common practice, but we'd have to have everything harvested by the end of January.

By mid-January, I began noticing the extra weight I was carrying. Hmm, could it be all the oranges I was eating along with the daily monster breakfast at Linda Mae's? I took to getting up at five and running the perimeter of the orchard. In fact, once I jogged to Linda Mae's, which earned me all kinds of teasing from the guys and Clay.

"Screw all of you," I said too loudly, and got a cross look from Linda Mae. When she came over, I put my hands up. "You're right, I know not to curse in front of the customers."

She walked off, shaking her head.

As soon as she was back in the kitchen, Clay and Melinda just about busted a gut laughing at me. I leaned over after checking to make sure Linda Mae was nowhere in sight. "Yeah, you two as well!" I whispered, which caused both of them to laugh so loud, they got the same look from Linda Mae as I had moments before.

When I finished my breakfast, I caught a ride back to the apartment with Melinda. After showering, I helped her sort the fruit and stock shelves. I was much better at that than harvesting oranges, but truth be known, I'd much rather be out in the groves, than in the store.

Regardless, I went where I was needed, and Melinda had lost her help.

"Why don't you hire someone full-time?" I asked Melinda. "It's not like you don't need the help, and you and Linda Mae are the only ones bringing in any income at the moment."

She just shrugged. "You've seen the bottom line, we barely make it as it is."

"What about marketing to the snowbirds that flock down here."

"We could, I suppose," she said. "But I don't have the manpower to deal with an upswing of customers."

"Screwed if we do, screwed if we don't," I said.

She nodded. "Yep, that's unfortunately the way of it."

"Okay, here's my offer. I'll come work for you full-time until we get the sales up to support a full-time person. If we succeed, you can hire someone to replace me."

Melinda looked at me for a moment. "No, that wouldn't work, Joshua. Your uncle specifically said he wanted you out in the orchards working with the men."

I held up my hand. "My uncle isn't in charge, and unless that's one of his conditions for me to inherit, I say let's do what we can to increase sales. If we're going to make it, I need to make a little more than what my uncle was living on."

She sighed. "I'll do it. But you work mornings with Clay and the guys and come to me after ten. That's when I see most of my customers, and you can help with the lunch crowd."

"Perfect," I said. "Now, how do we advertise to the snowbirds?"

Melinda and I hashed out a plan that included setting up visits from the local senior activity centers and RV parks.

Luckily, we got our schedule up and running quickly, because two weeks after setting our plan in motion, we were literally swamped with snowbirds. Even with me working full-time, we weren't able to keep up with the crowds and had to hire a full-time person and keep me working as well.

By the middle of March, when the crowds began to subside, we'd done an inventory of our citrus stock. We learned we had enough to last until June. Despite the fact it was about the same time the Valencia would start to ripen, we'd still be completely out of produce. Meaning, no oranges for Linda Mae, and nothing to sell in-store either.

Melinda, at my request, convened our first board meeting of the year, to discuss all the ups and downs we'd encountered during the season.

The board was an interesting group. Linda Mae and Melinda were present, of course, but there were four men I hadn't met.

Our meeting was more of a Sunday afternoon social than anything official. Mr. Clark had lived next to the groves for forty years. Before he retired, he was an administrator of one of our local hospitals.

Louis—he didn't like to be called Mr. Bennett—had been a banker, but he too was retired.

Reggie Smith was a wealthy man who'd purchased one of the groves just off the main highway that ran through Mesa, and currently, just kept it going for fun. He'd built an elaborate home on the property, and he suggested multiple times during the day that Clay and I might like to come over to go swimming in his pool. It only took me asking six times, before I figured out that he wanted to do *more* with us than just *swim.*

Finally, we had Dr. Jones. He had to have been close to ninety years old and could barely get around, but he used to be our biggest competitor. I quickly learned there was nothing about the business he didn't know.

After over an hour of talking and socializing, Linda Mae clapped her hands loudly, and told everyone to sit down. If we didn't get to business, she was going to miss her evening shows.

We all chuckled, and sat around one of the tables in the restaurant, where apparently, all the board meetings were held.

They all confirmed they were aware of my uncle's plan for me to inherit, and knew a bit about the hoops he'd set up for me, so I left that conversation alone.

Melinda gave everyone a copy of the financial status. "As you can see, we're still in the black, but we're headed toward the red if something doesn't change, and soon."

As we'd discussed, I began talking about the upswing in sales.

"Melinda and I have begun marketing to the snowbirds, and as a result, we've doubled sales this quarter. Unfortunately, that also means we have created another problem. Our estimates are that we're going to run out of produce before the summer's over."

"I wish you'd let me know," Mr. Smith said. "I basically gave away all my produce this year. I'd have happily given it to you."

"Maybe next year," Melinda told him.

"Clay and I can come over and take you up on that swim. You can show us your trees, and if need be, I can have our crew go out and tend to them." I inwardly cringed at what we'd have to do to avoid anything... uncomfortable.

Old Dr. Jones chuckled. "Boy," he said. "Why don't you let me reach out to a couple of the youngsters I know still working the groves around here?"

"By youngsters, you mean they're sixty?" Linda Mae said, winking at Dr. Jones.

"More like seventy, but you know kids these days, they need a strong upper hand," the older man teased her.

"Thank you, sir," I replied, before Linda Mae and he could go on with their digression. "If we can find a supplier, maybe we can continue to improve sales at the store. So, my goal over the next six months is to develop a strategic plan for the property as a whole."

It was Louis's turn to respond. "I hate to be the one to bring this up, but the reality is, the property is in the wrong place at the wrong time. You're being forced out of business, son. Maybe not today, but like I told Chris, at some point, you're going to have to face the music and either make the property a heritage site, or something that alleviates the pressure from the state and local governments, or you're going to have to develop or sell the property."

"As you all know, my uncle put restrictions on me, and therefore the board, so there isn't much we can do, at least not without a court battle. I don't know if we can save the property or not. And Louis, sir, it's very possible we can't, but I owe it to my uncle to try to figure it out."

This seemed to mollify the group, and they all nodded. We concluded quickly after that, having gained permission from the board to begin purchasing produce we hadn't grown ourselves, and allowing me to pursue other options for the property.

I was surprised the board wasn't more protective of the idea of not developing the land. I assumed my uncle had put these folks in place to protect the groves, but again, I'd underestimated him. Uncle

Chris's board was comprised of people who really could help with the business.

One week after we met, the first week of April, Melinda got a call from Dr. Jones. He had three men who wanted to meet us regarding selling us their surplus oranges. All three were still in the Salt Valley. One was on the reservation, and the other two weren't far away. "You'll have to send those boys over," he told her. "These men aren't going to do business with someone they haven't met face to face."

"You can tell he's pissed he's not able to go with you," she said.

"He may be old—" I replied, "—but that man is still a spitfire."

She laughed. "You have no idea, he gave Chris so much grief when they were in competition with one another."

"So, I'm guessing we're going to meet a few of the diehards?"

She chuckled. "I'd be willing to bet on it."

Chapter Sixteen

Clay

After the harvest, my life slowed back down to my normal fixing irrigation pipes and chasing our Jerk Russell Terrors around the property.

Joshua intrigued me. Now the initial reaction I'd had when I first discovered I was attracted to him, had settled some, I was able to keep myself under control.

Joshua was amazing with the dogs. He seemed to love working with them too. He'd come over to the house in the evening to pick Dude up, and as we waited for the foster parents to pick the pups up, he'd play with them all. When the others were gone, he'd spend about thirty minutes to an hour each evening playing with our three monsters.

All three were hardheaded, but it made Joshua laugh, instead of getting to him. He hadn't been bitten once since that first time, although Dude still tried to take my finger off from time to time. If Joshua saw it, though, Dude would end up on his back until he did whatever Joshua needed to see that said, the dog was ready to act right.

"You've got to learn to be the alpha," he'd told me, time and time again, and every single time he did, I imagined holding him, and kissing him senseless.

I would either walk away, or change the subject to avoid him seeing my arousal, caused by his innocent comments.

He was right about the dogs, though. All three of them respected Joshua in a totally different way than they did me. If Joshua called them, they came, and he didn't even have to use the whistle, *or* bribe them with food. Although, he always made a fuss over them, cuddling and kissing them when they did what he asked. All three little mongrels ate the attention up, like I never touched them. Guess the top dog's love was always a little sweeter.

Joshua set up a time to go visit the groves down along the reservation. He said Dr. Jones had recommended I go along too.

All three groves were run immaculately, but they were all less than a quarter the size of ours. All three got their water from the reservation, which helped cut costs compared to what we had to pay, so that did give them a little relief.

The first grove we visited was a recent acquisition, and although the owner's grandfather had owned the orange groves, he was still pretty green.

We inspected his surplus, and it was fine. There was very little grade-A, though. Most of his stuff would have to be used for juice, or sold as B in the store.

The guy didn't care much. He said he was still figuring things out, and would be happy to let us have it for what we'd offered. Mostly, he wanted to get it out of his cold storage, so he didn't have to pay the electric bill. "Putting the oranges out for compost just seemed wrong," he'd told us, after settling on the price.

The other two groves we visited were better quality. After we'd looked at the oranges they had in cold storage, the last family invited us to dinner at their place. We followed the older man, and were surprised to find the other family there as well.

"We figured, it would just be easier to deal with us both at the same time, hope you boys don't mind," the guy that had invited us said.

"Why do you have such a surplus?" Joshua asked.

"We usually run them down to Yuma to sell, but this year, the bottom fell out of the wholesale price. There was a glut in the market from California, and we couldn't compete, but we didn't want to give them away, either."

"What are your plans for them?"

"To be honest, it's a waiting game. We hope the California glut will thin out, then we can sell our product this summer."

I nodded. My late husband's family used to play the waiting game too. It was a game they usually lost.

"Well, we need the product," Joshua said. "Since you were honest with us, I'll be honest with you. I'd prefer to sell local products, even if it isn't ours. If you're going to have to wait anyway, and we can agree on a price, I'll buy what we can from you."

The farmers regarded Joshua warily. They wanted to believe Joshua could help them through this downward cycle of luck, but I knew from experience, there were more empty promises in this business than actual help.

Joshua must have sensed it too. "I can promise to take a certain number of boxes now, and I can give you the Yuma price plus twenty percent. Unfortunately, I can't do more than that, but I think that's fair, since I can't commit to all your produce, at least not yet."

The farmer we'd visited first stood up, reached over, and grabbed Joshua's hand. "It's a fair offer, and I accept. Call me Alfred, and we can talk about how you want to split the sale. Mr. Howard, you've done your uncle proud here tonight. We both respected him highly, and he was a tough negotiator, but he was fair. You seem to have inherited that same quality. You let us know if you need more."

Joshua sighed. "I understand I'm offering less than you made from Yuma last year, but we're struggling too. This is all an experiment to try to stave off the wolves."

Alfred just nodded and sadly looked down. "None of us are going to stave them off forever, son. At least you have a plan."

Joshua stood up, and I followed suit. "We'll be in contact. Maybe you can deliver the boxes later this week. We have room to store them, which might alleviate some of your storage issues as well."

As I listened to Joshua take the reins, negotiating prices with the farmers, and then finally hearing the offer he made, I realized I'd underestimated him. He'd done his research on what market value was, and had upped the price to make it fair. At the same time, he'd saved us money as well.

Alpha dog he was, and I was quickly learning that underestimating him would be a serious mistake.

Chapter Seventeen

Joshua

We'd set up a meeting with Mr. Smith, to view his groves and understand how to manage them, so next year's crop could be used in the store or restaurant. When I contacted him, I could tell the older man was tipsy.

"Oh, Joshua, I wondered when you'd call. I was beginning to wonder if you'd just said what you did to placate me."

"I'm sorry, sir," I said, trying to placate him now. "We ended up going down to meet with a couple farmers Dr. Jones knows. We've solved our need for more produce for this year."

"Oh, that's good, that's good," he said.

"Now, you and your boy, *Clay*," he said, with an indecent slur. "Can you two come by Saturday after next? I'm having a party, but the two of you can look through the trees," he hiccupped then, confirming he was indeed drunk. "Then you can come by my party, and maybe take a swim in the pool."

Dear God, I thought to myself. *What am I getting us into?*

"Sure, Mr. Smith, that'd be fine."

"Oh, you don't have to call me Mr. Smith. Just call me Reggie."

"Sure, thanks, Mr. um, Reggie."

The man chuckled, and hung up without saying goodbye.

I needed to meet Clay and pick Dude up, that had become my job since harvest time, and I enjoyed playing with the dogs, before they went to their foster families. Tonight, I was late, because of the call with Mr. Pervert.

I laughed at my own wit. I just needed to keep an eye on the man, I wasn't sure why my uncle had put him on the board, but since he had, I needed to give him the benefit of the doubt.

When I got to Clay's place, I was immediately attacked by several of the dogs who hadn't yet been picked up. "Sit!" I demanded, and most of them did as instructed. I reached into my pocket for the treats I'd brought with me, and gave a couple commands to each individual dog, calling their name first. I'd been working on them to recognize their name, instead of all of them attacking me for a treat at once.

No, I hadn't succeeded. Buddy came up each time I called a name, and when he didn't get a treat, he growled at me. Buddy was the hardest nut to crack, but I was a believer that patience always paid off, and continued my training every afternoon.

Finally, I made my way over to where Clay sat watching, or more accurately laughing at Buddy's refusal to follow my commands. "You just encourage him, you know that, right?" I asked.

He laughed again, so I playfully pushed him over, as I sat on the swing next to him.

"Hey, I've got, um... news." I said, knowing this was going to be as painful for him as it was for me. "Reggie Smith has asked us to go look over his groves..."

Clay moaned. "That man has more hands than an octopus."

I couldn't help but laugh. "I can't argue that, but if he's willing to let us have his oranges next season at a reasonable price, we may need him."

Clay just nodded, but didn't add anything else.

"Um, he also wants us to come to his pool party after we're done."

"Oh, no. I'll be wearing all my clothes when that man is around, and might even wear a chastity belt as well."

I leaned back, laughing, because frankly, I felt the same way.

"Well, we can probably get out of the party, but we do need to go see the trees."

Clay glared at me before smiling, and leaning into me for a shoulder bump. "As long as you're there to protect me."

I almost choked. "You're the butch one here. I think you've forgotten who you're talking to."

"Hardly," he replied. "You're a dominator when it comes to the dogs, and even that blockhead Buddy respects you."

I laughed, because Buddy didn't respect anyone, and we both knew it.

"You also impressed me with your work with the grove owners. Where did you learn to negotiate like that?"

"It's like I said, I grew up with a businessman as a father. I may not know how to be in a relationship, but definitely knew how to negotiate a deal."

"Would your father have been fair?" he asked.

I hated that he asked that question. I preferred people not to know what kind of man I'd come from. I decided it was best to be honest, so I looked at Clay and frowned. "No, he'd have raked them over the coals. My father is a ruthless businessman, and he'd consider me weak for offering them more than Yuma."

Clay just nodded. "You're a good man, like your Uncle Chris."

I just chuckled. "I have no idea who I'm like. I didn't know Chris, so I can't confirm what you say. You all have a different opinion of him than I do anyway." I drew in a breath, willing myself to shake off some of the bitterness before I responded. "It might be hard to hear, but my uncle put me in a really precarious position, and not for my interests, but for his. It's hard for me to see him as a generous person. The truth is, since arriving here, all I've seen regarding my uncle, is a man who is *exactly* like my dad. Apples don't fall far from the tree, Clay."

I stood to go. I didn't want to paint my uncle in a negative light. I still wanted to believe he was a good man, but dang, if that wasn't the opposite of what I'd seen. The reality was still the reality. I'd made the effort to call him, and as a result, he'd changed his will to make it more difficult for me to inherit. That wasn't a man who cared, that was a man who wanted to promote his own personal agenda.

"Wait," Clay said. "I'm still in the dark about what your uncle had in mind, and this whole charade you're stuck in, but I can tell you this much, he loved you."

"You don't know that. I hadn't seen him in years, Clay. The reality is he created this *charade,* because I reached out to him, wanting to see him. Had I just left well enough alone, his attorney said, I would've inherited the groves without any interference. I could do what I choose to do. I'm being punished for trying to know him." I realized I was being nasty, so I turned to leave, before I said too much.

"I know for a fact he loved you, because he told me," Clay said.

I turned around, unable to hold back the anger any longer.

"Yeah, Clay. He told *you*. He never told me. The man didn't even try to get in touch with me. Sorry, I know you cared about him, and I shouldn't be talking about it with you, but I can't pretend he was a good guy, at least not someone who cared about me. Not that anyone does."

Crap, did I just say that last part out loud? How wimpy am I?

I walked toward my uncle's old GMC truck, that I'd taken over when I had to turn my rental car in.

"Wait, I... *Joshua*, I can prove he loved you and cared about you.'

I kept walking. I'd done enough to embarrass myself. "*Keep your personal stuff away from business.*" Those were my dad's words. He'd shouted them at me the night he found me kissing Peter behind the pool house. Now they reverberated in my mind.

"I have a letter from him, Joshua. It says he loved you, and tried to see you, your dad wouldn't let him."

I turned back toward Clay. "What do you mean, my dad wouldn't let him? He tried to get in touch with me? When?"

Clay just shook his head. "I don't know. He didn't go into that much detail, just that he'd tried to see you, and your dad wouldn't let him."

"Show me!"

"Um, I'm not supposed to, it has instructions from your..."

I turned away again, headed for the truck. "Screw you... Screw all of you. Screw you, screw him, screw the crappy groves... I'm sick of the lot of you," I yelled over my shoulder.

Before I could get into the truck, I felt Clay's arms around me.

"Seriously, Joshua, I probably shouldn't have told you about the letter, but you can't keep thinking your uncle didn't care. He did care. I know him, and he would've fought for you. As it was, he practically adopted all of us as his family. You have to know the man wouldn't have thrown away his own kin."

"Why not?" I turned around and pushed Clay away from me. "I've been tossed away by family all my life. Why wouldn't he? You think I don't know what the world is really like? That I don't understand what having a kid you didn't want really means, or that tossing me aside to win a war with your uncle would've made me an asset to my father? I have no doubt my uncle did what you said, but answer me this. Why didn't he get in touch with me after I turned eighteen? What about when I graduated from college, and had to go to work for that monster, I call my dad? Where was he? I'm sorry you're wrong, and you can keep the stupid letter. I've got six more months to jump through hoops, then I'm going to do what I should've done. I'll sell this festering lump of desert sand and get the heck out of here. I'm sick of him. I'm sick of family in general! I'll be happy never to see my so-called *family* land ever again."

I climbed into the truck, threw it in reverse, and headed down the lane toward the apartment.

I was so happy no one was around, I'd ended up crying like a baby the entire night. I hadn't cried like that since I'd lost my mom, and my father had told me to stop acting like a girl, to get my ass out of the room, and get my chores done.

Luckily, my father was nowhere around, and as the tears fell, I was able to mourn all of them. My mom, a father who'd never loved or given a crap about me, and an uncle who apparently told people he cared, but that I'd never seen any evidence of.

I knew I couldn't make decisions while I was upset, and if I stayed here, I would.

In the wee hours the morning, I opened my computer and bought a last-minute ticket to Atlanta. Then I texted my friends Trevor and Peter, and asked if I could stay with them for a few nights. I needed to get the heck out of Mesa.

Peter texted back immediately, although it was only four in the morning in Atlanta. "You're always welcome, want me to pick you up at the airport?" he asked.

"No, I'll rent a car. Also, please keep my visit between us, I'd prefer my dad not know I'm in town."

I chuckled, realizing why Peter was up that early. "Hey, give a cuddle to my godson for me. I'm needing some significant Luka time!" I said, and in my mind's eye, I could see the rambunctious little toddler snuggled into Peter's arms, staring at him, and refusing to sleep.

It'd been six months since I'd seen him, and I could only imagine how much he'd grown while I'd been away.

My flight was scheduled to leave at five, which gave me an hour before I had to get down to the airport. I hadn't slept, but Trevor, Peter's husband's big home, had plenty of room, and I knew once I was there, I'd get all I needed.

I took a shower, packed, and left with plenty of time to spare.

When I got to the airport, I texted Melinda, telling her I'd be in Atlanta for a few days. She texted back immediately, asking if everything was okay.

> *Yeah, just need to get away. I'll let you know when I'll be back.*

Then, I turned my phone onto airplane mode and boarded my flight back to Atlanta, and away from the mess I'd found when I arrived here six months ago.

Chapter Eighteen

Clay

I didn't know if I'd done the right thing or not. Why did I feel like I needed to defend Chris? Truth was I'd thought since our meeting with Melinda, Linda Mae and Joshua, that if I'd been put in the same position as him, I'd have been pissed as I could be. Why did Chris think he had the right to force the guy to give up his entire life, to come here and run a business that was dying?

Yeah, Chris had been a surrogate father to me after my parents and husband died, and he'd help heal the wounds between Melinda and me regarding the adoption. He'd known Melinda at the time, and had seen what she'd gone through after giving me up. "She died for a while after that," he told me, and that was when Linda Mae refused to talk to her, so she didn't have anyone.

But, no matter what Chris had been to me, he wasn't that for Joshua, and it sounded like Joshua's father was a horrible man through and through. I also didn't know why Chris hadn't fought harder for him.

I'd almost gone after him, but every time I did that, it ended up backfiring on me. Just remembering that kiss could burn my insides to ashes, and turn me into a puddle of mush on the floor.

So, instead of following him, I'd given him space and decided I'd find him the next day, and show him the letter. Chris might still hold most of the cards, but I could at least do that for him.

Melinda called me at six the next day before I left for Linda Mae's. "Hey, do you know what's going on with Joshua?" she asked.

"Yeah, he had a bit of a blow-up last night about Chris. Why, is he okay?" I asked.

"No, apparently not. He flew back to Atlanta this morning. He didn't tell me why."

"Well, crap," I said. "Melinda, I've got to go and see if I can find him. I'll call you when I know something."

Before I could hang up, I heard Melinda say, "You better hope this hasn't got anything to do with you!"

"So much for familial support," I replied, before I hung up on her.

I called Joshua's number, but no one answered, so I left a message. "Hey, Joshua, I need to know where you've gone. I thought about it last night, and you're right. I'll overnight the letter to you, and you can read it for yourself."

When noon came, and he still hadn't called me back, I tried again. The message went to voicemail again. "Joshua, it's Clay again. Hey, give me a call, okay?"

I already knew the guy wasn't going to call me back. Around three, I texted him, asking for his address, because I wanted to send the letter from his uncle to him.

Melinda and Linda Mae were upset at me, of course, because it *must* be my fault, right? We'd all gotten into it that morning, and I finally slammed my fist on the table. "Listen, he was upset, and I told him the truth. It isn't my fault the whole thing is messed up, and he's been led around since it all started, like a puppy on a string. So Melinda, before you go pointing fingers, you might wanna look at your own self in the mirror."

I'd stomped out of the restaurant, and didn't look back. I was a snippy jerk for the rest of the day. I yelled at the workers for minor stuff, and had to apologize. Finally, because I was sick of myself and guilty for being a jerk, I'd sent them all home, saying we should all try a fresh start the next day.

I grabbed a shower, and when I came out of the bathroom, I found I'd gotten a text. It was from someone who said Joshua was staying with him, and gave me the address.

My initial thought was *I don't know this guy, and I shouldn't be sending personal correspondence to strangers.* I was just about to send that message back, when I had a hair-brained idea. I could just take the stupid thing to him myself. He wouldn't be in Atlanta if I hadn't intervened anyway, so it seemed like appropriate penance for me to hand-deliver the letter myself.

Luckily, I found a redeye leaving the next morning and booked it. I texted Melinda telling her I'd be gone for a few days and not to worry. The guys knew what needed doing, but if there were any problems, she could text me. She texted me back immediately.

You're going after him, aren't you?

I am, and don't try to talk me out of it.

Two seconds later, I got a call. "Yeah," I answered.

"Clay, are you sure this is a good idea? He said he needed to get away."

"Yeah, but you weren't there when he had his blowup. He thinks Chris didn't care, and the truth is, I'd wondered the same thing. Why would he put him through all this? Explain that to me, Melinda, why?"

"You know I can't, but it'll be clear in the end. I promise Chris wrote it all down."

"Then Chris is a jerk, and maybe we're all jerks too for playing his games, and putting that man through all this."

Melinda was quiet on the other end of the line. "You're right," she said. "He was a jerk about this. I feel guilty too, but if I don't follow the rules set out by the will, I could cause Joshua more problems. You have to trust me."

"I do trust you, but that doesn't mean Joshua does. It's time for someone to stand up for him, and for now, anyway, that's going to be me."

Melinda went quiet again. "Clay, don't forget to take care of yourself too. okay?" she asked.

I knew what she meant. It'd been months since the outburst at Luey's, and I had yet to talk to anyone about it, mostly, because I'd hoped the whole thing would be forgotten. I also knew, there was no one on earth at the moment with as much power to hurt me as the two women I was related to by birth and had become friends with by choice, and the only man I've had any feelings for since the loss of my husband almost six years earlier.

"I'm fine, Melinda. I'll let you know how he is when I see him."

I knew I was probably making a mistake. But I'd heard the finality in Joshua's words last night, I knew what that sounded like. I knew I'd sounded that way when I left Florida for the last time. It might be nuts, but if I didn't follow him, I was almost sure the guy wouldn't return, and even if he did, Chris's will and the stupid requirements, could make it too late for Joshua to inherit what was rightfully his.

Chapter Nineteen

Joshua

By the time I got to Trevor and Peter's house, I was exhausted. I'd had a little breakfast, thanks to Trever's Aunt Doris, who heard I was coming and came over to fix breakfast. Best of all, after everyone had eaten, I snuggled my godson Luka while he had his breakfast bottle. Two seconds after the bottle was gone, so was he, Peter following close behind him.

It was so funny watching Peter chase after the little tot.

"So, how has he been since I left? I swear he's doubled in size since I was here last."

Peter just chuckled. "He's growing like a weed. He's into everything. We've had to babyproof every room he has access to, and we worry about the ones he doesn't, since he has a knack of getting through any closed door."

I smiled as Peter brought him back into the dining room, and sat him on his knee while the little one wiggled to get free. Finally, Peter reached over and picked up a car, which Luka grabbed and said, "Dar!"

"That's right," Peter said. "'Car'."

"Dar!" Luka corrected, and scooted out of Peter's arms once again.

We all felt sorry for Peter, so we followed him into the music room that had been converted to a baby corral, with toys strewn around the floor.

It only took a few minutes before I began to fade and excused myself. "I'll take you up to your room," Peter said, handing the reins off to Trevor.

When we got to my room, Peter opened the door, and I hauled my luggage in. "So, you gonna tell me what's up?" he asked.

"Why do you assume something's up?" I asked.

"Cause, I know you, and I can tell when something's up!"

I sighed, knowing Peter was right. "Okay, well, I told you how my uncle slipped all these requirements on me regarding the estate. I sort of blew up at the hot property manager yesterday, and that was the last straw for me. I needed a break. Heck, I don't even know if I give a crap about the inheritance any longer. Even if I do survive all my uncle's ridiculous hoops, I still have the deed restrictions to worry about."

"So, you ran away?"

I just looked at Peter. "Did you not hear what I just said?"

"Yeah, I heard. And like I said before, I know you and when things get tough, Joshua, you tend to run for the hills."

"Peter, I don't have the energy for this right now. Seriously, I need a break, and I really need you to be neutral, at least for the moment."

Peter stood up, and pulled me into a huge bear hug. "You know I'm never neutral, but for now, I'll give you a break. That's all I've got to offer, buddy."

I chuckled. No, Peter was never neutral. He was opinionated and usually right, but hardly ever neutral.

"Okay, I'll take it."

"Smart man! Get some rest, and then come down when you're ready."

I felt better after I'd woken up, and although I'd only gotten four or five hours sleep, I figured I'd better get up, since I'd have to sleep again tonight.

When I came down, the house was empty, except I could hear someone in the music room. When I walked around the corner, Peter was working on his computer.

"Where's the rest of the hoard?" I asked.

"Aunt Doris took them all out, so you could rest."

"They didn't have to do that. I can sleep through a hurricane."

"I think it was an excuse for her to get her nephews out and show them off. Did you sleep well?"

"I did, thanks."

"Okay, so I agreed to give you a break, but you know I'm curious about your new life. Can you fill me in without it breaking my word?"

I just laughed, I knew Peter wouldn't leave it alone, and truth be told, I really did need to talk it out.

So, I broke it down in detail, telling him about all the insanity around my uncle's wishes, the pressure the state and local governments were putting on us, including escalating taxes and water costs."

"And the sexy manager?" Peter asked.

"You caught that, huh?" I asked, shaking my head.

"Oh, you know I caught that," he said, winking at me.

"He's one of the most handsome men I've ever met. He's got muscles galore, and he's usually calm, unless I'm around. He also has a really bad habit of grabbing and holding me when I'm in the middle of a meltdown."

"Oh crap, really?"

"Yeah, really, and you know how much I like to be touched."

"Well, do you really mind if he's as hot as you say?"

"No. At first I did, but that's when I thought he had some kind of angle, but to be honest, the last time, it felt so good to be in his arms, especially when I was blowing my top."

"You do tend to do that well, but god help me, I'd never think to touch you when you're going off."

I laughed. "Yeah, no one in their right mind would, not even my father."

"So, does he know you like him?" Peter asked.

"Well, that's complicated. I'm sort of his boss, although, technically, he's my boss, so when he kissed me, I sort of nipped it in the bud."

Peter's face lit up like a light bulb. "He kissed you?"

My face turned red. "Well, yeah, sort of. During one of my blowups, he was sort of drunk, and he sort of laid like the most amazing kiss on me I'd ever experienced before... *ever.*"

Peter laughed out loud. "You are a mess, Joshua. A total mess. So, have you kissed him again?"

"No, of course not, I put the skids on and told him to back off. My attorney even told me to make sure I didn't go there with him. It could cause all kinds of problems with the will."

"Like what?" Peter demanded.

"Like, I don't know, he could sue or something."

"It sounds like he kissed you, and you told me before you couldn't fire him, even if you wanted to. So, what's the big deal? It can only be deemed harassment if you can fire him, or make his working for you difficult, right?"

"I guess... I don't know, Peter. I keep hearing my dad going nuts over you and the idiot I'd gotten involved with before you. 'Keep your personal stuff out of the business'. He's right about that too... they don't mix, and when I've mixed them, it's just created a whole bunch of problems."

"I don't know, considering you are standing in my house, I think we worked it out pretty well."

"Yeah, after my father fired you!"

"Your dad's a douchebag. He wanted to fire me anyway, cause we disagreed about the structural issues on the Grant Building. I don't know if you've noticed, but your dad isn't real keen on being disagreed with."

I just laughed. This had been an ongoing discussion since Peter had been fired from my dad's company.

"Besides," he added. "I've landed on my feet."

I stood up and paced toward the window and looked out, before pacing back. "He called and left a message."

"Your dad?" Peter asked.

"No, blockhead. Clay, the property manager."

"Oh, and what did he say?"

"He's offering to send my uncle's note." When Peter looked at me like I'd missed several important details, I sighed. "I was having a tantrum because of my uncle's hoops, and even pulled my father's bad attitude toward me into it. Clay told me he had a letter my uncle had written him that said he loved me. I know it's ridiculous, but it matters to me that he did, you know, care, even though nothing indicated he did ever since I arrived, and ended up at his funeral."

Peter shook his head. "So, why not let him send you the letter?"

"To be honest, I have too much pride. I acted like I was Luka's age, Peter, and I still have to work with the man. I told him I didn't give a crap about his letter, and now I'm going to run over to him like a dog with his tail between his legs? That isn't very professional."

"You're letting your pride get in the way of what's good for you, and the fact that your uncle mixed everything up with your inheritance already made it personal. I say, let your pride go a bit and call the man back."

I shook my head and got up, ready to change the subject. "Hey, I'm going to run down the street to the little restaurant we used to go to. Want me to grab you something?"

"You aren't shaking me off that easy, Joshua Howard. Let's go together. I wanna hear all about how hot this man is."

When I gave him a friendly punch on the arm, he pushed me back. "Hey, I'm an old married man with a two-year-old! All I do is clean up poop and put his toys away. I have to live vicariously through my single friends!"

"You're madly in love. I'm not fooled by you, Peter Reed!"

Peter laughed as he put his shoes on, and we headed to the restaurant around the corner from his house.

Chapter Twenty

Clay

I rushed to the airport and got there just in time for my flight. I'd overslept, and had it not been for the dogs needing to go out, I might have missed the plane altogether. I had to ask myself, was this some kind of sign I was doing the wrong thing?

Oh well. Too late to back out now.

When I arrived in Atlanta, I decided not to rent a car. I might not be here for more than a few hours before I had to fly back. The first thing I noticed when I stepped out of the airport was the humidity. Dang, I didn't miss that. Sure, the heat was so intense in Mesa at the moment, that it could melt your shoes if you stood too long on the pavement. Still, I'd take the heat over the humidity any day.

I found a taxi sitting outside the airport. After giving the man the address, he took off like a bat out of hell. I'd swear, it didn't matter if you were in New York, LA, or Atlanta, taxi drivers all drove like they wanted to kill everyone in the car. At least the ones I hired did.

We pulled up in front of a large building. I paid the driver, got out, and looked up at the giant house sitting on the hill. To say I was intimidated was an understatement. Who was the owner of this kind of estate? I turned around where I stood and saw similar homes surrounding that one.

It was almost as if I'd gone back in time, except a car dashed behind me, causing me to realize I was still in the middle of the street.

I quickly rushed up onto the porch and rang the doorbell. It took several moments before anyone came to the door, and when they did, it was an older woman carrying a very wriggly infant.

"Can I help you?" she asked.

I cleared my throat, showing how nervous I was. "Um, is this where Joshua Howard is staying?" I asked.

The woman looked uncomfortable. "Who are you?" she asked.

I squirmed, not unlike the little one. "I'm Clay Masters. I, um... I work for him."

"I see," she replied. "Can you wait here, I'll see if he wants to see you."

Well, at least I knew I was in the right place. I sat on the little wicker swing that hung next to the door. It took several minutes before anyone came back, but when the door finally opened, I found a very grumpy Joshua looking at me.

He came outside, closing the door behind him "Clay, why are you here?"

"Um," I said, not ready for the confrontation. I swallowed and forced the words out. "Um, I thought you should have this. I thrust Chris's letter at him, then I got up and was about to leave.

"Wait, where are you going?" he asked.

I shrugged as I walked down the stairs and toward the street. When I got to the bottom, I turned and said, "I just wanted you to have that, and I didn't want to mail it without speaking to you first. When you didn't return my call, I decided to bring it here myself."

I turned again to leave. "Wait. You did not just fly all the way from Phoenix to give me this and leave. Come in, and I'll pour us both some coffee."

I was hesitant. I didn't want any more confrontation. I just wanted Joshua to know Chris had said he cared about him, and that even if I left, he had a right to his ancestral property.

"I think I should go," I said and turned again.

"If you leave like this, you are so freaking fired," he said to me.

That shocked me. If he were going to fire me, there were a lot better reasons, like grabbing and kissing him without permission, for example.

"Why? Why do you want me to stay?" I asked. "I've messed up since I met you. If anything, I've made things worse for you since you walked into the groves. I can't change that, but at least I can get out of your way, so you have a chance at finishing what you've started."

"What are you saying?" he asked.

I shrugged. I'd been thinking about it a lot. I loved the groves, sure, and I knew it was a refuge for me, but that had been years ago, it was time to let go and leave, time to give Joshua back what belonged to him.

"I'm going to head back up to New Jersey, where my folks lived. I own a house there. There's a renter in it now. I'm going to go up and check on it, then I'll figure it out from there."

"What? You're quitting on me?"

I was caught off guard by his anger. "Quitting on you? No, I'm getting out of your way. You left because of my stupidity. I'm not going to get in the way of your inheritance, Joshua. The guys can do the job with their hands tied behind their backs. They don't need me supervising anyway, and you are more than competent to handle the day-to-day stuff. It's best if I go."

"The hell it is," he said, the temper I'd seen flair before was beginning to ignite. "You're right, you've made my being in Mesa difficult. For some reason, my uncle put you in front of the inheritance, but that's on him, not you. Now, I'm not going to ask you again. Come in and have some coffee, so we can talk like civilized people, instead of making a spectacle in front of Trevor and Peter's neighbors!"

He turned to go inside, dismissing any further argument from me. So, I walked back up the stairs and into the grand entryway.

We walked into a large living area with a dining room attached. That side of the house was open concept leading back into a large kitchen space. Two men sat at the table, each had their hands full with the toddler. The woman who'd met me at the door was in the kitchen, and I followed Joshua until he told me to sit at the table with the other two men.

"I'm on breakfast duty this morning, so you can sit here and get to know Trevor and Peter. That little one is Luka." Then he disappeared into the kitchen.

I introduced myself to the men, noting that Joshua hadn't told them my name. Yeah, he was still pissed, I was here. Again, I had to wonder why I'd come.

Trevor and Peter were fun to talk to, even though they were inquisitive.

So, how long have you been at the groves?" the one named Trevor asked.

"Um, six years now," I answered.

"You're a professional orange grower then, so did you grow up in that business?"

I deflected the question. "Not exactly."

They continued to ask questions. I'd become so good at deflecting personal questions, they didn't even seem to notice I always brought the conversation back to the groves.

I noticed a couple times that when I deflected a question, Joshua would look over at me from the stove with a look of concern or frustration or well, I couldn't really read his expression, but it wasn't good whatever it was.

The woman and he brought out eggs, bacon, and biscuits to the table, then went back into the kitchen to grab butter and jelly and a pot of coffee. After filling my cup, Joshua refilled the ones around the table.

"So, you've met Trevor and Peter. Peter is my best friend," he said. "Trevor is his husband and that little tyke over there is my godson," he said.

Pride flowed out of him as he looked toward the little one.

Then he turned to the woman. "This is Doris, Peter's aunt."

I smiled and greeted everyone, then Joshua said, "This is Clay Masters. He runs the groves for me in Mesa."

Doris smiled in a way that told me I was in trouble. "So, what brings you to these parts, Clay." Her accent clearly exaggerated.

I cleared my throat. I hadn't been prepared to be questioned about it, and I wasn't quick-witted enough to dodge the question, so I answered honestly. "I was a shit to Joshua before he left, and didn't give him something that he has a right to see, so I came out to ensure he got it."

The second I finished, I saw the group flinch and look at the baby. It was then I realized I'd said a curse word in his presence. *Dang*, I thought, *I shouldn't be allowed out in public.* Luckily, the little one was so busy putting blocks in a big wooden box that he didn't seem to notice what I'd said.

"Sorry," I said, my face turning red. "It's been a long time since I was around a toddler."

Peter laughed. "We all slip up, but he's become a freaking parrot lately, so we have to be extra careful what we say."

To confirm that fact, the little one said, "Reaking pawwot!" as he continued playing with the blocks.

Everyone chuckled, except Peter, who just shook his head.

"At the moment," Trevor said. "He seems to only be mimicking his daddy, Peter."

Joshua looked at me then, and asked, "How did you know where I was?"

I shrugged. "Someone sent me your address."

Peter's face grew red, and Joshua narrowed his expression on him. Then he looked at the group, before standing up. "No guess who'd that'd be, huh? Peter."

"Well, you were in bed already, and I saw his message pop up about where to send the letter. You said you wanted to read it, so it seemed to make sense to give it to him."

Joshua pinned his friend with the disapproving look again, but there was no heat in it. "Well, he's here now, so y'all get to decide where he's gonna stay, and I'm not offering him my bed, since *you* are responsible."

"No, I'm not staying," I said, standing up too quickly and almost toppling the chair over. "I'm just here to drop off the letter, and—"

"You are not leaving yet, and that's final," Joshua said. "If they don't have room for you in this enormous mansion, then I'll get you a room at the bed and breakfast a couple doors down."

"No, we have plenty of room," Trevor replied. "In fact, we'll put you guys next door to one another."

I gulped. The last thing I needed was to be in a room with adjoining doors to Joshua.

"Um, that's generous of you, but I really..."

Joshua put his hand up to stop me and turned to the group. "I need to have a moment with my *employee*," he said, emphasizing the last word. "If you can put the dishes in the sink, I'll get to them when I come back."

He walked over, and all but pulled me out the front door. "Come with me, Clay, we're going for a walk."

Chapter Twenty-One

Joshua

I was mad enough that I was seeing red. I'd left Mesa to get away from my problems, even if for just a stinking minute, then Clay showed up and threw the entire mess back in my face. I'd have to deal with Peter later about boundaries, and sharing addresses with people I was avoiding.

I knew better than to react while angry, and at least while sitting at the breakfast table, I had a moment to collect my temper. As soon as we were outside the house, though, the anger rolled over me again. I did the only thing I knew would help, I speed-walked several blocks, only partially aware that Clay was behind me.

Finally, after arriving at a park where only a couple people could be seen walking around, I turned on Clay. "I'm so pissed at you," I said, although I still wasn't a hundred percent sure why.

"I know," he said. "I'm sorry, Joshua."

"You come all the way here, with the lame excuse that you were going to drop off a letter I'd already told you I didn't need to see, then you drop the bomb on me that you're going to quit, just like that. No real excuse, other than you've somehow made my life more difficult?"

Clay just stared at the ground, and the genuinely sad look on his face was like water on the angry fire.

I sighed, and sat down on a bench close to where we were standing.

"Clay, why did you really come out here?" I asked, tired of all the strange games the two of us had been playing. He shrugged like a teenager, and although he'd sat next to me, he kept his gaze downcast. "That's not good enough. You need to come clean. Is this some garbage you and my uncle cooked up?"

He looked up at me, genuinely shocked. "No, nothing like that, Joshua. You have to believe me. I only talked to your uncle about you a few times, and certainly not about this. To be honest, I was as clueless about my part in all of this as you were."

I looked at him skeptically. "Read the letter," he said. "That's the first time I'd heard about what he wanted me to do."

He pulled the letter out of his back pocket and handed it to me. I sighed, too tired to do anything, but what he said, and I began to read.

Dear Clay,

As I read the letter that was never intended for me to see, I couldn't hold back the tears. He had come after me, if what my uncle had said was correct, he cared about me, and I could totally see my father placing every roadblock in my uncle's path to me, for nothing else than to spite someone who crossed him.

I looked back up at Clay, surprised at how empty I felt. I sighed and stared at the small lake in front of us, a momma duck and several ducklings swam across, which under normal circumstances would've made my heart swell.

"Did you drink the whole bottle?" I asked.

"Huh?" Clay responded. "What bottle?"

I handed the letter back to him. "He told you not to drink the whole bottle of Jack."

Clay looked down at the letter and back up at me. "That's what you got out of the letter?"

I chuckled. "No, but that's the least loaded part of it. I'm not sure I know how to digest the rest. I told you I didn't want to read it."

Clay shook his head and looked at the ducklings. "At least now you know I wasn't a part of this mess. I'm a pawn just like you."

"That doesn't help. Now the only person I have to blame is a dead man, and Melinda, I guess, but it's hard to be mad at her."

Clay chuckled. "You're telling me. Try coming to terms with the fact she's your birth mom, and gave you away."

"You mad about that?" I asked.

"I used to be, but no... she was a kid and had no way of supporting me. My birth father was a drug dealer who was killed two months after being incarcerated. I shudder to think what my childhood would've been like if she'd kept me."

I sighed, no idea what to say, so I said what first came to mind. "I wish my dad had given me up for adoption."

Clay looked at me, shocked, then looked away. "Did he abuse you?"

"Not physically, although he gave me a few spankings that might have gotten him in trouble if social services had known. Mostly, to him, I wasn't even worth hitting. I was a pesky parasite that he was stuck with. Anyway, this isn't about me. I asked you why you came out, why you *really* came out. I deserve a straight answer, Clay."

He laughed, but there was a bitter tone to it. "I'm pretty sure you *really* don't want my answer," he replied. "Trust me, my honesty will not make this any easier!"

I think I already knew enough about what he was interested in. I leaned over before I could talk myself out of it, and kissed him gently on the cheek. "I'm attracted to you too. It's inconvenient, and it's tricky, and probably inappropriate, but if that's what's on your mind, then let's get it out in the open... and now is the best time, while we're on neutral ground."

"I kissed you like an idiot ass already, so there's no surprise, but it was sure a surprise to me, Joshua. I haven't kissed another man since my husband died. I thought all that was over for me."

I looked at him, somewhat taken aback. "You're what, thirty-nine? How can that be over?"

"You're a jerk. I'm thirty-one. I met my husband at university while going for my Ph.D., I don't look thirty-nine years old!"

I chuckled. "I see you're a bit vain, that's good to know."

"I'm only a few years older than you. I'm not a freaking daddy, for god's sake."

"You sort of are." I laughed. The banter seemed to be helping ease some of the tension.

Then it clicked that he'd said they'd met while pursuing a Ph.D. "You are Dr. Clay Masters?" I asked, letting the shock wash over me.

Clay sighed and nodded. "Not many people know that about me, at least not in Mesa."

"Does Melinda know?" I asked.

He shook his head. "I haven't told her, or anyone."

"Dang, Clay, why are you such a closed book?"

Clay stared at the water for a long time. "It's really hard for me to talk about, and I left that life behind me. I..." he stopped talking, and when I looked back at him, he looked green around the edges.

"Wow, you really are weirded out talking about yourself, you know, that's sort of messed up, right?"

He shook his head and stood up.

"What the crap? You are *not* going to walk away," I said, the anger coming back. "Sit down and fess up. What is going on with you?"

Instead of sitting, Clay began pacing around me. "I'm not sure I can..." he said, and before I knew it, he was over at the edge of the pond, puking his guts out.

"Um," I said, as I put my hand on his back, "It's that bad?"

He nodded and stood up. "I haven't..." he hesitated and spat, obviously trying to rid himself of the rest of the sick. "I don't talk about this stuff. I haven't talked, and..."

He looked like he was going to be sick again, and so I stopped him. "Okay, I get it, this is hard on you. You don't have to tell me about your past, but I need to understand what's going on between us. Can you explain that much, at least?"

He nodded. "Let's walk back to your friend's house. I need a moment to get myself together."

We walked quietly past the beautiful Victorian homes, and when we got back to Trevor and Peter's place, Clay excused himself. Taking his bag, he went into the downstairs powder room.

"What's going on?" Peter asked me.

"Beats me, the guy's screwed up about something."

"I see that. Trevor has Luka up in the attic room, and Doris has gone back to her place, so you two have this level to yourself. Let us know if you need anything."

I stood up and thanked Peter for understanding. "It's okay... remember you were here while we were going through our own drama, it's our turn to support you."

Just the thought of the nightmare Trevor's parents had put them through when Luka was little, made my stomach hurt.

"I'd have thought you'd never want to think about that again," I said.

Peter frowned. "It's part of our life together, as Whitney Houston said, 'You can't run from yourself, there's nowhere to hide'."

"That's your drag song, right?"

"Dang, I really do tell you too much," Peter said, before sprinting up the stairs, laughing.

Clay came out shortly after, looking significantly less green than when he went in.

Chapter Twenty-Two

Clay

Using the restroom had given me a moment to collect my thoughts. How much to tell? What to tell? I'd never been good figuring all that out.

As long as people didn't ask me to deal with them on an emotional level, my Asperger's didn't usually impede me from functioning in my day-to-day life. It did, however, keep me from having insight on some things, and it for sure made processing my losses much more difficult.

I decided, the best way was to spell it all out, and let Joshua work it out for himself.

When I found Joshua, the house seemed empty, at least, until I'd heard Joshua and his friend talking. I couldn't really hear what they were saying, but when I heard laughing, I thought that was a good indication that the mood was lighter and easier to navigate. Even when people were laughing at me, it meant the heavy emotional stuff was easier to deal with.

Joshua frowned when he saw me. I was not sure he meant to, but I noticed anyway. My mother had worked with me since my doctor told her I had a mild case of Asperger's Syndrome when I was in middle school. So, noticing when people made facial expressions, had become something I was well-trained to do.

"Let's go into the living room," he said, and I nodded and followed him.

Joshua started the conversation. "I'm not going to pressure you, Clay. This is obviously difficult for you, but I do need to know where we stand, before we go back to Mesa. This emotional roller coaster has to stop."

When I sat across from him, I blurted out, "I have Asperger's, or a mild form of it. That doesn't mean I don't have emotions. In fact, I do, but I've been told mine are often bigger than other people's, and dealing with them is hard for me.

That's what you need to know about me, before we talk much more."

Joshua nodded. "I had a friend in high school with Asperger's, so I know a bit about that, and how your emotions can get in your way."

"So, good, you know a little about it then. It's hard to explain to someone who's never had experience with it."

"I don't have a lot of experience, but I do know that when my friend needed to talk about something, it was better for him to just say it, instead of bottling it up. It might come out weird, but it's easier to manage once it's out. Is that the same with you?"

"Sort of. I don't usually talk about my emotions at all... I could, some, with my mom, but now that she's gone, I don't really."

"I see," Joshua said. "Well, answer me this... how did you lose your family? You don't have to tell me about your feelings. Just tell me the facts."

I thought about it for a moment, and that felt better, like I was looking at something objectively.

More like reading an article, like the article I kept in my house about it.

"There was an accident on I-95 headed into New York." I knew I was speaking as if I was reading about the incident, and I was about to call my parents Mr. and Mrs. when I caught myself.

"My parents and husband were driving to the airport when they were hit by an eighteen-wheeler going the wrong way. All three were pronounced dead at the scene."

Joshua's hand came up to his mouth, the way people did when they were shocked.

"I was in Scotland. I'd spent a couple months there earlier with a group of mathematicians who were working to solve mathematical equations that might help with technological advances in healthcare. It was a big deal, and I'd helped the group solve one particularly difficult equation that pertained to probability. I traveled back to Scotland to receive an award... they were all coming to meet me."

Joshua shook his head. "You lost all of them at once. I'm sorry, Clay."

I'd always been confused by that statement. When you were sorry, that was what you said when you needed to apologize. Of course, I understand empathy, but if you weren't responsible, why would you be sorry?

"Thanks, Joshua, but it took a long time to fall in love with my husband. That's not really true, I fell in love with him almost instantly, but I didn't really understand it." I chuckled. "I was a jerk to him. I felt something, and that pissed me off. I was snapping at everyone around me, including my parents. My mother finally sat me down, and after asking a few questions, figured it out, and told me she thought I was in love with him."

"So, you came to Mesa to get away?" Joshua asked.

"Well, not exactly. I went back to Florida, but my in-laws were, well, they were struggling with me being there. I sold our property in Florida, then went back up to New Jersey and emptied my parents' home and rented it. Melinda was my only family connection left on the earth, so I decided I'd go find her. That's how I ended up in Mesa."

Joshua sat back. "Tell me about your relationship with Chris. How did you end up in such an executive position?"

I sighed. I'd always believed relationships were personal. I didn't like to talk about them, even after I'd lost the person to death. It felt like I was betraying them and what we'd had by discussing it with others, but I also understood that I couldn't avoid talking to Joshua either. Too much had happened.

"Chris was just my employer when I showed up at the store. And when I met Melinda the first time, she immediately took me under her wing. When she asked Chris if I could stay in the Airstream, he immediately said yes. He even went with me to pick up some things to keep there."

Joshua just nodded. When he didn't say anything, I continued, "Over the next few weeks, I just sat in the Airstream, staring out the tiny window, unable to figure out what to do or how to function. Melinda would check on me every day, but I'd never told her about my inability to deal with emotional distress, so I think she just assumed I was depressed.

"Several weeks after I arrived, she showed up with Chris, who offered to have me work on his team. It was right before harvest, and he said he could use an extra pair of hands. My parents used to tell me you never took from anyone without returning the favor, and I knew I could help him with my labor. What I hadn't anticipated was how much I'd enjoy the work. Up until then, I'd only worked with my mind, solving equations, sometimes teaching, but I wasn't very good at that. Students required too much interaction and understanding.

"When harvest season was over, Chris offered me a full-time job. I worked a full year for him before he promoted me. That was after he'd got sick again. He spent about a month in the hospital, while they gave him radiation treatment. While he was gone, the guys tended to lean on me for guidance, mostly because I was so analytical. When Chris came home, he wasn't really able to function much, so I continued to run the team, and helped

Melinda care for him. After he recovered and was in remission, he promoted me to manager, although it wasn't necessary. I was happy to continue as I had been doing."

Joshua shook his head. "When I went through the documents, your name wasn't listed anywhere for payment. I asked Melinda about it, but she just said you and Chris had an agreement. What's that about?"

"I didn't need Chris's money. I received a large prize with my award. I also do consulting work from time to time for the tech company that sponsored the event in Scotland. With the sale of our home in Florida, I'm reasonably well off, and Chris didn't have enough money to really pay me. I refused to accept funds from him, because he provided housing."

I chuckled at the memory. It'd been really intense when Chris came down on me for the first time. I pulled myself out of the memory, and continued, "That's when Chris said he'd fire me if I didn't start taking an income. I really didn't want or need his money, but I did need that job. To be honest, it's what kept me stable, kept me from losing my mind." I looked at Joshua, hoping he'd understand. When he nodded at me, I felt better, like he got it... maybe, he was more like Chris than I'd given him credit for.

"I'd seen the old ranch house sitting on the edge of the property. Chris basically used it for storage, and it was fairly rundown. I liked the house, and thought I'd enjoy fixing it up, something that could help keep my mind occupied at night, and in the mornings when things tended to get harder for me. So, I made a deal with Chris. If he'd let me stay and work for him, I'd live in the house. He agreed to pay for all the supplies to fix it up as well. He started paying me too, but I refused to cash the checks. Again, I knew we were becoming financially unstable, and I didn't want to take money that Chris needed. Finally, Chris got angry with me. He said he'd get in trouble if I didn't accept payment for working there, so I suggested he just give me the house. So, he did. We went to the attorney, and he added me to his will."

I got nervous, then afraid that would piss him off, and quickly added, "Joshua, I don't need the house. I'll sign it back over to you. I know it was your family's house, and you probably want it back. I just agreed, so Chris wouldn't make me leave."

"I don't want it back, Clay. I just wanted to understand. Since coming to Mesa, I've been stumbling around, knowing there were lots of things happening, and no one willing or able to explain what's going on. When Arlington, the attorney, told me you were technically over me, well, I got suspicious, because, to me, it looked like you and Melinda were working together against me. I kept asking Melinda questions, but let me tell you, that woman is an expert at keeping secrets."

Joshua chuckled. "She's cool, but like her mom, when she gets her mind made up, you aren't going to convince her to change it."

I just smiled. Since moving to Mesa, I'd learned that I was more like her than I realized. The Asperger's was undoubtedly part of who I was, but I was also stubborn, and that, apparently, was genetic.

Joshua put his hand over mine. "When you add the other part, the part where you kissed me, well, that made me *very* suspicious. I've been taken advantage of before, Clay. I have a difficult time trusting men. Of course, my father is a jerk too, so that certainly hasn't helped either. I thought you were straight, or bisexual, and trying to take advantage of me, or trying to thwart the inheritance. Besides, Arlington told me you'd worked against him with my uncle about developing the property. So, it all sort of made sense. You could tell I was gay, and you wanted to take advantage of the vulnerable nephew."

I was shocked, to say the least. I knew I missed social cues. It was the part of Asperger's that caused me the most problems, but I'd never have guessed he thought I was trying to take advantage of him. I knew I needed to say something, but I could feel myself shutting down. I needed to shift directions, or I could lose my control, which I hadn't done since I'd blown up at my in-laws. That had led to me being kicked out and asked not to return.

"Joshua, I'm really not doing well. I need a break, okay? I promise to tell you more, but can I have a few minutes to calm myself down?"

He nodded and led me up the stairs to his room. "You can either stay in here, or take a walk, whatever you need. Just come get me when you're ready."

Then, he left me alone. *That* wasn't what I'd expected. People usually pried or pushed me. They never just walked away, at least, not unless they were my teachers or parents, or someone who'd seen me at my worst. I lay on the bed, doing the finger counting game I used as a kid to calm myself. I'd seldom needed it at the groves, but here I was without any of my tools to help. Here, I was like I used to be when I was a kid, and I needed the old game to self-soothe.

Chapter Twenty-Three

Joshua

After showing Clay his room, and leaving him there, I came back downstairs and sat in Trevor and Peter's music room. I liked this room, because, unlike the other side of the house, this one was intimate and personal. The rest of the home was open, and although conceptually, I preferred that, when you lived with other people, a smaller space was always a good place to get away.

This room was special. You could tell at one time it had been reserved for the family's more intimate gatherings. There was a beautiful bay window that curved out into the large front porch. Inside the window was a place to sit and look outside.

When I was staying with Trevor, after Luka had been kidnapped, Trevor tended to sit in this spot for hours, staring out toward the street, almost like he was willing the baby to come home.

Today, I sat where Trevor had, but I was sitting here digesting what Clay had told me. He'd never been out to get me, that was clear now. My uncle needed his butt kicked for leaving things as he did. Of course, he was dying. It was probably difficult to figure out how to put all his manipulations together without making mistakes. It still hurt to assume he thought I was too childlike to understand what he wanted, or that I wouldn't listen to his wishes, just like I'd assumed Clay was out to get me.

I could feel the frustration building again, so I decided to let those thoughts go. I needed to apologize to Clay. I bet he *did* need a break, I was forcing him to face stuff he'd been avoiding for years, and in reality, I'd treated him like he was a conman since I'd walked into his life.

I'd fallen asleep on the bay-window seat. The late-afternoon sun was pouring in and warming my legs. I'd always been a sucker for lying in the sun as it filtered through the window. My mom used to tell me I must be part cat.

When I woke up and looked around, I saw Clay sitting across from me, staring out the window.

"Clay, you should've woken me."

"No, you looked so peaceful, I figured you'd wake soon, since you were sitting up."

I smiled. "It's such a nice spot. It's easy to fall asleep here."

"There's a window seat like that one in the Mesa house. Do you remember it?"

I shook my head, not able to recollect the seat he was talking about. Then, the memory came to me, and I chuckled. "That's a little different from this one. You're talking about the one in the dining room?"

He nodded. "I like sitting there during the winter months when the sun isn't as intense. I put cushions like that one on it."

My mom had used it as a sort of buffet, but it was usually just full of stuff that changed with the season. In the winter, it tended to be where bushels of oranges would sit. In the summer, I had all my stuff on it, like toys or games. It was often too hot to do much outside, so that had often been my play area.

"I'd forgotten all about that!" I said.

'You should move back into your house," Clay said. "It holds good memories for you. Even I can tell your face changes when you look at it or think about it."

I could feel my smile getting bigger. "Those are my best memories. My mom cooking in the kitchen, my dad working in the big sheds behind the house. They're my happy memories. But, I like you living there. It's not my home any longer. My dad and I moved long ago, leaving it to sit vacant all those years. I can't imagine what kind of condition it was in when you got it. No, it's your house, and you've more than earned it. No matter what we do, I like the idea that the home will always be there."

"You're more like your uncle than you think. He wanted to leave thinking the land would be there, that oranges would continue to grow there. He used to talk about that..." Clay looked over at me. "He used to say, his ancestors took desert land that had been scrub brush and mesquite and transformed it into an orange grove. He told me his parents used to talk about it being a miracle that was created by blood, sweat, and tears."

I listened to him, comparing me and my love of my childhood home, with the groves that I'd now come to think of as my uncle's obsession.

"I never thought of it that way. I guess for me, these past few months have been me dealing with my uncle's obsession. I didn't think about the nostalgia."

"You've just been angry," Clay said matter of factly, then seemed to recognize what he'd said, and tried to backpedal. "I mean, not that you don't have a right to be..."

I just laughed. "Seriously, Clay, you don't have to try to protect my feelings. You're right, I've been mad. And since you're there and my uncle isn't, I've been directing my anger toward you. I didn't realize that until today. Clay, I need to apologize for that. I made a lot of assumptions about you, and they were wrong."

Clay sighed. "I didn't know how to fix it, so stupid me kissed you. I know I shouldn't have."

I laughed. "How many people have you kissed since being in Mesa?"

Clay looked at me, wide-eyed. "None!" then he quietly added, "None since... him."

I knew instantly who he was talking about.

"Clay..." I said, then hesitated. When he looked back up at me, I knew I needed to have this conversation. If not for me, he needed to talk, that was evident.

"What was his name?"

I saw the tears well up in his eyes immediately, and figured he'd need to take another break, but he surprised me instead, by saying, "Paul." Then, he closed his eyes and laid his head back on the large sofa.

I got up and sat next to him, careful not to touch, remembering my friend from high school's rule about not touching him, unless he said I could.

Clay opened his eyes and looked at me. "I loved him so much, Joshua. He understood me in so many ways, and when I was stupid, or didn't know how to act, he was okay and didn't tell me I was stupid."

I opened my hand, so Clay could put his hand on mine, and instead, he reached over and hugged me, tears falling down his face and onto my shoulder.

I held him for a while as he cried. When he pulled back, he apologized. "I'm not good with emotions. I've never understood them, especially not my own. I'm sorry I cried all over you."

I chuckled. "You have to know that's a normal response to losing your spouse, Clay. I'm glad you trust me enough to let me be here for you."

Clay just nodded and wiped away a few more tears as they fell.

"Can I make a suggestion?" I asked, afraid I was pushing too far, but not able to resist the desire to help him feel better. When he nodded, I continued, "I recommend you start practicing sharing things about Paul that you loved, and that you start saying his name again, to Melinda, even to Linda Mae, although she's likely to say something rude about it if you do, but also you can tell me about him. If you can get used to sharing stories about him, I don't think the feelings would continue being so big and difficult to deal with."

Clay shook his head. "I'm not sure I can do that." I could see the panic beginning to seep into his expression.

"Shhh, that's okay, Clay, you don't have to. But, emotions tend to be biggest when we haven't resolved them. When we bottle them up, they can become too difficult to manage. I know, I've been dealing with suppressed emotions my whole life. First, about losing Uncle Chris, then my mom, and then losing my dad, who became a statue after Mom died. That's why I've been a total mess around you and all this inheritance stuff. My father forced me to bottle my emotions up. So, you aren't the only emotionally stunted person." I sat next to him for a long moment, then turned toward him.

Clay still looked a bit green around the edges, so I said, "Okay, let's go do something fun. Enough emotions for one day, you agree?"

Clay looked at me, confused, but after a moment, he smiled. "I have a place I was going to go, but you might not like it?"

"I'm open, what is it?"

Clay looked embarrassed. "It's a museum about papermaking. Kazuo Haga has a project here called Mathematics through Paper Folding. I know you'd probably think it's boring, but I've wanted to see it since I heard about it."

I just shrugged. "Sure, sounds good to me." Although, truthfully, it sounded boring as anything could be. If it made Clay feel better, though, that would be worth it.

I drove, and Clay sat quietly staring out the window. I knew his emotions were probably all over the place, and I wanted to give him space while he processed them, so I drove in silence, not even turning the radio on.

The museum was interesting, Clay dragged me directly to the Kazuo Haga exhibit, and very eloquently talked about how Haga was a writer, and the exhibit demonstrated his geometric designs using paper art. In the six months I'd known Clay, I'd never seen his passion, never seen him light up, until we walked around the papermaking museum.

As we stood in front of a bizarre-yet-beautiful, bright-red book-like sculpture, I turned to him and asked, "You really love mathematics, don't you?"

"I know I'm probably boring you, aren't I?" he looked so vulnerable, I almost laughed.

"No, I've always liked math. I didn't want to major in it, and clearly, you're more fascinated with it than I am, but I especially found geometry interesting. Building must be in my blood, because I struggle with Algebra, but the moment I found the theorems in Geometry, I knew I'd found something that worked well for my mind."

Clay just smiled at me, and we continued through the museum. I noticed the historical elements of the museum were more interesting to me than him, but he waited patiently with me as I read the exhibits.

When the museum closed, we left and found a little bar. The woman who served us, brought us each a pint and disappeared to get our order, when an older man came over, and looking at Clay, asked, "Dr. Masters, Is that you?"

Clay looked up at the man, his face blank for a moment, then a tentative smile crossed his face. "Dr. Calhoun, nice to see you."

The man smiled and shook Clay's outstretched hand. "I've heard you're on sabbatical. Are you back in the swing of things again?" he asked.

Clay just smiled. "No, I brought my friend Joshua here," he said, pointing toward me. "To the Robert Williams Museum. We're just visiting, though. Are you with Georgia Tech now?"

"No," the man smiled. "I'm still at The National Mathematics Museum. I'm here as a guest for a lecture series they're doing on campus. Now that you're here, I'm sure they'd be happy to squeeze you in if you're available."

Clay laughed. "You always seem to be trying to get me into lectures, Paul. I'm on vacation, and I still hate doing lectures."

The older man laughed. "But you're good at it." He turned to me and asked, "Are you a mathematician?"

"Hardly, my background is in building, I also own a large orange grove in Mesa, Arizona."

When he turned back to Clay, I could tell he was trying to figure out how the two of us fit together, and after a couple seconds, I could tell it hit him—he thought we were boyfriends. This was too much for me, and I excused myself to go to the restroom, before I embarrassed Clay with my amusement surrounding the man's pretentiousness.

When I came back, the man had sat in my seat, and Clay was looking particularly uncomfortable. I came up behind the man and cleared my throat. He ignored me.

I came around the table and stood next to him, and he continued talking to Clay, still actively ignoring me.

"I really think you should consider the lecture. It will give you a better opportunity to re-enter the mathematical society."

Clay declined again, but the man seemed to be ignoring him. I searched my memory for the man's name, and when I remembered, I stepped in. "Mr. Calhoun," I intentionally left off the 'Dr.' knowing this often undid the academics. "If you don't mind, Dr. Masters and I were having a meeting. If he decides to lecture, I'm sure he'll be in touch. Clay, do you have Mr. Calhoun's number?"

The man looked at me in shock, that quickly turned to contempt.

I smiled back at him and waited for him to correct his title. When he didn't, I knew it was clear he didn't think I was worth the effort. Luckily, though, his contempt for me made him leave. He tried one last time, asking Clay to consider his request, and handed him his card.

When he left, I asked Clay if we should just go.

"No, I was never good at dealing with pressure. It's one of the reasons I wanted to leave that profession."

"Clearly, you're highly regarded, though. Do you miss academia?"

"Not at all," Clay replied. "I hated it. Well, I hated this part of it. I was always being pressured to lecture here, or go to a conference there, but I like the research programs."

"Well, *Doctor* Masters," I made sure to accent the doctor part. "It seems to me, you can do what you want, and you could've told the pretentious windbag where he could put it."

"It was more fun to watch you do that," he said, a smile crossing his face.

"You liked that, huh?" I asked, chuckling.

"My dad worked people in academia since I was a kid. Those folks can be really full of themselves. I noticed you kept calling him Mister. I was afraid he was going to hit you."

"Naa, he thought himself too good for the likes of me. He just thinks I'm your current piece of ass."

Clay's eyes grew big, and his face turned red. When his mouth opened and closed like a fish, I couldn't help but laugh.

"I'll take that as a compliment," I said, and poor Clay was rescued from having to comment, by the arrival of our food.

Chapter Twenty-Four

Clay

What were the chances of one of my colleagues finding me at Georgia Tech? Most of my colleagues were in New York City. Even when I'd got married and moved to Florida with my late husband... Paul... I made myself say his name in my head, remembering what Joshua had said, I had flown back and forth to New York when I was needed, but otherwise worked from home.

"Um, thanks for that. I never really know how to react when someone is so pushy."

Joshua shrugged. "You say no, and if they keep pushing, you say no again. And if they don't stop, you say, 'Please stop, I've said no'. The truth is, Clay, that man was being a bully, and he knew what he was doing. He was trying to take advantage of your situation. I'm guessing he probably would've gotten some kudos by having you speak."

"No, I know what he was up to. He's part of a group that recruits for large technology developers. I've worked for one of the companies, they get pretty big bonuses for getting people like me to sign up."

"Tell me about that, you've been moonlighting on me?" he said, then laughed.

"Yeah, well, Chris did know about it. I do consultation, especially around social media and that kind of thing."

"Oh, so you're one of the hackers like the documentary on *Netflix*?"

I shrugged. "I don't have Netflix, but no, I don't hack things. In fact, I'm not really even on social media, but I do help them build algorithms to analyze and predict people's buying habits."

"Impressive, I guess. Although, I hate that kind of thing. I don't use social media much anymore."

"Yeah, if you knew what I know, you'd probably avoid them anyway."

Joshua looked at me. "Yeah, don't tell me, it's too science fiction for me. Like we've entered into an alternative universe or something."

"Or something," I said.

We stood to leave and, unfortunately, had to pass Dr. Calhoun on the way out. To my surprise, though, it was Joshua who got recognized this time. "Joshua?" we heard someone say from Dr. Calhoun's table. At first, I thought it might be someone who was going to act like they knew him to get to me, but when Joshua turned around, a genuine smile crossed his face.

"Dr. Julia," he said, and when he walked over, the woman stood up and hugged him.

"What brings you to Georgia Tech?" she asked him.

"Oh, being tourists," he said. "Dr. Julia, this is my friend, Dr. Clay Masters. Clay, this is Dr. Julia Simmons, president of the mathematical research department."

I looked at Joshua and was surprised he knew her. When Joshua noticed my surprise, he smiled.

"I was on the team that did most of the work on their new research facility."

"And he was magnificent at it," she said, beaming. "How long are you back in town?"

"Just a few days, I'm afraid. I'm running my late uncle's estate in the Phoenix area," he said.

Then he looked over at Dr. Calhoun, and to my surprise, the old man looked embarrassed.

I also noticed the smile that crossed Joshua's face when he saw it, but he quickly hid it and went back to talking to his friend.

"Will you have time to meet me for coffee?" the woman asked.

"I can probably fit it in. What's your schedule like tomorrow morning?" Joshua asked. After noticing me, he said, "If that's okay with you, Clay."

I nodded, not sure what to say.

The woman looked at her phone, apparently looking through her schedule. "I have about an hour if I move some stuff around. Can you meet me at my office, around ten in the morning?"

"I think so. I'll text you when I know for sure."

"Please do. In fact, if you can copy my assistant in on that, it'll make it easier."

Joshua just laughed. "I'm an expert on scheduling time with you, Julia. Don't forget, I had to navigate your landmine schedule for three years after all."

She laughed as we turned to leave.

"How do you know the president of the research department?" I asked Joshua, as soon as we were out of earshot.

"You aren't the only one with secrets, *Doctor* Masters. I told you, my father is a builder. Well, he didn't want to do the Georgia Tech building, because it wasn't as profitable, so he gave me the reins. The benefactor made working with my father's company a requirement for the money, so it was really a mess from the beginning.

"How did you end up on the project then?" I asked.

"Well, Julia came to my father's office personally. I sat down with her on and off for a couple weeks, until we were able to come up with a plan that would appeal to my father.

When he agreed, he said since I was the one that worked it all out, I had to be the one who dealt with all the details. My father even won an award for the building, although he didn't even mention me."

Joshua laughed a bitter chuckle, then sighed.

We walked silently back to the car. I could tell Joshua was brooding a bit about the conversation. When we got into the rental car, he looked over at me. "Clay, I really want to make Uncle Chris's plans work out, but if we can't, promise me you'll work with me to come up with a viable alternative. I never want to go back to work for my father. I've met people I will always be friends with, like Julia, but I always felt inferior when it came to anything, I did for him. Even though the last six months have sucked, because of all Chris's manipulative crap, I have felt more independent there than any of the years I worked for my dad."

"If you can come up with a plan, I'm open to helping. I'd miss the groves if they were turned over to a developer. Although, to be honest, I have no idea how to prevent that from happening unless we figure out how to perform a miracle."

Joshua looked at me in surprise. "So, you think it isn't going to work out?" he asked.

I sighed. "I told your uncle the same thing. Since I've been there, the business has steadily lost money. You don't have to be a Ph.D. in math to know that if things don't change drastically, there will be no future for the business."

"The attorney made it sound like you were fighting for the groves to remain undeveloped. Something else I was misled about. Seems you and I needed to work this stuff out months ago."

We were both quiet the rest of the way home. When we got back, pandemonium was in full swing at Joshua's friends' house. The little boy was screaming his lungs out about something, and both Trevor and Peter seemed to be at their wit's end. We immediately went to the kitchen, where Luka ran to join us.

I reached down and picked the little one up, and he immediately calmed. By the time his fathers came into the kitchen, the little guy had his head down on my shoulder, sucking his thumb.

I stood still, totally unsure what to do. I was afraid if I moved, he'd start screaming again. I could see the curious look on his parents' faces. Then Peter came over and leaned against the counter. "He usually won't go to anyone but Trevor and me. He even screams when Aunt Doris picks him up these days."

"Looks like he has a good eye for the pretty boys," his other dad, Trevor, said.

I could feel my face turn red, and Joshua laughed behind me. "I know, I've felt the same way a couple times. Clay has good shoulders for crying on."

It only took a few minutes before I could tell the little one was asleep. Peter looked at him. "I'd take him from you, Clay, but if he doesn't sleep for a full fifteen minutes, he'll wake up. If you think the temper tantrum he was having when you came in was bad, you haven't seen anything compared to what he can throw when he's been woken up."

Trevor nodded. Both men had a look of fear on their faces, which spoke volumes about how their son could react.

"It's all good, I'm not going anywhere," I replied, trying to remain as still as I could, so as not to wake the little demon.

"Let's all go sit in the living room," Trevor said. "It's more comfortable to hold him when you're sitting down. He's as heavy as a brick."

I walked delicately into the living room following the men, but the little guy was clearly asleep and didn't seem to mind that I was walking around with him.

"Peter," Joshua said. "I've been asked to have coffee tomorrow morning with a friend, do you have plans or can I take her up on the offer?"

"No plans for me. I have baby duty tomorrow morning, because Trevor has to go into the office for a client meeting."

"Cool, let me text her to let her know."

"It's confirmed. I'll only be gone for a few hours. Clay, do you think you can entertain yourself? I'd take you with me, but if you think Calhoun can be a bully, you have no idea what Julia would be like if she gets wind that you're potentially a professor for her department."

I all but moaned at the idea. "No, I'd prefer to stay here. Thanks for thinking about me."

Joshua laughed, and patted my knee.

Trevor came over and took the little one from my shoulder and said he was going to take him up. "I'll see you all tomorrow sometime," he said, and made his exit.

Peter followed after him, saying he'd see us in the morning. "Clay, you're welcome to hang out with Luka and me. We aren't very exciting, but it'd be nice to get to know you. Maybe we can take Luka down to the park to play."

"Sounds... domestic," I said, making both Joshua and Peter laugh. "It's a date then?" he asked.

"Sure, it's a date."

Joshua came over and sat next to me after Peter left.

"It's still pretty early, wanna go out for a drink?"

I shook my head. "No, I'm still full from supper, how about sitting on the front porch in the big swing I saw out there."

"Humidity is about a million percent," Joshua said. "You okay with that?"

"It is a bit difficult to breathe, but I grew up in Jersey, just outside of NYC, it isn't the first time I've dealt with it."

"Yeah, but you've been in the dry desert heat for several years, you have to be dying."

I nodded, then smiled. "Let's do it anyway, I like the thought of sitting on a front-porch swing with you."

Chapter Twenty-Five

Joshua

Luckily, the humidity had lessened, and the stifling heat had fallen a bit since the sun had set. We sat on the swing, and Clay let his arm rest behind me.

"So, Clay," I began. "Something I want to talk about before we go back... you said I was the first guy you've kissed...well, in a while." I didn't want to bring up the uncomfortable conversation about his lost husband.

"But, you liked kissing me, right?" I asked.

Clay's eyes darkened a bit. "I liked kissing you a lot. It was hard for me at first, how *much* I liked it."

"Would you be willing to try it again, now that I know you aren't out to get me?" I asked self-consciously.

Clay leaned over without responding, and kissed me gently on the mouth. He leaned back and looked me in the eye, before I reached out and pulled him back to me, kissing him hard.

A thrill soared through me as we kissed, I'd already decided to take what Clay would give, and I didn't want to hold anything back. The kiss I gave him said all that, as I took everything I'd wanted since that luscious, dark, muscular body picked me up in the ATV. I stood up, pulling Clay with me, and hoping not to wake any of the other occupants, I rushed us up the stairs and into our bedroom. I thanked god Peter and Trevor were up in the attic room, because I figured this was going to get noisy.

I stripped off my shirt before the door closed behind us. Clay chuckled and reached for me, but I pushed him onto the bed before his hands could touch me.

"Hope you're ready for this," I said, as I straddled him, and kissed him with every bit of lust that was in me. Clay gripped my ass and squeezed, sending shockwaves to my already-throbbing cock.

"Take this off," I said, as I finished unbuttoning his shirt.

Clay complied immediately, and I pushed him back down and assaulted his muscular torso with my tongue. He moaned under me, as I licked and nipped his pecs and nipples. Finally, Clay flipped me onto my back, undid my pants, and pulled them off me with one quick tug.

I laughed at the ease of it, before he came back up to my mouth, and plunged his tongue inside. I moaned with pleasure as the heat I'd felt for him poured from me and matched his.

Clay ground into me,, and the stiffness of his jeans with the feel of his hard cock sent the same shockwaves through me as I'd felt before.

He continued to assault my mouth, as I moaned and spoke his name in whispers.

Clay crawled off me, pulling my underwear off. In the same quick motion, he dispatched my pants, and took my cock into his mouth.

"*Oh, Clay!*" I yelled into the darkness.

"Mmm..." he moaned around my cock, the vibration reverberating to my core.

I gripped his head, unceremoniously pushing in as he took me deeper and deeper into his mouth.

"Fuck, I'm gonna come if you don't stop!" I said, trying to warn him.

He lifted off me, letting my cock plop back onto my abdomen, then crawled back on top of me, his jeans rough on my exposed body.

"What do you want?" he asked, with way too much composure compared to my own out-of-control feelings.

"I want you fucking naked," I said, and tried to roll him off me.

Clay was stronger than me and didn't budge. "What do you want me to do to you?" he asked, looking me in the eye.

I immediately thought about how much I'd like to be fucked, and the thought shocked me. I didn't fuck someone the first time. There were rules, right?

Clay smiled like he'd read my mind.

"Do you have condoms?" I asked.

He shook his head. "But, I'm taking PrEP, and I haven't had sex with anyone in a...in a while. I'm negative every year when I get tested."

"Clay, I've never had unprotected sex. I don't know."

He smiled down at me. "It's okay, we'll save that for later."

He began to unzip his pants, and fell onto his back as he pulled them off, along with his underwear. I watched as he exposed his beautiful cock that was as rigid and hard as mine.

"That's what I want," I said, and rolled over him, taking him into my mouth.

Clay arched his back when my tongue worked around his head. The taste of his salty precum spread across my tongue, causing me to thrust my own cock onto the bed.

Clay rolled me over and we got into a sixty-nine position, so he could take my cock as well. "I'm not gonna last long," I warned him, but he ignored me, sucking me deep into his throat.

I moaned around him, and as he took me, I sucked him harder.

Clay reached around my ass, found my hole, and began playing with it.

"Fuck," I said. "I... I..."

Before I could stop myself, I was coming in his mouth. I heard him moan through my own ecstatic cries.

When I finished, I moved so I could give my full attention to him and sucked him while jacking him off into my mouth.

He came seconds later, gushes of come filling my mouth.

I leaned back, and as the post-cum spilled out, I looked him in the eyes, smiled, and licked up the last drop.

I plopped down next to him and curled into his body, all but purring with the afterglow that overtook me.

We lay almost motionless for several minutes. I dozed as Clay's masculine scent surrounded me, and probably would've drifted into a deeper sleep, if Clay hadn't roused me by rubbing my chest with his beautiful big hand.

"You okay?" he asked.

I couldn't stop the laugh that escaped me. "I'm so okay. I think I might just melt," I said.

He chuckled. "I'm sorry it was so fast."

"Not your fault, clearly," I said, and rolled over to look at him.

"It's been a long-damned time for me. I think I was a ticking time bomb. You're lucky to be alive."

Clay smiled. "It's been a while for me too. My hand does its job, but it's not the same as sex with a hot man."

I sighed and snuggled back into his side. "You aren't freaking out?" I asked.

"Not yet, but there's always tomorrow."

I smiled at his humor.

"Well, we'd better take advantage of the lull then," I said, and rolled back on top of him. I hadn't even jacked off for several days, so the moment I moved next to him again, I grew hard.

I rubbed my cock against his and kissed his neck and chest, taking my time to enjoy what I was in too big a hurry to do the first time around.

Clay rubbed my back as I explored him. When he kissed me, the heat rose again, and I felt his cock harden against my ass.

I leaned back and let him slide up between my cheeks. "I think we need to get condoms," I said, as I moved my ass up and down his cock.

"Yeah," he said huskily, and his big hand gripped my ass, and forced it down onto his cock.

I moaned at the feeling of him, and suddenly, I couldn't think of anything I wanted more than to feel him inside me.

I knew it was probably a lost cause, but I reached over to the bedside table, and pulling it open, *I found condoms.* God, my friend Peter was a perv, but bless him cause I want everything Clay had to give!

I pulled a condom out along with a bottle of lube, and smiling from ear to ear, I showed my finds to Clay. He smiled mischievously at me, and flipped me off him. He took the condom, quickly ripped it open, and slipped it on. He straddled me as he lubed us both up. Then he pressed his finger inside me. I was glad I'd already come once, or I was sure just having his big finger inside me would've caused me to blow. I rode his finger, getting used to the sensation. When he slipped a second finger in to scissor me, I arched. "Fuck, Clay, that feels so fucking good."

Clay continued watching me, and when I made eye contact, he leaned over and kissed me, while stretching my ass further.

"I need you in me, Clay! Please fuck me!"

Clay's expression was clouded with lust, as he positioned himself between my legs, and lifted my ass. He slowly moved his cock up to my hole. The sensation was amazing, as the contrast between his fingers and cock crossed my mind.

I immediately pushed down, wanting him inside me, needing to feel him there.

Clay moaned as his head breached my hole, and I arched just in time to force him further in.

"*Fuck!*" I cried, as he pushed the rest of the way.

"Damn, Joshua, you feel so good, so tight!"

I was struck dumb, the feeling of his cock filling me up. All I could do was look at him, as ecstasy overtook him while he fucked me.

His head was thrust upward toward the ceiling as he moved faster and faster. I watched him as he took me, overcome with the feeling of being fucked after such a long time, and how much I'd wanted it to be him that fucked me.

When Clay looked back at me and made eye contact, something inside me shifted. Something had happened, and I knew we were both experiencing something magical, something important.

He leaned over and still fucking me, kissed me passionately.

"Joshua, you are so..." He didn't get the words out, but I knew what he meant.

He pulled out of me then. "Get on all fours," he demanded.

The thrill of being taken doggy style overcame me, but I complied as quickly as I could.

Clay slipped his cock back inside me. This time he wasn't slow or easy, and immediately pushed my face into the mattress as he pounded into me.

"Fuck, Clay, fuck..." I kept repeating, my shouting muffled by the pillow my face was planted into.

Clay took me with all the pent-up sexual tension that was lingering between us. I met his passion with my own, needing his aggression like I needed to breathe.

When he hit my prostate, I came again, yelling his name.

I fell back onto my back, and Clay pulled the condom off and straddled my face, jacking off. He came in my mouth.

He shivered as the last of his come fell on me, then rested back onto his knees before leaning over, and licked the come off my lips,

"Fuck, that was hot!" I said, before I could stop myself.

He chuckled, went into the bathroom, and returned with a towel. I wiped the rest of the cum off my face, cleaned up the bed, knowing I'd be doing my own laundry tomorrow and fell onto the mattress, utterly spent.

This time Clay snuggled into me. His big arm lay across my chest, and his mouth whispered in my ear. "It's been so long, I think I might have gotten carried away."

"Yeah, and I can't wait until you get carried away again. My poor ass might need a little time, though."

Clay chuckled. "I like your ass. We can give it a break, but not for *too* long, okay?" he asked.

I rolled back over and kissed him. "I doubt it'll take long before it and I are begging for you again."

Chapter Twenty-Six

Clay

I woke up early the next morning and searched myself for regret, fear, or any emotions that reflected the loss of my first and only love, up until that point.

What I found was the absence of all those emotions. I allowed myself to contemplate what that meant. Was I losing perspective on what it meant to love Paul? No, since Joshua made me say his name, the angst that used to be there had diminished. Saying his name out loud didn't end in me going into a complete meltdown. That allowed me focus on how much I'd loved him. How I'd always miss him.

I lay in the antique bed and pondered my past. I'd been so angry that he was gone, that my only support group, Paul, Mom, and Dad, were *all* gone.

And for the past almost-six years, I'd lived in a constant state of hypersensitive loss. Just like I'd hidden the article under the floor, I'd hidden what they all meant to me. During the past twenty-four hours, I'd begun feeling them again. I understood they were gone, but they were still in my heart.

So, how did I feel about Joshua? Silly and giddy all at the same time.

I sighed. That was probably bad. Before she died, I would've talked to my mom about it. She could've helped me navigate the feelings... well, if I'd been brave enough to talk to her about lust that was this intense and overwhelming.

Did I love Joshua? Not enough time to say. If I were honest with myself, I'd been drawn to him since the minute I saw him standing over Chris's grave. Now that I look back, I'd been angry with him for being there, for filling a spot I wanted to fill for Chris, but even then, I'd been attracted to the man. No, not attracted at that point, drawn to him... the attraction had come later.

First thing, I had to stop 'perseverating', a word my therapist used to use, on my emotions.

"Psychoanalyzing emotions aren't the same as managing them," she would say. I always thought she was wrong about that. For me, understanding them was my first defensive tool for managing them.

I rolled over and asked myself, would we be able to figure out how to work around each other? Or, would this be the end of my career at the groves?

Joshua had a level head, much more so than I did. He overreacted occasionally, but always at times that made perfect sense. I couldn't help but chuckle, as I thought about how I would've handled being in his situation regarding Chris's will, not knowing any of us and feeling like he'd been dealt a losing hand.

I went downstairs to give myself something to do, then after drinking a glass of water, I came back up to the bedroom and sat down in the loveseat that sat next to the window across from the bed.

Joshua woke up about half an hour later, and when he saw me he came over to where I stood, yawned, kissed me, and asked, "What's up?"

"Just thinking about how insane I'd have been if I'd been stuck in your situation. I'm sure I'd have had multiple epic meltdowns."

Joshua opened both eyes and leaned up. "If I recall, that's exactly what I did."

When he sat next to me, I leaned over and kissed his forehead. "You didn't have a meltdown. I could show you a meltdown."

Joshua chuckled. "Let's just keep that for the imagination, shall we? What time is it, and why are you awake?"

I pushed Joshua onto his back and crawled on top of him. "I was thinking about how much I wanted you. It's hard to sleep when you have such a handsome man in your bed."

"Mmm," he purred. "Show me."

I reached into the drawer and pulled a condom out, Joshua's eyes grew big. "I'm not sure..."

"Shhh, I'm sure you'll be ready for this," I said.

He didn't complain when I led him back to the bed, then after opening the condom, I slipped it onto his hard cock.

He looked at me in surprise as I lubed him up. After prepping myself a little, I slipped his cock into my ass.

Joshua moaned and rocked into me, slowly letting me get used to the feel of him. I smiled down at him, and knowing he was still afraid of hurting me, I forced myself down onto him and thrust his cock all the way into my hole.

Joshua moaned with the sensation of being inside me, but I still had all the control. Where he bucked, I sat and just smiled at him.

He cocked an eyebrow at me, and I laughed. "Bottoms can be bossy, didn't you know?" I asked, making Joshua laugh out loud.

"You're telling me you're a bossy bottom?"

I nodded and slowly moved up and down on his cock. Joshua's eyes clouded over, and I began moving over him faster, letting the sensation overtake me. I rolled my head back and lifted up enough that Joshua could fuck me from beneath.

He surprised me on one of the thrusts, he tossed me onto my back and crawled between my legs.

"Now, who's bossy?" he asked, causing me to laugh.

Chapter Twenty-Seven

Joshua

It hadn't occurred to me that Clay might be a bottom, or versatile even. He just struck me as a top, but when he crawled over me and fucked himself with my cock, something inside me came unglued.

He enjoyed my shock and the whole bossy bottom thing, making me laugh. Time to shake this up a bit, though. When he was caught up in the sensation, I threw him onto his back and took him from there, lifting his big muscular legs over my shoulders.

I rammed into him, and he arched against me.

"Josh..." he moaned, but couldn't finish my name, before I pounded into him again.

"Fuck," he whispered, and I knew I'd undone that cool exterior of his.

I picked up speed, and as Clay closed his eyes, I took over.

The speedy sex sessions of last night gave us enough endurance to enjoy this one for longer. I took advantage of it by plowing him and watching his face as he enjoyed my taking control over him.

When he made eye contact, I leaned over, and he met my kisses as I continued fucking him.

We were covered in a sheen of sweat as we rocked in unison. The move to kiss him must have put me in line with his prostate, because he thrust back and came all over my stomach and his.

I pulled out of him, and he grabbed my ass to stop me. "Just give me a moment," he said.

I watched him as he shuddered with one last thrust before he rocked back and forth on my cock again.

"Really?" I asked, and he kept his eyes shut. He nodded and continued moving on my cock. I was afraid I was going to hurt him. Once I'd come, I couldn't handle being fucked any longer, but he was determined. When it became clear he was enjoying it, I let myself get back into the rhythm we'd found before he came.

I could feel my own release building, and I pulled out, yanking the condom off and came all over his stomach.

"Fuck," I cried again, and collapsed on top of his muscular frame.

I couldn't talk, didn't want to talk. I just wanted to be right here, on top of this muscular body, with those big rough hands on my back.

I finally rolled off him, reached over the bed, found the towel from the night before, and wiped us both off.

Neither of us spoke. We snuggled as we had before, enjoying the feeling of each other in our post-sexual haze.

As I lay next to the muscle man, I searched my thoughts to see what level of neurotic worry I had going on after having sex with Clay. Much to my surprise, it was just a low-level hum. Nothing more than I usually had swirling around my mind.

After another couple hours of blissful sleep, I woke up happier than I'd been... well, maybe happier than I'd ever been. I leaned over and kissed the sleeping man next to me, before getting up and heading into the shower. I'd just lathered up when I heard the shower door open, and Clay's large hands slipped around me.

I hummed again with the feel of him touching me, his sexy cock pressed up against my buttocks.

"How can you have anything left in you?" I asked.

Clay leaned next to my ear and hummed. "I always want shower sex, Joshua," he said, sending electric shocks through me.

He soaped me up and played with my ass. I swear my poor spent cock actually jumped at the idea.

I turned and playfully pushed Clay off me. "You're going to make me late, and one never shows up late for the magnificent Dr. Simmons."

We messed around in the shower, lathering each other up and rinsing off. By the time we were done, I was hard as a rock, again.

I toweled off and got dressed, before I was tempted to jump the big man again, and rushed down the stairs. Clay was so delicious. It was a wonder I'd been able to keep my hands off him this long.

Chapter Twenty-Eight

Joshua

I hummed all the way to Julia's office, and felt happy as I opened her office door, expecting to be greeted by her assistant. Instead, Julia was actually ready to go.

"What's up?" I asked her. "I usually have to wait at least fifteen minutes for you to finish whatever you are doing before we leave."

"I want to see you and catch up. That's the priority this morning," she said, and surprised me by giving me a kiss on the cheek.

"What was that?" I asked, causing her to giggle.

"That's for being so happy," she said. "You were practically glowing in the company of your handsome mathematician."

I laughed. "Well, up until last night, I sort of hated the guy."

She coughed. "That's bull, and you know it. That man has had you wrapped around his little finger for a while, and good for him. You've needed a good loving for a long time, Joshua!"

I laughed. Julia and I had grown close while I worked for her, then once the project was over, we became closer over the lack of emotional capacity my father had. We were good friends, and she'd wanted me to find someone to date, saying I was a marrying kind of guy, which was why I hated dating so much. She was right when she told me I was too domesticated to play the field.

I hated to admit it, especially to someone who loved the field, and navigated it like a champion.

"So," she smiled. "I want the gossip. Dr. Clay Masters has been on everyone's radar for ages, but he disappeared several years ago. We all thought he was a recluse, then you of all people show up with him on your arm."

I sighed. "Well, it's a complicated story, but let's just say he's been hurt, and our meeting was simply by chance. I do like him, though."

"Any chance I can talk him into working here?"

I laughed. "No, that isn't very likely. I think he's pretty much given up the academic hat. He's not what you'd call a fan."

She sighed. "I heard that too, but you can't blame me for trying."

"That's true. But, as my friend, let me say this, hands off sister, this one is mine!"

Chapter Twenty-Nine

Clay

I stumbled downstairs behind Joshua and watched him dash out the door. Probably good that he left in such a hurry, or I'd have probably done my best to get him underneath me again. It felt so good to touch him. I'd wanted him since I'd met him, and everything about him set me on fire.

I found Trevor and Peter sitting in the kitchen, while Luka played with toys on the floor.

I greeted them and grabbed another cup of coffee between the couple's questions and the little one's needs. They were both so good with the toddler. It seemed effortless as they shifted him between them all the time, while continuing their conversation with me.

I learned that Joshua had been there for Trevor when Luka was still an infant and had been taken by his parents. "If it hadn't been for Joshua, I'm not sure I'd have made it," Trevor admitted.

"He's been a best friend to all of us," Peter added.

"Is that why he's Luka's godfather?" I asked.

Both men smiled. "We decided he was the perfect godfather, because we knew if push came to shove, no one would stand up and fight for Luka the way Joshua would. He's fierce when someone he cares about is being hurt," Peter said.

I thought about that for a moment, and nodded. "I can see that. Joshua can be fierce at other times too."

The men laughed. "Just don't push him too hard, or you'll see just how fierce he can be."

I smiled, but behind the humor, there was a great deal of truth to what they were saying. I'd been exposed to how the man could react under pressure. He didn't lose control, but he didn't back down either.

After we'd finished our coffee, Peter and Trevor talked me into going to have breakfast at a neighborhood café just around the corner.

We had a lot of fun talking about Joshua. Peter had known him the longest, and although they'd tried dating, it was a disaster from the beginning. They'd decided to be friends instead.

"I'm curious why someone like Joshua hasn't met someone long term?" I asked.

Peter shrugged. "Well, Joshua is not one to go chasing tail if you know what I mean. He's a slow mover, and when he dates someone, he's pretty quick to put up boundaries. I think his domesticity turns most gay men off."

I nodded. "I'm the same way. I don't have any interest in someone until I know what kind of man I'm dealing with."

Peter smiled and leaned over. "That's probably why you and he are such a good match."

I thought about that for a moment. Were we a good match? I wasn't sure.

We got back to the house, just as Joshua pulled into the driveway. When he got out of the car, he came over and kissed me. Although the kiss felt possessive, it felt good as well. I liked being claimed and wanted by this man.

Joshua took me out for dinner later that day, and we chatted about the groves. He had a lot of questions, which struck me as odd. Things about Mesa and the surrounding area, businesses and such. Unfortunately, I didn't really get involved much outside of the groves, so I wasn't much help. I could tell he was onto something, though.

Chapter Thirty

Joshua

I needed to meet with Peter today to discuss an idea I had about the groves. I'd had it after Clay agreed there was no way we could continue to run the groves as they were now. With him on my side, I thought we had a better chance at development.

I knew my uncle's dream was for everything to remain the same, but that wasn't going to happen, not in today's world. Now that I'd done a little more research to find that our competition in California was wicked, my hopes were even less.

But where there was a will, there was a way, right? I hoped so. I didn't want the groves to be another subdivision any more than my uncle did. I wanted them to be preserved for future generations too.

After getting my shower, I came down the stairs to find Peter sitting next to a happy toddler down in the music room.

"Any coffee yet?" I asked, causing both the man and the toddler to startle. "Sorry," I said and went to pick up my godson. "Sorry, little one," I said to him specifically.

"Yeah, you want me to get you a cup?" Peter asked.

I put Luka down. "No, I'll get it, but I want to talk to you. Are you busy?"

Peter shook his head. "Nope, I just finished a big project for Leonardo. You remember, Doris's new husband?"

"Um, how can I forget Leonardo?" I asked.

Peter chuckled. "So, yeah, my only duty currently is Luka, while Trevor gets caught up on some of his detective work. He sort of got behind while I was working on the *big project.*"

Curiosity struck me then. "Where is Leonardo's latest project?" I asked.

Peter shrugged. "We're building in downtown San Francisco. This is his first project out West, but there's a huge demand for our style of architecture in that area. When this one is done, we are headed down to Los Angeles then up north to Portland and Seattle."

"Good. That fits my plans perfectly."

Before Peter could push me any further, I darted out of the room to get my caffeine fix. If my idea worked out, it would take time, and I needed to have all my ducks in a row before I presented the idea to Clay, my board, and Mrs. Lucy James.

By Thursday, both Clay and I were ready to get back to Mesa. We booked our tickets and flew back together.

I'd told Clay I was toying with an idea about the business, but I needed to do some more research before I committed to anything, and as soon as I did, I wanted to meet with him to see what he thought.

Clay just shrugged, kissed my cheek, and said, "I trust you, that's how your mind works." Then he put his head back onto the seat and fell asleep. So much for the drama I thought he'd give.

I'd also let Melinda and Linda Mae know I wouldn't be available for a few days after we got back. And that I needed isolation while I was working on my project.

I'd taken over the entire floor of the apartment with papers I'd printed for my research. Luckily, the only person who showed up was Clay, and usually, that was late in the day. We'd have dinner together, he'd shower, then we'd make love. I think our nights together actually caused me to be more creative in my strategic planning.

During the day, I'd crunch numbers, do research, and make notes on my findings.

Finally, two weeks later, I emerged from my den. As I left, I hugged Melinda, which shocked her. "So, you're done being a recluse then?"

"Pretty much. Got one more stop to make, then I'll pull you all together and tell you my ideas."

As I pulled up at Lucy's place, I noticed another part of the building had suffered a cave-in. That poor woman. It had to be torture to watch. Maybe I had a solution, but it would take all my wiles to convince her of my plan.

Two hours and two bologna sandwiches later, I came out. The woman was a harsh negotiator. She didn't let anything slide by her, and when we were done, I had all the ammunition I needed to approach my team.

I thought to broach the subject with Clay first, but after meeting with Lucy, I decided I needed to meet with all the core players. Clay, Melinda, *and* Linda Mae. They were my real decision-makers, and if I didn't have them on board, I wouldn't be able to make this all work anyway.

I'd called a meeting for Sunday afternoon after the restaurant closed.

I'd talked Linda Mae into making us scones, which she did begrudgingly and not without a lot of complaints. Of course, she followed all that up with a kiss to my cheek. "You're up to something, and I'm excited to hear about it," she said.

After I had my audience seated, I smiled and started my pitch.

"So, as the three of you know, I've had a tough time figuring out all of my uncle's wishes and navigating the roadblocks he put in front of me." I noticed Melinda wanted to say something, and I put my hand up to stop her. "Let me finish. Trust me, I think I may have a plan to accomplish what he wanted and what needs to happen. Anyway, I need to thank each of you for having patience with me."

I looked at Melinda first. "You and Uncle Chris knew you couldn't have survived the last few decades with the grove as it was before. That's why you and he developed your store. Before that..." I turned to Linda Mae. "...you were part of an expansion to include a restaurant. In the fifty years before that, there was no need for a restaurant, and I'm sure my Uncle Chris's parents would've resisted it with gusto *if* the need hadn't been there. Unfortunately, times have changed again, and I think if my uncle hadn't been so sick, he'd have realized it. We really have no choice except to develop the property, but with a little creativity.

Maybe we can develop it in a way that doesn't destroy what makes it so special."

I reached down into my briefcase, and pulled out four folders I'd prepared just for this discussion. I handed one to each of them and kept one for myself.

"This project only works, because we have a neighbor who's willing to sell. If you open your booklet, on the first page, you'll see a contract to purchase Mrs. Lucy's property. Until Larry died, that place was mostly full. I've looked over the records. They didn't close because they'd lost customers. Even now, if they could get the permits, I have no doubt they could get customers to return for the hot springs."

Linda Mae's face was contorted so much, it made me stop and laugh. "Linda Mae, you look like you're giving birth to a twenty-pound turd."

She gave me a look that said she appreciated me, and could whoop me at the same time. "What does that crappy property have to do with the grove?" she asked.

"Well, give me a minute, and I'll get to that. As I was saying, the motel and hot springs are still a viable business. The fact that it's attached to our property gives us what we need to make it work and be a major success."

I went on to explain how we could overcome the water problem by using the hot springs. Linda Mae's expression changed from tortured to curious, and I knew I had her.

"If you turn to the next page, you'll see how I propose to renovate and upgrade the hotel property. I propose we create a convention center. Since that's something the city already needs, I think we may even get some public funding to help. Of course, much of this comes down to Mrs. Lucy's generous offer, and the fact we currently own the land around the proposed building site. You should also notice, I'm including a large section of our dead groves as a seasonal RV park. No reason why we can't also take advantage of some of the snowbird traffic as well."

Melinda looked up from the proposal.

"How are you going to fund all this?" she asked.

I sighed. "Well, it takes a bit of faith, and that's why I need you on the same page as me. Before we get into that, though, Melinda, I need you and Linda Mae to play a big role in this project. Hotels, restaurants, and even the groves don't make money the traditional way. Even restaurants like The Cracker Barrel have learned it's retail that brings in the big money. Linda Mae, if we had a business loan on the restaurant, we'd be in the red, so debt is a problem."

She nodded, but didn't respond.

"So, we have to think outside the box even if we expand as I suggest."

Melinda looked over my numbers for a considerable amount of time. Then she looked up at me and said, "You have to understand two things. One, you'll have to hire a lot more employees, and that could be a significant headache. Second, your costs for supplies are too high. You didn't take into consideration the savings associated with volume purchases. I think we could increase those bottom-line numbers by about a quarter." I smiled, and she nodded, before adding, "Don't forget the headache of hiring extra staff."

"I haven't forgotten."

"Linda Mae, the next part is on you. I'd need to create a high-end restaurant, but it needs to include some of your best recipes from the Square Biscuit. I'd need to lean on you to help me get that started."

She smiled, but shook her head. "Baby, I'm old. I'm not going to start a new restaurant, and in fact, we all know you'll need to find someone to replace me soon enough. If you pull this off, I will support you one hundred percent, but you'll have to find someone else to do that part."

I sighed, but had anticipated her reaction. "I ain't happy to hear that Linda Mae, but I do understand. So, that'll be something that has to be figured out."

I asked them to pull the paper out of the back of the proforma.

I turned to Clay with a smile. "This next part isn't really something that makes us money, but it's something I think you'll... well, something you'll be aware of how to do."

Clay looked at me skeptically, which made me laugh.

"I've come to love the little monsters that you've incorporated into our system. Jack Russells are one of the most surrendered dogs, as you already know. Because our groves need them to keep all the land from looking like the third lost by the voles, I'd like to use the area around your house as a Jack Russell rescue. I think the people coming to visit the groves would love it."

Clay just shook his head. "You know I'm not the best at making them behave."

"Yeah, I'm aware of that, but I'd be here to help."

"I'm not committing to that. I need a lot more convincing."

I just laughed, because anyone who'd had a Jack Russell Terrier could testify to the fact that they were one of the most difficult stubborn breeds to ever exist.

The excitement of my proposal propelled me to conclude with a flourish. Almost like I was presenting an idea to investors or to a board. "As you can see, this would shift us from a grove to a tourist attraction. In essence, we'd become agritourism, but because there are several growers still in the Mesa area, I'm convinced we could get most of our citrus needs met here."

I drew in a breath and walked over toward the place Linda Mae had put her orange marmalade scones and brought them over to the table. "I'll give you a moment to think it over and talk about it without me watching you. Can I get you any coffee or anything before I leave?"

"You aren't going anywhere, young man," Linda Mae said, surprising me. "This doesn't require a discussion, it's incredible. You've thought about everything, but Melinda had a good question, how do you come up with the money?"

"Oh, sorry, Melinda, I forgot. I already talked to a commercial lender, because the property is worth so much, we not only qualify for a commercial loan, but we also get a really low interest rate. If you go back to page eight, you can see the numbers."

"So, you've got to borrow the money?"

"Unfortunately. I'm not rich, Linda Mae."

The woman shook her head. "I don't like debt. It almost always leads to problems."

She was right. I couldn't argue with her, but I did have a quick payoff option in the paperwork.

Clay spoke up then. "Is that number on page eight the amount you plan to borrow?" he asked.

I nodded.

"I can look over the numbers and do a probability analysis if you want. That way, you'd know the likelihood of your success as well as the potential for return on investment."

All three of us looked at him. "That would be amazing," I said. "Yes, with a famous mathematician giving his blessing, I'm sure that'll help with our loan application."

Linda Mae nudged him. "What are you two going on about? You are the foreman of a citrus grove."

Clay laughed. "Well, I'm also a mathematician."

"That's right," I added. "This foreman also happens to be Dr. Masters. I was lucky enough to run up on a few of his colleagues while we were in Atlanta."

"Speaking of Atlanta, what was going on? You ran off like a drama queen, and then you're back. Next thing we know, you're pitching this huge expansion."

"I went to get a man," I said, causing Clay to blush an exceptionally deep crimson.

Linda Mae looked at Clay, then over at me, and sighed. "The old woman is always the last to know."

"They haven't really announced it until now," Melinda said.

"But you knew, didn't you?" Linda Mae asked.

"It's easier to figure it out when you work next to where the make-out sessions happen."

"Hey, I'm not ashamed. Look at him," he teased the women. "Joshua's totally hot!"

Linda Mae shook her head, then looked over at me. "So you worked it out? You figured out you wanted to kiss on my grandson, now you're ready to commit to this place?"

I put my arm around her. "I decided before that, but when Clay came clean about all he knew regarding my uncle's will, that helped me decide. Clay was always a big part of this. My attraction to him was a problem actually, but now that we've had a good long talk, it's a problem I'm willing to deal with. As far as him being your grandson, be careful, I'm happy to start calling you granny!"

Linda Mae pretended to hit me on the arm. "I'll whoop your butt if you do."

I looked over at Melinda. "Meanwhile, you need to look this over and see if anything we're doing will disrupt Uncle Chris's requirements. I need to have Arlington look to see if this violates the deed restrictions."

Melinda looked flushed. It appeared as if she was about to say something, but instead, she just nodded.

"So, if you don't have any questions, or want to talk about it without me, I think I'm done."

Linda Mae came over and hugged me. "You did good son, you did really good," and she walked back toward her kitchen.

Clay leaned over after Linda Mae had left, and whispered in my ear, "I have a reward for all your hard work later."

The sexual promise made my hair stand up on end, not to mention the quick jerk of my cock.

Melinda waited until Clay had walked away before she moved closer to me. "Chris wanted you to spend a whole year, before you were given the reins, but I think after looking at this, you've far exceeded his expectations. I need to make sure I don't do anything wrong, but if I can, I have some things to share with you. Let me look the plans over, and I'll let you know tomorrow."

I really didn't understand what Melinda was saying, but if I could get to the bottom of all Uncle Chris's requirements, and do what needed to be done, it would go a long way in helping secure a loan.

As promised, Melinda met me the following morning at the dining room table in my apartment. "I've gone over all your uncle's requirements, and the stipulations are still what they are. You have to be here an entire year before you can do any development, but, he did anticipate it would be inevitable. I think it's time to bring you into the clearing. No more games, and if your uncle doesn't like it, he can fire me!"

I laughed, but Melinda remained serious.

"Melinda, I've forgiven Uncle Chris. You don't have to be so down on him. It's been hard, but I really do understand his motives. Besides, the situation where we have to wait until I've been here an entire year, that's fine. We won't be anywhere near ready to start for at least that long. Truth is, it'll probably be even longer, because we don't want to disrupt our harvest season, and I'm going to really need all of you on my team if I succeed at this."

She sighed. "Well, here's what your uncle gave me before he died. It's a step-by-step guide regarding how you're to take on the reins. You've accomplished everything up to now. The rest of the year was you helping Clay, meeting the neighbors, going to a citrus convention held by the Arizona, California and Florida's extension offices. You'll see when you go through it, there aren't really any big things left for you to discover. He didn't have me handing over the books until the end of the year." She laughed. "Had he known your analytical mind, he'd have seen the folly in that requirement. You'll see he has a closed folder with an amended will. That isn't supposed to be opened until the end of the year. However, you might as well see it. Mr. Arlington has a copy of the amendments as well. But it was his partner who drew these up. Not even Mr. Arlington himself is aware of the modification. You'll need to look at that sooner than later, because it will impact how you proceed. There's also a letter in there, Joshua. I haven't read it, because it was meant only for you. He didn't want you to read it until you completed his requirements. I'll leave it up to you to decide when it's time."

Melinda handed me a folder that held my uncle's last wishes. She stood up and pulled me into a hug. When she pulled back, she had tears in her eyes.

"What's wrong?" I asked, keeping my arms around her.

"Your uncle was the love of my life. Yes, he was older, and he was a total player, so there was no way I could ever take him on as a full-time partner, but we became best friends and were for many years. This..." she put her hand on the folder I'd placed on the table when she hugged me. "This was his final request of me, as long as I was helping him...helping you navigate the requirements, it was almost like he was still here."

The tears fell, and she shook her head to clear them.

"I didn't really know him, but it almost feels like I did, because I've learned how much he loved this land and these trees. I feel him here. Sometimes, just the way the breeze blows, it's almost like I'm a little kid again, and he's behind me laughing." I put my hand next to hers on the folder.

"I know he didn't come up with all this until I called him two weeks before he died. Mr. Arlington told me that, and to be honest, that's why I struggled with it as much as I did. These requirements, they don't represent him, not really. It's just what he set up to give me time to fall in love with the place, right?"

Melinda nodded. I hugged the woman again, and held her until the tears subsided.

"He'd be so proud of you," she said. "Or, to be honest, he would still be proud of you. He never stopped loving you, never stopped talking about you."

She walked toward the door, and turned to me before she left. "I'll keep the coast clear to give you time to go through all the paperwork. If you have questions for me, I'll be out in the store."

Of course, I already knew that, but I understood it was hard for her to let go. Maintaining some semblance of control was probably needed to manage all the emotions coursing through her.

As soon as she'd left, I opened the folder and looked at all the stuff. I read through all Chris's requirements for me, and recognizing the ones I'd completed, I chuckled. Uncle Chris had obviously been thorough in his planning. I thought about what it must've been like, knowing he was dying, but planning for my arrival.

It still didn't make sense to me that he'd done all this, because I'd called him before he'd passed, but maybe it'd become clear as I worked my way through the paperwork.

As soon as I'd finished reading all the requirements, I looked up the convention he wanted me to attend. It was less than three weeks away, so I assumed Melinda had already signed me up. If my uncle thought it was that important, I wanted to make sure I accommodated his wishes. Besides, it might be fun to go to Tulare, California. I looked up where that was and found it wasn't far from the Sequoia National Park, it might be a good vacation for Clay and me. I hadn't been camping in years, and I'd never been to the park, but it looked like there were some beautiful hiking and camping options from my quick search of the web.

Clay and I, *that* was a concept. It'd been less than a month since we finally started dating, and it already felt so... well, so *right*. I had to admit, I still worried about how he felt about it all. Would he tell me if he was having second thoughts? There was no way to know, and getting him to have a conversation about his feelings was...well, it was difficult.

I came to the sealed package that held the amendment to the will. I sighed and picked it up. I had no idea what to expect. Would my uncle have more restrictions? Probably not, he'd pretty much made it impossible with the original restrictions to do anything other than allow the grove to continue on as it was. Even so, the thought of seeing what my uncle had in store for me next, filled me with dread.

No way around it though, I had to face what he'd written, and I had to do so before we could fully set the strategic plans in place to save the groves.

It was early afternoon, still too early for a whiskey, but screw it. I'd bought some Jack Daniel's Fireball earlier. Thinking it required more than a little alcohol, I poured myself three shots. I downed them, gave myself enough time for the buzz to settle in, then went back to the table and broke the seal on the amended will.

Chapter Thirty-One

Clay

Joshua wasn't very affectionate the night he'd met with Melinda. I'd seen the packet with Chris's information on the table, but I didn't ask him about it. I figured he'd tell me when he was ready.

He remained distracted through supper, and kissed me goodnight early, saying he wanted to get some rest.

The next morning, before I found my crew, he texted me, and asked if I could meet him at the apartment for a chat.

"My uncle waived the restrictions on the property," I said, the moment I sat down at his kitchen table. "I just have to finish the things he laid out. Mostly, he wanted me to go to a conference, which Melinda has already signed both you and me up for. As you know, he wanted me to remain on the property for a full year, but when the year is up, the groves are mine to do with as I choose."

I looked at him, not sure how I should react.

"So, are you going to sell out?" I asked.

"No," he said matter of factly. "If anything, it's made me more determined to make this work."

I nodded, not sure if I was happy or not with the news. On the one hand, it would probably allow me to keep doing what I loved. On the other, it meant a huge responsibility for Joshua.

"So, do you need anything from me?" I asked.

He smiled. "Not really, I just needed to tell someone what I'd learned. I assume Melinda already knows, and Linda Mae, well, she isn't the best person to confide in." I chuckled at the thought of trying to tie Linda Mae down for a heart to heart that didn't involve her kicking my butt in some way or another, I looked back up at Clay and smiled. "I just needed to say it out loud, so it would be real and not just in my imagination."

Joshua came over to where I sat and pulled me up into a hug. "I know you, Melinda, and Linda

Mae told me, over and over, how my uncle didn't hate me, that he had a plan, but it's different when you see that plan laid out. I couldn't help but think he had a problem with me personally, that he didn't trust *me*. I think it comes down to the fact that he didn't trust my dad. He mentioned something to that effect in the will. 'Joshua should take into account the advice and guidance of those who are in my employment while running the business. It is highly advisable that he takes guidance from those who are aware of the nuances of the business, instead of outside influences that could lead him to make a mistake that can't be undone.'."

"Yeah, that sounds like Chris." I chuckled. "He wasn't one to attack something directly, he'd often talk around an issue and let you figure out the best way forward."

"I can understand his concern. My dad is a jerk. I'm sure he broke Chris's heart when he left, and he let me suffer loneliness instead of having my uncle. That's just selfish, you know?"

"Yeah, it wasn't fair for either of you."

Joshua leaned up and kissed me. "Clay, I'm so thankful you've been there for me these past few weeks. It's easier to face all this knowing I get to have you."

I laughed. "You're just using me for my looks."

"Dude, I am gay. Seriously that's a given. But, I just want you to know, you're the only guy I've ever wanted, like...this much."

I kissed him. "Yeah, that's how I feel too."

"Okay, enough mushy stuff," Joshua said and stepped out of my arms. "Let's get to work. I have some more planning to do before we go to the convention. Oh, don't forget, we have Mr. Smith's party this Saturday."

"Oh, god," I whined. "Can we just decide to miss that?"

I laughed again. "No, he'll be one of the board members we need to convince, and he also has a good relationship with the banker, since it was him who referred me."

"You're really going to make me go to the octopus's house?"

"Yep, but I'll protect you."

"Psst, who's going to protect you?"

Joshua laughed, but kissed me again. "I'm sure we'll be okay."

The week went by fast. Joshua spent most of his time working on his plans, but occasionally, I'd see him helping Melinda, or he'd come by the house to play with the dogs. When I'd get home in the evenings, Joshua would meet me at the door, often with a hundred questions. I liked the routine. It felt good to be wanted again.

I started picking him up in the mornings, and we'd always ride together over to Linda Mae's for breakfast, and to chat with everyone. My team had come to accept Joshua as one of their own, and they'd often tease him about wasting away in the store, when he could be out in the trees, building muscles.

He seemed to enjoy the banter as much as them, and would always come back with some smart-aleck comment. The last was that if it built so many muscles, why did he only see flab?

The men hooted at that one, of course. They were all built tough, but as age had come over them, they all had good beer bellies.

When Saturday came, we went to the dreaded party. I would've rather gone back to Luey's and announced all my past emotions, but Joshua insisted. Before we went to the door, we wandered through the trees. Luckily, most of them were in good shape. You could tell there hadn't been a routine watering system applied, and several of the trees were showing that.

"He'll need to revamp the watering system and keep it running. In fact, we'll probably just needs to assign one of the guys to him full time if he wants the fruit to be of any value," I told Joshua, as we walked along.

The property was supposedly twenty to thirty acres, and it backed up to the canal, so acquiring water wasn't a problem. The voles had done a number on several of the trees, so that would have to be dealt with too. The thought of having one of my little monsters running through the grounds made me laugh. Mr. Smith wouldn't stand a chance.

After we'd made a good assessment of the trees, I looked toward the car-filled driveway, and then up to the house, and walked toward the truck.

"No." Joshua grabbed my arm before I could reach the truck. "We said we'd come by the party," he said, as he pulled me toward the house.

I sighed. "You know we're going to regret this."

We weren't disappointed. When Mr. Smith opened the door, the place was overrun with older men, dressed in an array of clothing, some not much clothing at all. Mr. Smith seemed to be the youngest man there.

"Um," Joshua said. "We said we'd let you know when we were done with the trees."

"Oh good," the older man said. "You're just in time, come in and join the party."

I started shaking my head, and Joshua put his hand on mine. "I'm afraid we can't, we're getting ready for the convention, and Clay has to get everything in line before we go. We'll call you tomorrow to set up a time to talk about the grove."

Joshua all but pulled me away from the party, and I could hear the older man laughing, as the door shut behind him.

"Why do you need him on the board?" I asked.

"Because, he was selected by my uncle, and he's smart and wealthy, and he owns thirty plus acres of citrus trees we could use."

"I'm sure we could find other growers who don't have creepy-old-man parties."

Joshua chuckled. "But, what fun would that be?"

I looked at Joshua with fascination. "You think that was fun?"

"Well, not the party, but watching your expression will surely go down as one of my life's fondest memories."

I shoved him playfully, and he laughed as he climbed into the passenger side of the truck.

Joshua teased me as we drove back to the apartment, and when we got there, he rushed into the store, where Melinda was working in her office. I followed a few minutes later, hearing their laughter.

I walked over to them and could hear Joshua telling Melinda about our encounter with Mr. Smith

I loved how close the two of them had become. The fact that Joshua would want to tell her about this encounter, immediately confirmed that he was beginning to see her as a close friend.

Melinda was wiping tears from her eyes, as he described the look of panic on my face, when the older man opened the door displaying in all his glory. "Then Clay looked up, and saw all those older men, most of them in various degrees of undress, walking in the background, and his face went pale."

I smiled, enjoying Joshua's animation.

"You'd have gone pale too, because the man wanted us to come in. We'd have been like chum in the water!" I said, causing the two of them to burst into another fit of laughter.

Unfortunately, the bell from the front door chimed, telling us a customer had arrived, so we had to break up our little party. Melinda said we had to come by after the restaurant closed tomorrow, and tell the story to Linda Mae. "She particularly dislikes Mr. Smith, so it'll make her day," Melinda told us.

The citrus growers' convention was more fun, because Joshua was there. I'd gone the past few years with Chris, but sitting through the dry lectures, although very informative, wasn't always the most fun.

Joshua hung on every word of most of the lectures we attended. He was a total sponge when it came to the business of citrus production, and there were several speakers who were talking about agritourism. Those were of particular interest to Joshua.

The speakers talked about wine tastings among the trees, banquets, and other events that accented the farm without jeopardizing the crops. I knew Joshua asked the most questions afterward and was actively taking notes throughout the entire lecture.

After the conference, we drove up to Sequoia National Park and hiked among the trees. I hadn't been to the park before, and the trees fascinated me.

If they fascinated me, Joshua was obsessed with them. He dragged me through miles of backwoods trails. Every time we came upon one of the giants, he'd inhale sharply and rush toward it, often embracing it like another human.

I think it was there, I first accepted the fact that I was in love with him. My Asperger's often got in the way of my emotional awareness, and the feelings I had for Joshua were so different from those I'd had for Paul.

One morning, Joshua dragged me out before the sun came up. He rushed us down a three-mile hike before we came to the trees. I was exhausted and a little grumpy, since I'd have preferred to sleep at least two more hours. When we came upon the trees, however, Joshua nudged me, curled in, and gave me a huge hug. That demonstrated his excitement, and he rushed over to the massive sentinel a hundred feet away. I just sat down on a fallen tree, and waited for him to gush over the trees, and get it out of his system, so we could go back and have some breakfast. I totally missed Linda Mae's cooking, and more than that, I missed my routine.

I was feeling sorry for myself when I looked up. Joshua was leaning against a giant trunk, eyes closed. We were the only people anywhere around, and the sound of early morning life sang in chorus with him. The sun peeked around him and gave the optical illusion that he and the ancient tree were illuminated by light.

I couldn't take my eyes off him. My heart pounded, and sweat broke out all over my body. That was the moment I knew. I'd always love my late husband, I'd always have him in my heart, but Joshua, he was the love of my life.

Chapter Thirty-Two

Joshua

I looked over at Clay, and I could tell he was studying me. It was too far for me to interpret his expression, but I assumed it was a mixture of frustration and desire to get back to the tent.

I'd dragged the poor man all over the National Park and Forest since we'd arrived. I'd never experienced anything as remarkable as the giant, ancient trees, and something about them serenaded me. It was almost like I was a different person while I was in their presence.

I closed my eyes and enjoyed the feeling of the morning sun on my face with the giant tree to my back.

When I looked up, Clay was standing over me, and I had no trouble interpreting his expression. Luckily, we were way off the main track, exploring a part of the forest seldom visited by other tourists. Clay knelt down next to me, unzipped my pants, and took me into his mouth.

As we made love under the giant tree, something stirred in me, shifting, and locking in emotions that up to that point had been scattered like seeds. Maybe it was the trees. Maybe it was the sound of the forest and the smell of the pines. Whatever it was, making love to Clay in that spot solidified the love that had been growing in me since he'd first held me, trying to comfort me when I was upset about my uncle.

"Clay, I'm in love with you."

I didn't know what I'd expected. Maybe the darting of his eyes like he sometimes did when he didn't want to face his feelings, but instead, a smile spread across his face. "I'd just come to the same conclusion," he replied. He pushed me against the tree, and put his hand on the side of my face. "I think I've been falling in love since the first moment I saw you, mourning the passing of your uncle. I didn't understand it, and still didn't until just a moment ago, when I saw you leaning against the giant tree." He looked up at the sequoia and smiled down at me.

"Is it too early to ask you to marry me?" he asked, and I just about swallowed my tongue. I was so shocked, I couldn't answer for a moment, causing a look of concern to cross Clay's face. "We don't have to if it's too fast," he said worriedly.

I couldn't help but laugh. "No, it's not too early, because we both love each other, and I know I'd like to spend the rest of my life with you. Yes, Clay! I'll marry you!"

Clay immediately began dancing around the grand old tree, yelling and hooting.

Next thing I knew, he was pressing me against the sequoia again, kissing me deeply. "I promise to be the best husband I can be," he said, and at that moment, I knew he really would be!

Epilogue: Joshua

Things sped up the moment we returned to the groves. Clay was significantly wealthier than I'd realized, and since we were getting married, he told me he wanted to use his savings to create the resort.

It's too risky," I said, resisting the idea. "We're better off taking a loan from a neutral party."

"No, you're looking at this from an emotional perspective."

Clay sat me down, showed me the probability of our success, and how investing in our venture improved his chances of doubling his investment.

"I see your reasoning, but seriously, there are too many unknowns."

Clay laughed and showed me statistics involving individual owners who had a commitment to a project, compared to corporate ownership of property investments.

"Statistically, you have a much greater chance at success if I'm involved, versus a bank," he said smugly.

I hadn't meant to bring it up this early, but if I was going to agree to take Clay's money as an investment, I was going to use it for leverage.

"I'll concede, and you'll be my equal partner in the groves. That's non-negotiable, since you're basically putting up the equivalent value."

He nodded, and I smiled. "That's not all. You have to agree to stop hiding in the groves, and to work with Dr. Julia on the Phoenix Mathematics project. It's mostly nonprofit work, and it doesn't require you to teach or lecture. It does, however, force you to stop being a hermit, and get back into a field you loved."

Reluctantly, Clay agreed, and using his investment, we broke ground on the anniversary of my uncle's funeral. Also, the first anniversary of my arrival at the orange grove.

It was both a memorial and a celebration. Both Melinda and Linda Mae swore it was appropriate for the gregarious man. "He'd be so proud of you,"

Melinda told me, as she hugged me tightly, after the ceremony was over.

The mayor and several councilmen joined the celebration. Each told me they could see the stubborn resolve in me that they'd been at war with all these years with my uncle. I laughed. "So, you mean you approved all this, because you knew I'd never quit?"

They all laughed and nodded. "What you're doing will help Mesa in so many ways. We've all wanted the old resort to be rescued, and we've desperately needed a convention center. The fact you've tied it in with our history so beautifully, can't be any better for our community," the mayor told me, before disappearing into the crowd.

I'd moved into my childhood home with Clay. After ripping the crappy vinyl siding off, and returning the structure to its original adobe exterior, I was happy to be back. It didn't feel like the home I grew up in, though. The entire place was full of Clay, and he'd done a remarkable job bringing new life to it.

Since I'd vacated the apartment, we'd moved Mrs. Lucy into it, after the completion of the sale of her resort to our company. She immediately began helping Melinda with the store, saying she refused to sit in that lonely space all the time, without something to keep her busy. Although Linda Mae and she were still bitter rivals, Mrs. Lucy began joining us at the Square Biscuit for breakfast every morning.

She came up to me, and pulled me into a hug. "Larry would be so proud that his legacy isn't going to be destroyed. He loved that place." A tear slipped down her cheek.

I hugged her back. "I wish I could remember Larry better, but like Uncle Chris, I can feel him here. It's so awesome that we could bridge the two properties to create the resort." I felt emotion swarming through me as well.

She patted my hand and turned away. "Now, where did that Linda Mae go? I want to lecture her on how to make a proper meringue pie." She winked at me, and scurried off to cause some mischief. I chuckled as she left, and then shook my head at how well this all seemed to be working out.

That evening as we sat under the stars, me curled up in Clay's arms, I was amazed at how wonderful our life together had turned out. We hadn't set a date, both of us appeared to have an unspoken agreement to get the project completed, before we made our lifetime commitment. Married or not, Clay Masters was the love of my life, and I'd happily go wherever he wanted me to go. Luckily, he and I had the same interest, and that was an orange grove and resort in the deserts of Mesa, Arizona.

Epilogue: Clay

The project took over three years to complete. Joshua's analytical mind and my mathematical precision, along with his ability to manage a large building project, ended up being exactly what was needed to keep costs under control, and the timeline on schedule.

The convention center was booked several years in advance, and the RV resort and cabins that had been restored, were mostly booked during the winter months as well.

The actual numbers for the property were significantly better than we'd planned. Joshua demanded the surplus be used to pay me back for the investment I'd made. I just chuckled. He didn't realize I was invested in this place as much as I could be. The money didn't really mean much to me other than I could live without working if I chose to. The fact that I loved the groves, and my crew, meant I'd never stop working, or at least, not until they buried me. Not unlike Chris, I thought.

It was amazing to watch Melinda and Joshua create the commercial elements of the resort. We sold out of all our orange produce every year, about as fast as we could harvest it. Linda Mae retired as the head of the Square Biscuit, and passed management on to Lola, the server who'd been with her the longest. Clearly, Linda Mae had rubbed off on her, because she ended up being as tough as the old woman ever was.

Linda Mae, however, told us over and over that she wasn't going to get involved in the development of the new restaurant, but the moment she found out Mrs. Lucy was going to help design it, she butted right in.

Although the two argued like sisters, they bonded together, to ensure the restaurant was top of the line. The most amazing thing they did was hire a gourmet chef, recently out of culinary school. They proceeded to teach the young woman how to prepare food the way they thought it should be. As a result of the two women's direction, and the young chef's willingness to learn from the two seasoned experts, the place ended up being one of the top restaurants in the greater Phoenix area.

It only took a couple months before we had to start taking reservations, because the place was packed every night.

Melinda, of course, ran the large retail shops. Despite complaining about having to manage the new staff, she did so with as much precision as her mom had run the restaurant all those years. The resort had several small businesses, including a boutique salon, and massage center for the hot-spring baths, her storefront, which she moved to the resort, a culinary shop that included several new products we manufactured ourselves, and several small shops we rented out. The result was a fully inclusive, trendy place, for both our guests and customers to enjoy.

Once a manager was hired to oversee the entire resort, and Joshua was confident the young woman was comfortable with keeping things running in his absence, he surprised me with the resort's first wedding... *ours*.

I'd complained about how I hated all the planning that went into my first wedding, and how my mom and Paul had pretty-much planned the whole thing. So, when he showed me the setup, and asked me if I'd be willing to tie the knot now that we were up and running, I pulled him into a huge hug. "You are the best fiancé ever!" I said, and wiped a tear, surprising myself with the emotion.

He laughed. "You're alright?" he asked, and kissed me hard. "You aren't upset that I planned it all without you?"

"*God, no!*" I exclaimed. "I've been dreading all the planning for, well, for years," I admitted.

I wasn't sure how he convinced everyone to keep the secret from me, but the next day, the entire crew, our friends—including Joshua's friends, Trevor and Peter—sat in the audience. Their five-year-old, Luka, causing an insane amount of chaos among the guests.

The oranges were blooming around us, and the smell was as intoxicating as ever. Not everyone liked the aroma of the oranges in bloom. For me, it always felt like new beginnings, and like life was full of possibilities. The fact that Joshua planned our wedding under the blossoming trees, testified how much he and I thought alike.

Linda Mae met me at the groom's area, and informed me she was walking me down the aisle. When Joshua came out of the other area, Melinda was on his arm. I wasn't sure why, but the fact that my birth mom and grandmother were the ones who officially stood with us, caused me to become emotional. I couldn't help but wipe tears away, as we walked to where the minister stood waiting.

It was funny, I was the emotional mess through the entire thing, and Joshua was the cool and collected one. He held me through most of the service, though, and I apologized in a whisper for being so out of control, which made him chuckle. "I thought it was going to me doing all the blubbering," he said, before he squeezed my hand, and whispered, "I love seeing you all choked up about marrying me."

"Do you, Clay Masters, take Joshua Howard to be your lawfully wedded husband?"

"Heck, yeah!" I said, and blushed when the audience laughed.

The minister smiled. "Do you, Joshua Howard, take Clay Masters as *your* lawfully wedded husband?"

Joshua smiled from ear to ear, a tear slipping down his cheek. "With all my heart, I do."

As the minister, a friend of Linda Mae's, pronounced us husbands, my heart leaped. I pulled my new husband into my arms, kissing him with everything I had.

To my surprise, I met Joshua's father for the first time that day. He'd been standing awkwardly at the back of the audience, but when we came out, he circled around to us, shook my hand, and welcomed me into the family. He hugged Joshua, which clearly shocked both of them, then promptly disappeared. We didn't see him again, and Joshua said, "He probably just flew back to Atlanta. It was a small miracle he showed up to begin with."

Despite that, I could tell it did Joshua a lot of good that his father had come.

After the ceremony, we cuddled under the blooming trees, as he told me we had to go make everything legal now. Which meant, we'd have to get a license, wait the appropriate time, then have another small ceremony. He hadn't wanted to mess up the surprise by telling me about the ceremony beforehand.

"We sort of did it all backward, didn't we?" I teased him, and he laughed. "Yeah, but we're gay men getting married, we don't have to follow anyone's rules, right?"

I smiled at him. "However it happens, I'm just happy you're mine."

After everything was official, we flew to Seattle, rented a small RV, and drove down the coast to San Diego. It was the perfect honeymoon, as we were able to just enjoy each other, without our business getting involved.

Of course, I was happy to get home, but having Joshua with me, and knowing he'd be mine for the rest of my life, made home so much more than I'd ever imagined it would be. I loved Joshua with all of my heart, and I looked forward to making his life as fulfilling and as happy as I could.

For extended scenes, including recipes,

go here:

https://BookHip.com/DNDAABJ

Continue reading for an excerpt from

Love's Legacy

By

Blake Allwood

Flex

The electric pulse surged through me as I touched the handle of the motel reception door. "What the hell?" I said to myself, then shook my head when I touched the handle again. This time there was no shock.

"Must be static electricity," I said, and although my heart was beating significantly faster, I ignored it and pushed through the door.

I walked into the front room and turned back to see if maybe there was some explanation, but there was none I could see. I was about to say something to the front-desk person I'd heard come in behind me, but when I turned around and saw the man behind the desk, the same electrical sensation that'd hit me before surged through me again. Just this time, it was more... intense.

The man looked to be in his mid-twenties. He was short and lithe, with long lashes accentuating gorgeous brown eyes that would've made any female model jealous. His arms were strong and muscular from what appeared to be work-related exercise, and not time spent in a gym.

He looked up and smiled, which made his entire face glow and my knees go weak. "How can I help you?" he asked. I froze for a moment and subconsciously reached up and rubbed the place above my heart where the electrical discharge still stung a bit. Finally, I came to my senses, and told him my name.

"I'm Fletcher Henry. I'm traveling with Eric Anderson," I said. "We should have adjoining rooms."

The man typed in our names and then smiled. "You have the honeymoon cottage. Is that good news? Should I be congratulating you?"

I laughed. "No, we didn't just get married. That's why we wanted the rooms to be separate. We're friends from years back. We ran away from home and wanted to visit Big Bend before it gets too hot." It wasn't a complete lie.

"Well, Mr. Henry," the man said in a sexy, southern drawl that put images in my mind of hot cocoa being stirred. "Your accommodations are ready. I hope you and Mr..." He looked at the computer. "You and Mr. Anderson have a good time here in Alamito."

I winked at him before I knew what I was doing. I was not the type to flirt, but something about this man triggered me.

I pulled the rental car over to the cottage, and Eric and I began to unload. The place was as cute as it could be. Like the rest of the motel and campground, you could see distinct signs of renovation. The interior was what you'd expect to see on an HGTV series. It was modern with clean lines, and the bedding was obviously new and looked particularly chic.

I turned toward Eric and shrugged in surprise. "I guess we won't be roughing it after all."

Eric smiled and agreed. The two rooms were separated by a door. When the cottage was being used as a honeymoon suite, one room could easily be used as a living room and kitchen, and the other a master bedroom. As it was, Eric and I flipped for the bigger bedroom, and he won. I didn't mind though, the reviews for the room had said the hideaway bed was as comfortable as the main bed.

We went back to the car and unloaded each of our dogs. Puddles, a poodle, of course, belonged to Eric. I had the rambunctious Jack Russell, Ace. We were lucky, because Ace and Puddles enjoyed each other's company, and got along very well.

"I'll take them out," I volunteered, and grabbed both dogs, putting them on their leashes. I headed out the door before Eric could comment.

As I walked them across the courtyard, Ace immediately spotted a chicken pen, and began pulling me that direction. I was intrigued enough that I decided to let Ace lead us over and check it out. As we neared the chickens, Ace began lunging at the pen. I pulled him back and began to rein him in, when I heard barking at my back.

Before I could turn around, Ace darted toward the barking. Unfortunately, between him and me, his leash got caught against a rusty fence pole, that was just sharp enough to snap it.

When I finally managed to turn around, a Chihuahua was bounding toward Ace, and by the time I got to them, they were sniffing each other. The Chihuahua's lips curled back, his hackles raised, and I could tell the little dog wasn't friendly and was more likely than not going to bite Ace. I hurried over just as the owner came out of her mobile home screaming, "Lucca, Lucca." The dog turned to look at her owner as I grabbed Ace up and turned to pick Puddles up as well, just to make sure neither dog got attacked before the Chihuahua's mom got to him.

"I'm so sorry," the woman exclaimed. "I opened my door to put some things in my car, and he dashed out."

"No worries," I assured her, holding up the broken leash. This got cut on a piece of rust. She smiled as I introduced myself.

I was just about to leave, when I heard Eric call, "Is everything okay, Flex?"

"Yep," I said over my shoulder, letting Puddles down, so I could hand her leash to Eric.

When I faced the woman again, her expression had changed completely. She looked at me in disgust. "You need to keep your dog contained," she huffed, then headed back to her mobile home.

"What was that about?" Eric asked.

"I'm not sure," I shrugged. "But I'm guessing she thought we were a couple."

"Well, we aren't, but we could've been. Guess she's the anti-gay not welcome wagon, huh?"

"Guess so," I shrugged again, and we walked back to the cottage.

We'd only been back a few minutes when the phone rang, and the handsome man I'd first met behind the desk when we arrived, said, "Mr. Henry. I'm sorry to bother you, but we've had a complaint about your dog. Can you come to the front desk, please?" I answered in the affirmative, but I was already angry enough to spit nails, even before walking out of the room.

I knocked on Eric's door. "Hey, can you keep Ace? I have to go deal with the bigot. She's trying to get us kicked out of the motel."

"Seriously?" Eric asked in surprise.

"Apparently," I said, then headed toward the office.

When I got there, the disgruntled old woman was stomping around in front of the main desk, waving her hands and basically having a hissy fit. She stopped when I walked in, and put her hands on her hips, tapping her right foot.

"Mr. Henry, thanks for coming," the man said, with some hesitation.

"What seems to be the problem?" I asked, turning my own glare at the woman.

"Um..." the man began, but was interrupted by the woman.

"You know what the problem is, your dog was off his leash and tried to attack my dog."

I was shocked by the blatant lie, and I had to catch my breath before I responded.

"Don't you mean, your dog was off her leash? You admitted to me that you let her escape when you were loading your car. That's when she rushed my dog. You and I both know, the only reason my dog was off the leash is because when he turned to meet your terror, his leash snapped."

The woman crossed her arms, and I could tell she was about to call me a liar, or possibly worse, so I interrupted her as I turned toward the young man. "I think we all know this isn't about our dogs," I said, then looked her square in the face. "This woman was quite pleasant to me until my friend Eric came over. She thought we were a couple, and as a result, she decided to use this farce as a way to get rid of us."

I could tell I'd hit the nail on the head by the way the woman flushed. She dropped her arms, but knowing she was in an impossible situation, she crossed them again and turned away from me to stare at the guy behind the desk.

I noticed the man's jaw was locked, and his expression became angry. Despite the pleasant greetings when I'd first arrived, I had to assume he'd side with the woman, so, I waited for the words that told me I needed to leave. Instead, he looked at me, and said, "I'm deeply sorry, Mr. Henry. If I had known this was a homophobic stunt, I wouldn't have bothered you. Please, apologize to your friend for me as well."

Both the woman and I stared at the young man in shock. I turned to leave without saying a word. I didn't have the words, really. We were in West Texas of all places, so I didn't think anyone would be defending the rights of a gay person, no matter how in the right we were.

Mitch

Before Mr. Henry left, I was already dialing the number of the park across the street. "Yes, is Lia there? Hi, Lia, this is Mitch Armstrong at the Alamito Motel. I'm good, thanks. Hey, I have a mobile home who needs another place to park tonight. Do you have room? Perfect, I'll send her over."

I looked at the woman standing across the desk, and ignored the fact that she appeared to be so angry, her face looked like it could explode. "Mrs. Stanfield, I've already warned you to stop being nasty to the other residents, and I told you that if I had to say something to you again, you'd be asked to leave. I'm afraid lying about a guest who literally just got here, because you don't like his or her lifestyle is simply the last straw. As you heard, Lia said they have room across the street at the Events Campground. You can pull your mobile home over there."

The woman stared at me for a moment, before the tears began to fall. "But all my friends are here. The Events Campground is nasty."

I ignored the crocodile tears. "I'm sorry, but again, I did warn you."

I turned to go into the backroom, almost afraid of what damage the woman would do once I left, but fortunately, when I came back out, she was gone. About an hour later, I saw her mobile home leave the motel and pull in across the road.

I figured there was going to be hell to pay. Mrs. Stanfield was one of eight widows who lived here full time. When I inherited the motel from my grandfather, they were some of the campers who rented from him. I'd allowed them to stay on the ridiculously low-cost rent he'd charged, which honestly didn't cover the cost of utilities, but there was more than money involved when it came to these things.

The eight women were more than a handful. They tended to be busybodies who poked their noses in everyone else's business. Luckily, I only had to chastise them occasionally when they crossed a line. Usually, I just found their antics amusing.

Mrs. Stanfield had gotten worse over the past year, however. It wasn't only the usual annoying things the women tended to do. One evening, during the weekly Bunko game they held in my kitchen, Mrs. Stanfield had gotten upset with one of the other ladies, and pulled her hair. Of course, the other woman was livid and slapped her. I walked into the kitchen just in time to see Mrs. Stanfield pull her fist back and nail the other woman right in the nose. I yelled before the punch landed, and shocked Mrs. Stanfield enough that there wasn't much weight behind the punch, but still, things had gone too far. When the other ladies left, I asked Mrs. Stanfield to stay back and told her to find another campground.

She'd cried then too. Unfortunately for her, I learned long ago not to be influenced by crocodile tears. My mother had been a master at using them to get her way.

When she left, I thought I'd seen the back of her, except that the other ladies, including the one who'd been attacked, came and asked me to reconsider. Of course, I had, and here we were once again. No good deed goes unpunished, I thought, but at least the grumpy old coot was now someone else's problem.

Flex

I got back to the cottage and knocked on Eric's door to retrieve Ace. "How'd it go?" he asked.

"You won't believe it, but the guy actually took our side. I'm going to guess this could get him fired, though. I doubt the owner will be thrilled that he took my side over a damsel in distress."

Eric frowned sadly. "I hope not. It sucks when people doing the right thing get punished."

"Yeah, I agree. I'll go back down there later and check on him."

"Good idea," Eric said. "When do we need to be out at the ranch tomorrow?" he asked.

"We're expected by ten in the morning. The Real Estate agent is supposed to be there by noon, but I wanted to get a good look at the place before she arrives."

Eric looked at me. I'd never been particularly good at hiding my emotions, and I figured he could see the grief and sadness warring inside me, but Eric was a sensitive guy. Instead of pressing the point, he nodded knowingly and turned to his side of the suite.

"I think I'm going to turn in early. I'm exhausted after last week and the trip down from Oregon. I'll catch you around eight. That should give us enough time to eat, then get to the ranch."

I nodded. The ranch was about a thirty-minute drive from Alamito. I was tired too, so I decided I'd get Ace fed, then head back to the office and speak to the poor man behind the desk, to see if there was anything I could do to help save his job.

I left the cottage just as the old woman I'd had the run-in with rounded the corner in her camper. She locked eyes with me and flipped me the bird. "Wow, that one's a piece of work," I said out loud.

I waited until she pulled out of the parking lot, then walked over to the office.

I found the man thumbing through paperwork. He didn't look concerned, so I hoped maybe things weren't going to be as bad for him as I'd thought. When I entered, he looked up. I could see the weariness in his eyes before it was hidden by a genuine smile.

"Hello again, Mr. Henry. What can I do for you?"

"I... I'm just checking on you, actually. I hope you didn't get in trouble defending me from Mrs. Evil Britches."

The man chuckled. "I didn't get in trouble. In fact, since I own the establishment, there really isn't anyone to get in trouble with."

I was shocked by that fact. "Wow, really? You don't look old enough to own a business," I blurted out, then turned red in the face. I'd never been good at catching myself before I said stupid stuff.

He laughed, "My grandfather left me the motel in his will, along with enough money to do some repairs. I was going to renovate it and sell up, but I admit, I've gotten rather attached to it since I moved back last fall."

I quickly ran through the timeframe in my mind, and thought out loud, "So, you've been here for almost a year then?"

The man looked up, and the weariness seemed to settle on his face again. "Yes, it doesn't seem that long, though. There's still so much to get done."

"From what I've seen, you've done an incredible job. The cottage is beautiful."

That brought a smile to his face. "It was my first project. I wanted a comfortable place for newlyweds to escape to. As you know, since you're here, there isn't anything around for miles. Every town, even those in the middle of nowhere, deserves a nice place to... honeymoon," he said, and the sweet smile turned a bit mischievous.

The look, although fleeting, was delicious, and my nasty mind thought of a variety of ways I'd like to get that smile back on his face.

"Well, Mr..." I looked at him and shrugged. "I'm sorry I never got your name."

"My name's Mitch Armstrong," he said, causing that same strange electrical current to course through me, that had when I first arrived. What was it about this man that made me feel so... weird?

"Mr. Armstrong, it was nice of you to come to my aid earlier. I'll be honest, I wasn't sure that would be the case. I was all prepared to leave, but I was equally prepared to leave a nasty review for you online."

The man laughed. "I bet you would've, not that it would've mattered, since I'm pretty much the only motel around. But," He quickly back-pedaled. "We do what we can to make things nice for folks, though."

"Well, what you did mattered a lot to me and to Eric. Although, he's as straight as an arrow." The man looked at me again, this time with a bit of curiosity that he let go, without asking whatever it was on his mind.

"You thought we were together, didn't you?" I asked, wanting to find out more about the man, but not knowing how to ask without appearing nosy.

He continued smiling as he nodded. "I know you said you were friends, but that's usually how gay folks talk about their lovers around here."

"Are there many gay people around here?" I asked skeptically.

"More than you'd think," the guy said, with no malice in his voice.

"I wouldn't think Alamito would be a very gay-friendly place."

The guy nodded again. "It wasn't when I was growing up, but after the Supreme Court made their marriage ruling, even the churches seem to have found other things to go after. We've finally just sunk into the routine of the community."

There I had it, he was gay, but even with that information, I had to push further. I just had to. "So, you're gay too?" I asked, waiting, not sure how he'd respond.

"Yep," he said. "Been out since I was sixteen. I left here when I was eighteen, and swore nothing short of gold and silver would get me back. Seems I wasn't as stubborn as I thought. All it took was inheriting an old motel that was about to fall apart."

"I can imagine how awful it was. My grandparents lived down the road. Not too far from the national park. I spent my summers here, but we really never came into town unless my grandma needed supplies. For the most part, I just spent the whole summer riding horses and doing every possible chore my grandparents could think to give me."

Mitch chuckled with recognition. "My grandpa owned the motel, and my mom and I lived with him. I've been cleaning sheets since I was old enough to walk."

I was chuckling then myself. "It seems we both had grandfathers who thought an idle mind was the devil's playground."

"Well," Mitch replied. "He sure told me that enough. Good thing my mind was never idle very long, so I guess the devil has left me alone."

"Yeah, I'm pretty sure I was safe too... at least while I was here during the summer."

Mitch looked at me. "So, why didn't you stay at your grandparents' place? Not that we aren't happy to have you," he quickly added.

"Well, that's a long story," I said, and the sigh had the young man looking at me with sympathy. "My grandpa died about five years ago, and my grandma long before that."

"I see," he said. "I'm sorry for your loss. Even though my grandpa was a mean ol' bastard, I loved him and I miss him something fierce."

I nodded in agreement. "Yeah, mine was mean as well... what do y'all say out here? He was mean as a snake." I chuckled at the saying. "But, he never hesitated to tell me how much he loved me. Even after I came out, he said it was weird and he couldn't understand why anyone would want to touch a hairy man, when you could snuggle up to a pretty woman, but the next words out of his mouth were that it didn't matter what he thought. It only mattered that he and my gran loved me, no matter what I wanted, no matter how weird it was."

I smiled, but the backs of my eyes were stinging with unshed tears. It had been a long time since I'd come out to my grandfather. But, that simple, matter-of-fact love that he'd shown at that moment still burned a brand on my heart. Like Mitch said about his grandfather, I missed mine something fierce.

I knew I needed to change the subject, so I didn't end up bawling my eyes out and embarrassing the shit out of myself.

"Are you the one who did the desert gardens?" I asked.

"The smile that'd never left Mitch's face beamed then with pure happiness. "Yep. Felt like the old place needed a little sprucing, and I couldn't afford to put in a bunch of non-native species, nor could I afford to irrigate them if I did. Most of the plants came from around the property. I just had to reposition them."

"I saw some of those cacti. I bet that was... precarious."

Mitched laughed. "You have no idea. Those cactus thorns go through leather like it was silk. I had to remove most of the thorns to move them. What you saw is the new growth. Most of my cacti were quick to regrow the thorns. I guess it is their only protection, but dang, I hoped I wouldn't see them again for at least a couple years."

I smiled, and was enjoying the passion he was showing for his gardens. "I already took a ton of photos and posted them on Facebook. My mom loved them, and since she pretty-much hates everything to do with this area, her compliment is something you should be proud of."

The conversation stalled, and I realized I needed to let him get back to work. I turned to go, and Mitch quickly asked, "How long are you going to be in the area?"

"Just a couple of days, then I have to fly back to Houston to manage some business stuff. Eric has to get back to Portland too. He has classes on Tuesday."

"Is he a student?" Mitch asked.

"No, he's a teacher at a high school there. Although I have no idea why. We both hated high school. I guess the guy is a glutton for punishment."

Mitch chuckled. "Yeah, I sure wouldn't want to do that. I got my degree in business management and thought I'd be running a large corporation in Houston. My gramps clearly had other ideas," he said, as he gestured around the room.

"So, would you like to come by for dinner one night?" Mitch was blushing, which made him even cuter. It seemed impossible, considering how cute he already was.

"Sure, we'll be back tomorrow night. Why don't we go somewhere for dinner."

Mitch just smiled and looked at me like I was a simpleton. "Honey, there is nowhere to go in this one-horse town after lunch. Kimmie's is only open for breakfast and lunch. If you want dinner, it's pizza, or one of us will have to do the cooking."

"Oh," I said. My face turning red now. "I can't put you out like that. Unfortunately, I can't really leave Eric, since he came on this trip for me."

"No problem, I assumed he'd join us. I don't mind cooking. It'll give me something to do besides slave behind this desk, or deal with grumpy old women."

I smiled. "Okay, if you're sure. Can I bring anything?"

"No, I have everything we'll need. Do you prefer steak or chicken?"

"Both," I said, and he laughed.

"Sounds good, then I'll just let inspiration guide me."

"Um, I'm guessing we'll be out at the ranch until four or five. Can we plan to be at your place by six-thirty or seven? I'm sure we'll both want a shower before we eat. It's dusty and dirty out there, and I haven't been in the house since my grandparents died. It's probably pretty nasty."

"No problem. See you at seven, how's that?"

I grinned. I was secretly jumping up and down inside at the thought of him inviting me over for a meal, even if Eric was going to be with us, which was probably best, because the crush I was developing on this man was intense. I was sure I'd be trying to attack him before we cut into the steak or chicken.

"I'll see you at seven," I managed to say, and walked out of the office.

Purchase now to continue reading at:

https://amzn.to/3gmo3b6

Looking for more stories by #ownvoice authors?

Go to LGBTQownvoice.com

Books written by

LGBTQ+ Authors

for

LGBTQ+ Readers

Titles by Blake Allwood:

Aiden Inspired
Suzie Empowered
Bobby Transformed
|
Romantic Renovations
|
By Chance Series:
Love By Chance
Another Chance With Love
Taking A Chance For Love
|
Big Bend Series:
Love's Legacy: Book One
Love's Heirloom: Book Two
Love's Bequest: Book Three
|
Novella:
Tenacious
(Available at blakeallwood.com)

Made in the USA
Monee, IL
19 July 2021